MW01616031

Also by Caron Kamps Widden

RESTORATION

2/19

Dear Cathie,

Our Stories begin
at home.

Best,
Caron

THE LIES WE KEEP

CARON KAMPS WIDDEN

HILLIARD HARRIS

HILLIARD HARRIS

P.O. Box 84
Boonsboro, Maryland 21713-0084

The Lies We Keep Copyright © 2015-2016
By Caron Kamps Widden

Second Edition—2016
ISBN 1-59133-418-7
978-1-59133-418-7
Book Design: S. A. Reilly

Manufactured/Printed in the United States of America
2016

For Richard
The Love of My Life

Acknowledgements

An author must create an entire world of characters for works of fiction. Thank you to all the people who inspire me around town, at the coffee shop, sitting near me on the plane, standing in line at the post office. I see characters everywhere and draw from so many to create protagonists and antagonists from sometimes dozens of people I meet along the way.

I visited Sedona several times to collect research for this novel, as well as, New York City, Cleveland and the surrounding areas. Thank goodness for public libraries, town halls and the lovely people who work there. I should know you all by name, but I tend to research in stealth fashion, so thank you for pointing me in the right direction.

I am blessed in my life to have wonderful friends and family who support my writing. Thanks to Chris and Whitney Savage for the use of their dining room table for several chapters and loads of revisions. Thank you to Rick Widden for his gracious hospitality during my visits to Arizona, not to mention all the pep talks. Thanks, Joe Widden for your encouragement all these years, and for being patient with my writer's brain. And speaking of brains, thanks to these well-read ladies, Barb, Eileen, Kathy, Ann, Marsha, Mary, Ann and Sue. You have taught me so much from the point of view of the reader. Thank you to Linda Altemus for cheering me on. Deep appreciation goes to Jan Dennis, for teaching me years ago how to kill my darlings. Thanks to Pam Duignan for keeping me up on writing and publishing news, and for your kindness. Deepest gratitude goes to my younger brother, Chris, who continues to help our family by helping our mother. You are a blessing, fine sir. And to my mom, Cali, my biggest fan, who tells everyone she meets to buy my books. My longtime girlfriends who embrace who I am, and know I am perfectly happy sleeping on the sofa. Many thanks to Avery Grace who brings such joy to my life, I will always treasure my writing sessions with you napping nearby, and how you'd open one eye to see if I was still there, then smile and go back to sleep, precious moments, indeed.

Writing and publishing a book can only be accomplished with the help of great editors, and book champions. I'm deeply grateful to Sue Clark for her insightful help with editing and revisions, a true thought partner and a dear friend. I'd also like to thank Stephanie Reilly for supporting me as an emerging author, taking a chance on me with my first novel, and now again.

I'd also like to thank you, dear reader, for choosing to read my novel. It's a bit like leaving the house without clothes on to share my writing with the world—scary, exhilarating but also deeply gratifying. I truly hope you enjoy the story.

And finally, deepest gratitude to Richard who knows my whole story, my every secret and continues to love me anyway.

Chapter 1
Alex

Late afternoon in Sedona, Alex Gershom examined the rouge-tinted sky as sunrays radiated from a point in the atmosphere where the sun rested upon the horizon, and sunbeams projected silhouettes on vine-covered stucco walls and clay tile rooftops.

As he lit the first of two cigarettes for the night, Alex couldn't help but notice the enormous, cross-like shadow resting against the steep-pitched roofline above the service entrance to the restaurant where he worked. Behind him, a wooden utility pole jutted out from the asphalt, metal arms extended wide, power lines zigzagged the alleyway suspended above overstuffed dumpsters and stacks of empty pallets. Alex turned to exhale a wraith of bluish-white smoke toward the dusky, ethereal crucifix.

As a boy in the tree-lined Shaker Heights suburb of Cleveland, Alex had knelt before the sacred railing for communion hundreds of times. The crucified Christ suspended over the altar, the pastor's robes draped like angel's wings, the heavenly Father above, all knowing, all seeing. Alex often prayed the thin wires that supported the massive cross would hold until after he sipped from the chalice.

Lately, his mind often drifted into the past like that. Something that never happened before, since he was careful to stay busy.

Stretching tall, Alex twisted his head, and cracked his neck to relieve the pain between his temples. The shadow above the door had already shifted, the sun dipped behind the shops and galleries like a kite without wind. Wide brushstrokes of deep, midnight blue would soon conceal the red-orange canvas of Sedona, the heavens lit by thousands of tiny stars, like the glow of miniature holiday lights.

His favorite time of day, the air began to settle and cool in the Upper Sonoran Desert as the earth continued its rotation from west to east. During the evening hours, when stillness blanketed the red rocks and coyote falsettos floated on the wind, Alex glanced toward the galaxies, where beyond the earth's atmosphere all fell silent in outer space. If he closed his eyes, he could feel the breeze carry him away, into the stars, miles above the world, where peace embraced the soul and all sins were absolved.

Alex massaged the ligaments at the back of his neck. His body felt sore from head to toe, and he'd become aware of the weight of his skull teetering atop his cervical spine. His shoulders were weak from the slack in his posture. He tried to straighten, rolled his shoulders square, but pain shot through his head, and he cringed, his eyes watering.

"God damn," Alex said, and tried not to gasp. The painkillers dulled the intensity for a time, but left him weary and blurred, so he'd skipped the dose before he headed to town. Alex cleared his throat of the bitter aftertaste of tobacco, like the sacrament.

The dry, unleavened wafers—the body of Christ—soaked in tart, red wine—the blood of Christ—stinging his tongue, giving eternal life.

Alex hacked a stream of spit toward a drain cover in the middle of the alleyway, missed by several feet.

Forgive my sins, he'd ask God in silence as he rose from the railing. Alex then followed his father, Dutch, down the aisle, the pews cushioned in maroon velvet. They'd both wait for Alex's mother to sit down first. Jean always wore her pearls on Sunday, her hair styled into a neat flip. Dutch would unbutton his blazer once they were seated. He kept his thick, grey hair slicked back with sweet smelling styling lotion, and often smeared some on Alex's unruly curls before they left for church. Alex couldn't remember ever sitting with Michael, his brother, who stayed in the back row with his friends. Alex would glance over his shoulder, wedged between his parents, envious of the older boys.

His mother would pinch his thigh. "Turn around and pay attention." Alex would obey, but he'd only pretend to pray when they all kneeled again.

Alex hadn't attended church services since he left Cleveland. Not in ten years. But sometimes, when the chorus inside his mind increased to an unbearable range, Alex would slip inside the chapel at the village, not far from the restaurant. The whitewashed adobe walls and stained glass windows calmed Alex the moment he entered the sanctuary. He'd sit in the back row, the pews leather, and ask God to quiet the voices.

"Lord, I wait for you," he prayed. "I know I'm not supposed to say I'll pay you back for these wrongs. But with all my heart, I wish I could. I'll work with my hands, like I've read in the scriptures. I'll work hard, so you might forgive me."

Alex stayed at a handful of dusty, worn-out motels when he first arrived in Arizona. The seedier the place, the more likely he'd find a Bible tucked in the nightstand. For the prostitutes and drug addicts, the sinners, the downtrodden, Alex supposed. In time he found work, built a new life. But even so, the voices returned, spoke out of turn, shouted over one another, crowded against the walls of his mind. They taunted him, frustrated him, and angered him. Alex would sit inside the chapel until the voices were quiet again.

He'd be okay then, for a while.

Alex clenched his teeth now, and released a final drag of smoke and then flicked the butt near the trash containers against the wall. He ground it out beneath his heel and bent to brush the dust from his boots before his shift. Alex also tended horses for a wealthy L.A. couple a few miles from town. He was no cowboy, only a caretaker, but his boots were as worn and his skin as leathery as a man who'd ranched his whole life.

Alex hauled the backdoor open and let it bounce against a large bucket that kept it propped halfway. He grabbed his timecard, punched-in, the time clock sometimes required a swift whack, but it worked fine today. He was early, not a big surprise. He'd often arrive up to thirty minutes before his shift. Except this afternoon, he'd rested on a bench under a lofty sycamore, too shaky to notice when a bus stopped in front of him. After he glanced up, Alex kept his boots planted in the red dirt.

"Sorry," he shouted to the driver. "I don't need a ride."

He'd tried to shake the vertigo for days. The dizzy spells felt debilitating when they came on.

"You sure?" The driver kept the door open.

Alex waved him off. "I'm fine," he said. But, the driver waited. And once Alex realized he was in no shape to walk any further, he climbed aboard.

At the restaurant, Alex still felt a bit shaken, but better now. The kitchen was abuzz. He'd missed the familiar clang of pots and pans on the grill. Glad he got there on time, Alex grinned when he heard the jovial laugh of his boss, Carlos, coming from the chef's kitchen. Thick, spicy scents of cilantro and red peppers floated above the greasy, stagnant air inside the dishwasher's station, and melded together to create a pungent odor that stuck to everything. Whatever brushed against the peppery haze, clothing, hair, absorbed it. And even after washing up, sometimes there'd still be a faint reminder, from deep inside the pores especially after a busy night.

"Ain't nothing compared to the foulness of a barn when the livestock ain't been let out," Alex said one night, using his best cowboy voice, half joking, half trying to impress the pretty young hostess who'd complained. He'd sniffed the back of his hand. "Can't even smell it."

Strong odors of work didn't bother Alex. He only noticed the difference when he came upon something sweet smelling, like fresh blooms on desert flowers after the rain or a woman's perfume in line at the grocery store. Otherwise, Alex was a working guy, and he didn't mind sweat and getting dirty, as long as he had work.

Alex grabbed a clean apron from a hook as he passed the sinks. A man who once bused tables, hands crooked with age, stacked clean plates onto a cart, his silver hair covered by a white bandana.

"*Hola*, Miguel," Alex said, the older man only spoke Spanish.

Miguel straightened up and motioned to Alex. "*Cómo te sientes?*" He asked Alex how he was feeling.

4

Alex touched the gauze bandage on his forehead. "Good, no *hay problema*." He rolled his eyes, tied the apron tight around his waist and headed down a short hallway toward the prep kitchen. When he glanced back, the old man still had his eyes on him, so Alex smiled, and Miguel went back to work.

The dinner crowd would arrive soon. Friday nights, customers often waited up to an hour for a table. Carlos, head chef and owner, was known for his delicious, authentic, Mexican-style cuisine.

Alex idled near the chef's kitchen, where his boss adjusted the flames on the grill.

"Hey," Carlos said over his shoulder. "Fresh tomatoes in the walk-in." Carlos seemed stumpy against tall, thin Alex. In fact, Alex stood out from everyone who worked there, give or take a few local college kids on summer break. Otherwise, Alex worked aside a handful of Mexican immigrants, a few with questionable green cards, but Carlos with his big-heart didn't always follow the rules. Alex liked most of them, but he only socialized with Carlos outside work.

"Some peppers, too," Carlos said. "Organic supplier was here, left you a mess of clean containers on the counter." Then Carlos tossed a dozen or more marinated chicken breasts onto the grill. The sizzle of the flames released a smoky haze up into the whoosh of the exhaust fan.

"Got it," Alex said, as he tied a bandana around his head, careful to tuck his long braid underneath.

The main kitchen connected to the dining room by a narrow cutout in the wall. A stainless steel ledge held warm plates for waiters to serve. Alex worked across the hall, nearby if Carlos or the assistant cooks needed supplies. At the end of the galley between the two kitchens, the busboys shouldered their way through a swinging door to clean tables.

"Dude, you need a haircut," Carlos said, leaning away from the steam off the chicken, his grin affable, but also a bit probing. But Alex expected as much since he'd come back so soon.

One of the assistant cooks chuckled. Alex expected that too, his hair always a topic of conversation amongst the cooks. They'd called Alex, *chica*—the Spanish word for girl. Everyone would have a good laugh, but Alex never cut his hair. And Carlos said fine as long as he kept it covered. The assistant cook turned back to the grill and flipped a rib eye over the flames. Alex barely knew him. He was more skilled than the other assistant working that night, a short, wiry guy, more Alex's age, early forties, who always talked baseball. He looked like he wanted to laugh now, too.

And Carlos was still grinning. "You look like some old, hippy guitar player."

Alex smiled and played a few chords on his air guitar. But, Carlos turned around focused on the grill again, turning chicken.

Hectic nights were just fine with Alex. He wasn't a fan of idle time, the busier the better. He slipped inside the prep-kitchen, cleared the large island of plastic containers, and stacked them on a set of metal shelves under the window.

Now and then, if they were both off the same night, Alex would have dinner with Carlos and his family. That's where he injured his head. He'd followed the doctor's instructions, rested a few days, but though his head still ached, Alex couldn't afford to miss another shift. So he was back. And nobody needed to know otherwise.

Alex flipped the latch on the window with a mop handle, and the rectangular frame of etched glass fell open on a thin chain. One of ten windows created by a local artist set and flashed into the building's stucco sidewall, the only window inside the prep kitchen. The other nine lined the same wall high above the dining room tables. Similar misty vineyard scenes on the picture windows lined the front of the building, shaded by a vine-covered overhang above the outdoor patio. Before Carlos bought the place, the previous owner ran an Italian café and the prep kitchen had been part of the bar. Carlos enclosed the space and moved the bar along the opposite wall, with no windows, since the wall stood flush against the neighboring building. Alex thought it a waste, the beautiful etched glass hidden away where nobody could see it, although the window served him well on hot days. The chef's kitchen felt like an inferno at times, the air-conditioner never enough. Alex would take the tiny window in the smaller kitchen any day.

The room spun around Alex after he opened the window. Steady again, Alex rinsed his hands, and then began to sharpen the knives he'd use that night.

At the end of each shift, Alex scrubbed the counters, sink, utensils, knives, and then mopped the floor. His work area was tight, but adequate. He kept a fan going while he chopped and sliced. The rhythm lulled him into a near hypnotic state.

"Hey, baby," a woman's voice, sounded from across the room.

Startled, Alex dropped the chef's knife on the butcher-block. The knife bounced onto the island, and clanged against the stainless steel counter, but Alex caught it, grabbed hold of the polymer handle before the knife ricocheted onto the floor.

He pointed the sturdy carbon blade in her direction. Sonia. He thought he'd gotten rid of her weeks ago.

Chapter 2
Margaret

Margaret remembered her car as she stood outside the door to her hotel room. But she wouldn't go back for it, not right now.

She tightened the pale-grey shawl around her shoulders, the desert air cooler than earlier in the afternoon when she first arrived from Flagstaff.

"I'd like a quiet room, please," Margaret said, when she'd made the reservation. She found her room in a peaceful spot, tucked away from the main lobby and spa, far from the pool. She planned to sleep late, and explore the area in the afternoon if she felt compelled. Otherwise, a massage and a few laps in the pool, her only agenda.

The resort was surrounded by red rock formations, easy to see from Margaret's balcony. A pathway beneath her room followed the curve of the property down along the edges of the resort. At first, when driving up, Margaret slowed down captivated by the illusion of beautiful, well-designed subterranean structures built right into the hillsides.

She had taken the scenic route through Oak Creek Canyon to Sedona, a beautiful drive abundant with wildflowers that blanketed the forest of lofty pines. With all the ripened foliage, it seemed as if someone had scattered vivid floral-patterned rugs along the grounds of the woods.

She stopped several times to snap photos in the Coconino National Forest, trees the color of mature limes and olives, shifting to blood orange and ginger, a balance of intense hues juxtaposed against the spectacular sandstone hillsides.

Autumn, in all its glory, surrounded Margaret the entire way, something she'd taken for granted in the Midwest, and sometimes even now, living in Southern California. On her journey through the canyon, Margaret found it impossible to ignore the colors. She never expected such a spectacle in the desert. But in the upper Sonoran Desert, mountain ranges jutted up from vast desert plains with streams and rivers cutting through valleys thick with vegetation.

After a series of hairpin turns, the route settled into a winding road alongside Oak Creek. Margaret opened the sunroof to take in the fresh air, let her long, blondish-red hair flow free in the breeze. With each mile, she felt more relaxed. Her husband, Henry, was right—she did need a few days to herself.

But now, outside the door to her hotel room, digging through her purse for the key, she wasn't so sure. Margaret still felt shocked by a man she saw in town. Shaken and unable to calm down, she dumped the contents of her purse onto the ground. She found the key, and then jammed everything back inside her bag before going inside.

Her bed had been turned down and the drapes drawn. Quiet music filled the air. Margaret closed the door behind her and stood in the middle of the room as if trying to remember why she was there. The scene from the alleyway ran over and over in her mind. Her hands trembled. She folded her fingers together, massaged her palms, and then slipped her wedding band from her left hand and placed it on the desk with her purse.

Like with yoga, Margaret took a deep breath and blew it out as she made her way to the bathroom. She twisted the tub faucet to warm. The water ran as she used the lavatory. Then she leaned against the sink, and read the labels on the sample-sized shampoo and conditioner. She found one for body wash and squeezed the container under the rush of water. She closed the door, dimmed the lights, slipped off her dress and sandals, unhooked her bra, and then shimmied out of her lace panties into the tranquil suds. She heard the muted ring of her cell phone inside her purse on the desk.

"Not now, Henry." She'd call him later.

Margaret stretched her leg toward the faucet and used her foot to shut it off, then rested her head against the back of the tub, surrounded by amber-colored tiles. She glanced at the sink area, noticed the same pattern, and then the oversized mirror framed in heavy oak. She wondered if the rich tones would look good in their master bathroom. Margaret already had the floors stained a dark finish. Most of their furnishings were made from rustic, salvaged wood, a bit dramatic but a décor she loved. She'd have to ask about those tiles.

Wait. What am I thinking?

Margaret closed her eyes, and tried to clear her mind. She needed to focus on what had happened in town, not decorating.

Oh, God. Henry, come get me.

Margaret knew she was in trouble. She'd done this before, noticed men who reminded her of her first husband, Daniel Waterson. But it was never Danny. He was dead. He died ten years ago, a victim of the World Trade Center attacks in New York City.

Now, in the hot tub, steam fogging the mirror, she played it all back in her mind, and realized she'd only seen a glimpse of him at the restaurant. And outside in the alleyway, the dim light kept her from getting a good look. Margaret cringed thinking about how she'd acted like a maniac, grabbed for the busboy, interrogated him before she rushed outside.

Go see, go see, a voice kept saying.

The busboy told Margaret the man who worked in the kitchen, was called Alex, and he was on a break. But when Margaret found him, she stopped short and hid in the shadows, and witnessed him in the middle of a heated encounter with a young woman. Margaret saw him blow smoke in the air, the same way Daniel did when they were together.

Was that really Danny?

She hadn't thought about him in so long. Which seemed strange, because for years, Daniel was all she thought about. But since moving to California, she'd been so busy and her new life had helped her move on from his death. Yet, that man she saw in Sedona stopped Margaret dead in her tracks.

Come get me, Henry. I'm in trouble.

Chapter 3
Alex

Sonia acted as if they were still together. She shifted closer inside the kitchen. Alex gripped the knife, white knuckles. A small cramp formed along the inside of his wrist. Sonia stopped on the other side of the island, and rested her palms on the countertop.

Alex relaxed, placed the knife back on the butcher block, and turned to pull the handle on the walk-in. Halfway inside, he propped the thick insulated door against his boot as he reached for the tomatoes. He let the door slam shut, his eyes fixed on the sink. For a moment, Alex fantasized about shoving Sonia inside the fridge and holding the door shut until she froze to death.

"Why didn't you call?" she said.

Other violent ideas had crossed his mind lately, not just about Sonia. He'd wondered what it would feel like to be hit by a bus when the local transit pulled up to him at the bench. Onboard, he felt the urge to shove through the folding door, and dive into oncoming traffic. He'd closed his eyes, leaned back against the teal blue vinyl and imagined the cool steel bumper of a truck crushing his torso, as the broad tires pulverized his body.

There were nightmares, too. Visions of falling from a cliff, jagged rocks, the angry grey ocean dragging him out to sea. Enormous beasts with sharp teeth chased after him in darkened woods. Another buried alive. The scenes so vivid, he couldn't go back to sleep.

Last night, he'd taken the rifle from the locked tack room and shot several rounds into the air when he'd heard coyotes off in the distance. If he could have, he would've shot them all dead. The howling drove him crazy, his headache so painful he nearly turned the gun on himself. He'd taken extra pain medication, and passed out until first light.

At the sink now, Alex used his elbow to flip the valve on the faucet, and sunk the container of tomatoes deep into the basin under the rush of water. He continued to ignore Sonia. Her constant pursuit, her insecurities, impervious to anything other than her own misguided reality.

When he finished, she had gone. After the tomatoes, Alex sliced yellow and red peppers. Then prepared salsas, filled bins with salad greens, combined ingredients for soups, chopped onions, minced garlic and steamed rice adding fresh-cut herbs.

Deep into the groove, Alex noticed a busboy headed toward the fridge. He'd told Diego to stay out of the prep-kitchen and before he could tell him again, Diego spoke first.

"Man, you deaf or something?" Diego's thick accent made it difficult to decipher if he'd said dead or deaf. "Need more guacamole," he said, a thin veil of perspiration covered his brown face, as if he'd walked through a cloud of mist on his way into Alex's workspace.

Carlos said he planned to install a cooling system above the tables out on the sidewalk, since summer got hot. But, he hadn't done it again this year, and it was already September, anyhow.

Alex grabbed a container from the island and handed it to Diego, and then nodded to the younger cook across the hall waiting on the fresh batch. Within seconds, Alex was back to work, slicing chicken for fajitas. He didn't stop until his break two hours later.

Outside, behind the restaurant, Alex leaned against the stucco wall, one boot up behind him. The sky seemed to be splattered with stars as Alex searched the constellations. He pulled out a pack of cigarettes, his second and final of the day. He'd quit years ago, too expensive, but he allowed himself one before his shift and another on his break.

From the back exit Carlos stepped down next to Alex. "How's it going?" He looked like a sausage squeezed inside his chef's jacket.

"Good," Alex said. "Got through most of the produce. Still some beef and pork to cut."

Raising an eyebrow, Carlos kept his dark brown eyes on Alex. "Dude, you know what I mean."

Alex tried to smile, but knew Carlos would see through it, so he lowered his head, and tapped the pack of cigarettes inside his palm. "I'm fine." He knew what Carlos meant.

"You shouldn't be back so soon," Carlos said, and used the back of his sleeve to wipe his brow. He kept his dark, thick hair trimmed neat below his white chef's hat. "That was a hell of a fall you took."

Alex had gone for a test ride on an old Husqvarna out behind Carlos's house. He rode fast, trying to run the dust out of the lines. The sunset blinded Alex to the sudden dip in the desert floor, and when he struck the deep gap, he flew over the handlebars. It all happened so fast he couldn't remember much of anything.

Carlos had lifted Alex, unconscious for a time, from a prickly pear cactus. The scratches on his lower back were still tender, but the serious gash on his forehead had required several stitches. He tapped his finger against the gauze, the tape still secure. Alex refused the CAT scan, so the doctor instructed him to return to the hospital if he experienced nausea, dizziness, or headaches, which Alex ignored. He paid cash for the visit, the money he'd saved for the bike.

"You were flying," Carlos said. "I didn't know that bike could go so fast."

The engine seemed to be in good shape, but needed a new carburetor. "It needs some work, but I don't have the money now."

"Dude, take it and pay me later." Carlos didn't have the same heavy accent as Diego. He'd lived in Arizona for years.

"I don't know," Alex said. He didn't like to owe people money.

"It's okay," Carlos said. "Angelina wants the garage cleaned out." He lifted a trash can lid from the ground nearby, and covered a can, then shoved it closer to the wall using the side of his stocky leg. "You take the bike," he said. "Pay me when you can."

13

Carlos wiped more sweat from his face with the bandana around his neck. "Seriously, dude, you'll be doing me a favor."

Alex knew he wouldn't win. Maybe he could do the repairs, sell it fast, and give Carlos his cut. He had a stash of money in a coffee can hidden in the barn, enough for some parts. Alex didn't have a bank account. Didn't like to be in the system. Carlos paid him under the table, which he appreciated, but he wasn't sure he wanted more favors from his boss.

"Guess I could pay you when I sell it." Alex pulled a cigarette out of the half-empty packet and lit the end with a plastic lighter he kept in his front pocket.

"Deal." Carlos grabbed the pack, and lit one on the end of Alex's. He blew smoke into the air and then shook his head, smiling. "Clean out the garage..." Carlos said, with a chuckle. "Stop smoking." He laughed even harder. "*Aye yi*, Angelina is on my ass lately."

"Smart lady." Alex tried to suppress his own laughter, which started him coughing. Every hack vibrated inside his skull. He stayed against the wall to control the spinning.

"Maybe you should quit, too," Carlos said, and snorted as he laughed. "Don't tell Angelina," he said, waving his cigarette. "She'll kill me."

Alex liked Angelina. She was way too good for Carlos, but Carlos seemed to know it. Tenderhearted and graceful, Angelina's shiny, black hair hung to her waist. The customers loved her. And when sometimes she worked at the restaurant, she'd treat everyone like family. Carlos, a first-generation Mexican immigrant, had done well. He'd married an angel. Owned a successful business. Had five kids, and his widower-father, eighty-six, lived with them.

The other night, while Carlos rolled the motorcycle around from the garage, Alex spoke to the old grandfather in the backyard. The kids kicked around a soccer ball on the lawn, bounced it off their heads and knees, while Alex practiced his Spanish.

"*Jefe*," Carlos' father said, as he patted his chest.

"Father?" Alex knew. He'd heard the word before.

"*Si*, yes," he said, and smiled at Alex, missing a bottom front tooth. The old man sat in an aluminum folding-chair, and

14

peeled a tomato, sprinkled it with salt, taking a big bite while he watched the kids for Angelina.

"*Gringo*," Alex said, pointing to himself as he sat down next to the old man.

He wore his silvery hair slicked back the same as Alex's dad. "Ha!" the old man said, and then squeezed Alex by the shoulder. "Friend."

"*Gracias, mi amigo.*" Alex glanced over and tipped his head.

"*Muy bien,*" the old man said. "You talk good."

Angelina had something simmering on the stove inside the kitchen of their modest home. The delicious aromas wafted out through the screen door onto the patio where the two men sat.

"*Huele bien,*" Alex referred to the wonderful, peppery scent.

"*Ella es mejor cocinero que mi hijo,*" the grandfather said, and then chuckled, nearly dumping the peeled tomato.

"No *comprendo.*" Alex didn't understand.

"Angelina better cook than Carlos." The old man grinned, and raised a finger to his lips. "Don't tell," he said, the same way Carlos did about the cigarette.

But the old man was right. Angelina owned the recipes. Carlos had talent, but Angelina was the real chef with secret ingredients handed down in her family for generations. Carlos hit the jackpot when he married her.

Alex glanced toward the sky outside the restaurant, nearly finished with his cigarette. When he lowered his gaze, there stood Sonia again.

Chapter 4
Margaret

Margaret closed her eyes, and listened to the music floating under the door from the other room, muted tones from the opera, *Carmen*. She hummed along until the end, and then waited for a selection from Mozart's, *Figaro* to begin.

She felt herself begin to relax, the lavender scented water helped calm her nerves. Again, she thought about the man at the restaurant. In complete contrast to Daniel, the man had a thin muscular build, yet something about his movements reminded her of Daniel.

It's so peaceful here.

She tried hard to change the channel in her brain, to forget, and sunk deeper into the water.

Sedona with its red sandstone formations and the absence of heavy traffic like along the Pacific Coast Highway in Laguna Beach seemed ethereal to Margaret, relaxing, the landscape, mystical. Yet, Laguna Beach with its steep hillsides, craggy canyons, coves and ocean views had its own magical qualities. Both settings were natural inspiration for artists. Hundreds of art galleries crammed the streets of Laguna Beach, the same way as galleries in uptown Sedona. Margaret had decided to spend a few days in Sedona because she'd heard about the calming affect of the Sonoran Desert. But she didn't feel calm now, not after seeing that man.

Margaret had hidden in the shadows, like a spy and fled when the man spotted her, afraid to look back that he might follow.

Margaret rushed through town, forgot all about her car, as she hiked back to the resort.

"What is wrong with you?" Margaret's voice echoed against the tiles as she lathered her arms with soap.

She knew better than to go into a darkened back street in a strange town. She'd acted foolish. But danger never crossed her mind at the time. The sudden impulse of that man being Daniel drove her straight out the door to the alleyway. She could have been attacked. The busboy could have set her up. After all, almost flirtatious in the way he spoke, the skinny, mustached man had made her uneasy with his creepy little smirk. But she hadn't cared. She only wanted to get a better look at the man she'd seen inside the kitchen.

Margaret shuddered. This was all so crazy. She needed to pull herself together. She put the soap down, and wrapped her arms across her waist and stretched her legs in the tub.

Stop it. Stop this right now. Danny is dead.

No matter how many times she thought she'd heard Daniel's voice or spotted his double, it wouldn't bring him back. She'd decided long ago to ignore those impulses and face the truth. Daniel Waterson died in the north tower of the World Trade Center ten years ago. Period. The computer records proved he'd signed-in with the receptionist not long before the first plane hit.

Margaret had encouraged the family to plan a memorial service, even though she'd had a strange feeling about his death. But who wouldn't? There was no body to bury, not even a scrap of his clothing. She'd placed their wedding photograph and some small mementos in his coffin. It was like he'd vanished into thin air. Which is what happened to so many on that fateful day. Thousands had disappeared, evaporated into the earth, buried under tons of rubble.

Was it unreasonable to wonder if he'd really died or not? Maybe. Was she being irrational? Maybe. But, the physical resemblance to Danny, the mannerisms, both felt real.

With the anniversary of 9/11 two weeks away, she'd decided against attending the events in New York City. She had no intention of visiting the nightmare of that day ever again. She had a different life now, she'd moved on. But that man in the kitchen was not a figment of her imagination.

Margaret sighed.

I'm remarried, for God's sake.

Her name was Margaret Pierson, now. She owed so much to Henry. He'd saved her, provided the love and security she needed.

Henry.

She'd head home first thing in the morning. But it was weird. The busboy said the man she saw was called Alex.

Why would he change his name? It couldn't be Danny.

Margaret wasn't able get the swinging door at the restaurant out of her mind. The door swung wide open on its hinges, open and close, open and close, open again long enough for her to see a man, like in a silent film, his movements debauched, stilted. He tied his apron in a tight knot. He wore a beard, and long hair tucked under a white headscarf.

Daniel always kept his hair short and neat, visiting the same barber every three weeks.

It's not Danny.

Besides, that man had a deep tan, browner than she'd ever seen Daniel, even in late August at Lake Michigan's shore. Daniel's cheeks were never so hollowed out, like the man in the kitchen. But still? His movements. Uncanny the way he held himself—like Danny.

I'm losing my mind.

Outside in the alleyway, the lamp above the door shone down upon the man, and Margaret could see his profile. He leaned against the building, his foot up on the wall, and held his cigarette beneath his palm, like he did when they were married, to keep the smoke away from her face.

She'd hated Daniel's smoking. His occasional cigarette had grown to a pack a day. He stopped kissing her to avoid her complaints. Margaret always thought he'd quit, but the sand ran out, and all the problems in their marriage were buried with Daniel near Battery Park.

"Danny," Margaret murmured, as she ran her soapy fingers across her chest, tears spilling onto her cheekbones, as if Daniel had died all over again.

Margaret slumped down in the water and washed the tears away, as she cupped a handful to rinse her face.

Maybe the man is Danny's twin.

Once, at a food court, an elderly man sat down at Margaret's table and began eating his lunch before realizing she wasn't whom he thought.

"Oh, my," the old man said, his cheeks warming to a pink, coral color. "You're not my daughter."

People were always saying everyone has an identical twin somewhere in the world, so why not Danny?

Daniel being a twin, maybe, reminded her of the Twins Days Festival her parents had dragged her as a child to in Twinsburg, Ohio. She wanted to be a twin that day. Maybe the hottest weekend of the entire summer. Throngs of mosquitos had nipped at little Maggie's ankles, the red marks lasting for weeks. She was ten years old and fascinated by the sea of twosomes moving around the grounds in a synchronized choreography, gathering in a grassy area. She felt sorry for them, yet self-conscious of her tidy family of three. She stuffed her fists inside the pockets on her gingham shorts, feeling conspicuous without a sibling to walk with, hand-in-hand.

Her parents were at fault. Both college professors, they always traveled to odd places, grown-up places—art festivals, poetry readings, the Amish country, and to see the tall ships. They'd scan the cultural section of The Plain Dealer, and off they'd all go to see award-winning quilts or a new exhibit at the museum. The only interest for Maggie, the ice cream she'd been promised.

A glassblower, once, tried to convince Maggie to help him, but she'd hidden behind her father, afraid of the fiery wand. She'd wanted to be at Amy Carmichael's, roller-skating to 72's on a portable record player attached to a long extension cord plugged into the wall of Amy's garage.

"Can we please go, Daddy?" she'd pleaded, but by the time they arrived home, night had fallen, the extension cord rolled-up and stored inside Amy's closed garage.

In those days, Margaret wished they'd go on vacations to Florida or the Jersey Shore, like other families. But they stuck to assorted daytrips around northeast Ohio. She didn't mind when younger, but as a teenager, she felt ridiculous. Her parents detested hotel rooms, thought they were a waste of money. "We have plenty to do right here," her father had said when Margaret suggested Niagara Falls, which wasn't even that far.

Nevertheless, in September, when Margaret started the fifth grade, her teacher, Mrs. Harrington, asked the class to write a story about something they did that summer. Margaret sharpened her pencil, flipped her braids over her shoulders and proceeded to fill an entire page about longing to have a sibling. She told about how those children, and especially twins, would never be lonely, never fall asleep by themselves, never ride alone in the back seat, never have to keep their own secrets, or read stories aloud to an empty room.

Margaret took a deep breath, the water cooler now. She'd get out soon, but just a bit longer.

Her parents had phoned Jacob before leaving for Arizona to wish him good luck at college. Margaret hadn't had time to talk to them while packing the car for the trip. Why did she always forget them lately? She couldn't blame it on being busy. Her parents had simply slipped to the back of her mind since she left Cleveland.

Losing Daniel was tough for them. They'd loved him like a son, often looking the other way when he drank too much. She hadn't told them how bad it had become. When Margaret couldn't leave her bed at first, so distraught after Daniel died, her parents tried to help. But they weren't strong enough to shield Margaret. On 9/11, the world seemed to have entered a sinister place, a horrid, violent era where people blew apart other people's lives, where everything seemed out of control with hatred and vicious aggression. And Margaret had only wanted to hide from it all.

As the weeks dragged on, Margaret realized she had to be the strong one, for her parents, and everyone. But she couldn't keep worrying about them. In order to heal, she needed to think about herself for once.

Her parents were retired now and every March they traveled to California for a weeklong stay, each time their ankles swollen from the flight, their world overwhelmed by the traffic. They were crazy about their grandson, squeezed into the bleachers to watch Jacob play volleyball. They loved strolling along the shoreline collecting shells at sunset, the sand sticking to her mother's gabardine slacks.

Margaret thought about the Twins Day Festival again, about eating lunch at the Cracker Barrel afterward. She'd tried to focus on her book, a Trixie Belden mystery, but kept spying the sets of twins coming and going, while her parents debated curriculum or some such thing.

She wanted to call Jake now, to ask if he'd been lonely as an only child. But, she'd left her phone in the other room.

And besides, he was fine. More than fine. Jacob was independent and strong, and not worried about her one bit, that was for sure. When he'd left her in the university parking lot, Jacob headed straight toward the dorm without looking back. She'd sat in her car for a while, with tears in her eyes, before heading to Sedona.

"Oh, Jacob, your mom's a mess." Margaret laughed at her silliness. She was just having a slight nervous breakdown over her only child going off to college. That had to be it.

Chapter 5
Alex

Sonia sauntered toward them like a black cat sizing up her prey, slow and deliberate, the seductress, but kept her eyes on Alex. She wasn't giving up easy. Her behavior didn't surprise Alex, but he was with his boss. Couldn't she see that?

He knew he needed to talk to her, but not right now, not there.

"Dude, seriously," Carlos said. "Tell her she can't walk in the backdoor like she works here." Carlos grounded out his cigarette under his high-top sneaker, and kept an eye on Sonia as he went inside.

Alex smirked at Carlos playing the tough guy. But he dropped his grin when he glanced back at Sonia, and then blew a final line of smoke in her direction.

Sonia stepped through the haze, a few feet short of Alex, hands on her hips. She wore tight black shorts that skimmed the top of her lean legs, and a white t-shirt with the name of the restaurant where she worked printed across her chest. Generous cleavage spilled out from the V-neck. She looked young — too young.

"I only came inside because I was worried about you." Her red lips formed a pout, her black cropped-hair tucked behind her ears.

"Don't worry about me." Alex wasn't sure how she knew about the accident. He didn't talk to her anymore. Didn't meet her after work and walk her home. Not for a while, now.

Sonia was one of those girls who wasn't pretty in the face, but grew on a man after he noticed her great body, which Alex had done right away. He wasn't interested in a face he could look at for a lifetime.

Her place wasn't far from town, an apartment over the garage of an artist's home –- one room with an antique iron bed, her white cat lounging on a chair in the corner. She cooked him breakfast in her makeshift kitchen—hot plate, microwave oven, small fridge like in motel rooms, sink in the closet-sized bathroom.

Ever since he broke it off with her, she stalked him. Once he caught her near his place outside town, grabbed her by the arm, told her to go home. She wasn't out for a walk, like she'd said. Nobody goes out there since the highway leads to nowhere really, just past some hilly areas with fancy, gentleman's ranches for folks who kept livestock, but didn't ride much. And Sonia didn't ride at all.

"I care about you, Alex."

He flicked the butt of his cigarette toward her, missed her ankle by a few inches. "I like being on my own." Alex hoped she'd get the message this time. He'd begun to notice how ugly she was.

Sonia turned, flipped her bobbed hair and headed back toward her work. Alex tried not to think about her naked body sprawled across the bed in her tiny apartment, or how the street lamp from outside danced along her pale skin, highlighting every perfect curve.

Sonia slowed down on her way across the alley and glanced over her shoulder with cunning eyes as if she'd read Alex's mind. "You don't have to be alone anymore," she said, sounding sultry and dark like the black cat she was.

Then she stopped and turned to face Alex, as if she'd hit her mark on a stage. The light from the rooftop had a cover to shield the rays from the sky. But bright enough to shine against Sonia like a soft spotlight in a theatre. She turned her forearm over in full view. Alex could see a new tattoo, scripted words. He thought her tattoos were sexy. She had a delicate dove on her opposite arm, and angel wings stamped across her lower back. And he couldn't resist the small red heart on her lower pelvis.

23

Whoever the artist was, they were far more talented than the guy who'd inked Alex's arms, the images distorted and out of proportion.

But what do you expect when you're shitfaced in a tiny border town?

Alex shook his head now, enough for the pain to return as he tried to focus. He could see the words now. In black ink, clear enough to read from where he stood.

I LOVE ALEX

Alex stepped forward. "What the hell?" He felt a flash of hot rage, a sudden impulse to grab Sonia by the head and smash her face into the ground.

But she slithered away without a word, and slipped back inside the door where she worked.

Alex almost lost control and went after her, but took a deep breath, instead, and reined in his temper.

She's crazy.

The moon had risen over Sedona and the sky had faded to dark blue. Alex turned around and kicked the bucket holding the back door open, sent it flying into the air to land against a dumpster.

"Hey," Diego said, as he caught the door and pushed it open.

Alex shoved past Diego, who grabbed at his sleeve, but Alex pulled free. Diego let the door slam shut as he followed Alex inside.

"Hey, you have problems?" Diego yelled loud enough in his bad English for Miguel to notice and glance over his shoulder from the sinks.

"Only with you," Alex said, humidity emanated from the warm spray at the sinks as if he'd stepped into a sauna. Miguel, dripping with sweat, stopped the water and stared at Alex like he was crazy.

"Was to tell you about the lady," Diego said. "She knows you." Diego turned back toward the exit, kicked the door wide open, and pulled a handkerchief from his pocket to wipe his forehead as he stepped out into the night.

Alex had hit his limit, and caught the door before it closed. He didn't care if he knocked Diego clear off the stoop. But the busboy was already seated on the bottom step.

"What are you talking about?" Alex said, as he leaned out the door. "What lady?" he demanded. "Sonia?"

"No, not that dirty whore." Diego stood up to grab the bucket.

Alex wanted to hit Diego, not because of what he said about Sonia. He didn't like Diego, that's why. Never did. Diego always kissed Carlos's ass and jumped into conversations that didn't concern him. An illegal immigrant, Alex hated his type, stealing jobs. Diego's poor English took up Alex's time. And Alex didn't have time for Diego's idiot way of pronouncing things.

"I've got work to do," Alex said. "Just tell me who she was."

"Some lady eating dinner." Diego walked back to Alex, turned the bucket over, propped it against the door, and then sat down on the step again.

"How could she see me?" Alex said. The prep kitchen remained closed off from the dining area, and Alex had stayed busy inside there all afternoon into the early evening. "Maybe she meant one of the cooks."

Alex didn't know many women in Sedona, other than Angelina and a few waitresses he'd slept with before. He kept to himself, worked at the restaurant, and tended the weekend estate owned by a couple that only travelled to Sedona a few times a year. The place remained quiet most of the time.

Alex shrugged, decided Diego hadn't understood the woman, and then headed back inside toward the sink area. The dishwasher nearly sprayed Alex in the face as he worked the overhead hose on a sink full of empty containers.

Diego yelled something else from outside. Alex wasn't sure if he'd heard him right over the rush of the water and his damn accent, so Alex stuck his head out the door again.

"What did you say?"

Diego whistled a tune from where he sat, but then stopped and glanced over his shoulder at Alex.

"She said you looked like someone she used to know."

"Yeah, I heard that part," Alex said, as he motioned to Diego to repeat what he'd said before.

"Daniel Waterson," Diego said.

Alex had never heard Diego speak so clear before. He was stunned.

"Told her your name's Alex," Diego said, picking at something on the bottom of his shoe.

Daniel Waterson.

Alex hadn't heard that name in ten years.

"Where is she now?"

"She left."

Alex stood under the light above the door, his head throbbing. He glanced between the buildings and noticed someone in the alleyway, an image lurking in the shadows.

A woman.

Margaret.

He'd know her anywhere.

Chapter 6
Margaret

Everyone went through this, letting go of a child. Margaret knew she'd make the transition, like other mothers did. But right now, she wished Jacob was still a little boy and they were both at home with Henry. But Jacob was at the university in Flagstaff and she was 17 miles south in a hotel room, crying over his dead father.

It's just a nervous breakdown, Henry. I'll tell you all about it sometime.

Margaret worked lather through her hair, and thought about the Daniel she had known. His restlessness, his short fuse, and how he'd begun to drink more. Danny had become quieter, edgier over time, his sulking a loathsome habit. He'd hide away in the den, come home late. She'd been worried about him. He wasn't the Daniel she knew anymore.

This other Daniel she saw at the restaurant, his double, had aged, but not in the way other people's faces mature with time, more of a weathered appearance, someone who'd had a tough time, a lonely life. She found herself drawn to this other Danny, whoever he was, if only because of his demeanor. She hadn't thought about how mean Danny had become in a long time. It seemed funny how people pushed away the bad memories and remembered only the good about a person after they died. But, this man at the restaurant had stirred Margaret's memories of the real Danny, the man who had made her cry all the time, ignored her, and often lost his temper.

Margaret recognized the same mannerisms, and rejection of others, which Daniel had begun to exhibit during those final years before 9/11. The way that man dismissed the woman in the alley and shoved his way back inside the restaurant, something about the way he behaved made her remember Daniel. He'd blown her off so many times and yelled at her, stormed out, slept in the den.

Daniel had broken her heart hundreds of times in their final years together. Watching that man bully people in the alleyway was as real to Margaret as the touch of her skin.

Lying back, submerging her entire body, Margaret rinsed away the shampoo, her lengthy strands floating in the bath water like a forest of kelp skimming the edges of her face in a shallow sea. Margaret let her body float. She imagined her eyelids, the bridge of her nose, her cheekbones and the tip of her chin as tiny islands above the surface. She thought about Maui and her honeymoon with Henry, how they stood together at the edge of the shore.

"It's strange," Henry had said. "These islands are like a tiny dot in the middle of the Pacific."

Margaret wasn't afraid, even though she slipped her arm through Henry's like an anchor. He kept her steady as she glanced out across the ocean, the horizon feeling a million miles away.

She gazed up at the ceiling and remembered when she'd given birth to Jacob. Danny had held tight to her hand as their son took his first breath. Nervous with Jacob at first, afraid of making a mistake, Margaret felt relieved when Danny came back to the hospital the next morning. The nurse was instructing her on how to get the baby to latch-on. It's all very natural, she'd said. Danny had hung back near the door. Margaret smiled at him, waving him over. But he stood his ground until the nurse left.

"Danny, you need to hear this stuff, too. I don't know what I'm doing, so I hope you were listening." Nursing like a champ now, Jacob had latched on just fine with the nurse's help. But during the night, Margaret felt certain Jacob might starve with her lack of breastfeeding skills. "He's so tiny and I feel like I'm going to break him."

"You're doing fine. You worry too much. Women have been having babies forever. You'll get the hang of it." But Danny went to the window, distracted by something outside. "I hope they don't tow my car. I left it in short-term parking. How long till you're ready?"

Margaret watched him stare at the parking lot.

"Well?" He'd sounded impatient, like he needed to be someplace else, which made Margaret sad. But he didn't notice.

Once they were on their way, after Danny left the room several times for coffee and to move the car to long-term parking, and when they were all strapped in and heading home, Margaret sensed something had changed. Danny acted different now, distant, and faraway somehow. But she didn't say anything. Instead, she kept an eye on Jacob who slept the whole way home.

After Danny died, Margaret spent the first year breathing so shallow, her fingertips were numb and her chest often heavy with pain. She'd only wanted to sleep, for it was in her dreams where she found peace. During the day she found herself tangled in mix of emotions. The pendulum inside her heart shifted between the love she felt for Daniel and a deep weariness from never feeling loved in return.

Margaret sat up, leaned her head against the back of the bathtub and covered her forehead with a soaked washcloth, letting it drip over her eyelids. She wished she could stop the cloud from rolling over her now. There was no use for it anymore.

Henry, please come.

Margaret pictured Henry in his office at home, preparing for his conference, the windows wide open, a breeze drifting up the steep hillside from the ocean, the desk lamp glowing, coffee mug on his right, his warm brown eyes fixed on the computer screen.

I love you, Henry.

"You should take a few days to relax before driving home," Henry had suggested. "Go to one of those spas," he'd said, clearing a strand of hair from her face while they stood outside on the deck, watching the sunset. "You're a great mom."

"Thanks," she'd said, kissing his hand. His hands were one of her favorite things about Henry. Strong and warm, the same hands that saved lives when he performed surgeries. She always felt safe when he held her hand in his own. And she loved when

Henry said she was a good mom. It meant the world to her that he noticed. "You know, I think I will stop in Sedona."

Margaret felt open to new possibilities those days. She enjoyed the warmer weather and busier lifestyle in California. Her life in Cleveland had been predictable, dictated by the seasons— the winters wore thin on her nerves. She loved being outside all the time now. She walked and exercised year round. Life was good. Every morning, she'd sip her coffee on the deck, and viewed the white water break along the shoreline.

She'd thought about going back to work, maybe part-time at first, or to graduate school. She wasn't sure, but Henry had told her to take her time, do whatever felt right.

The last of the life insurance was invested into Jake's college fund, and the little savings she had, from before getting married again, had run out. She thought she might like to earn a wage, contribute to Henry's and her retirement account.

Margaret worked as an administrative assistant for a school district in the Cleveland area during Jacob's primary and middle school years. She earned a Bachelor's Degree in Business, but the marketing position she'd held before Jake came along, never felt like a good fit. If anything, she thought she might want to teach, like her parents.

"Whatever you want to do, whatever you need," Henry said, as they gazed at the shimmering, orange sun melting into the ocean.

Daniel would never have said the same thing, always impatient and demanding with Margaret. But, she knew with Henry, she could take her time and find her way.

When she thought she saw Danny at the restaurant, she felt her heart race as the door swung closed and opened one final time, and he was gone. He'd vanished again. The same familiar wave of panic washed over her, as she chased after him.

Margaret shivered. She unplugged the drain, grabbed a towel, and wrapped it tight around her body. She stepped from the bath and noticed her reflection in the foggy mirror above the sink.

I hope you'll understand, Henry.

"I know it was Danny," Margaret said, aloud, droplets beaded up across her shoulders, her eyes glassy and bloodshot. "He's alive."

Chapter 7
Jacob

Jacob only had one decent memory of his dad. They'd gone to an Indian's game together one summer afternoon when he was seven years old. His dad came home early from work for the 1:00 start time. They ate hotdogs, bought t-shirts and caps. The expensive hats, not the adjustable ones, the type of hat where you had to buy your actual size. His dad showed him how to curve the lid, tuck it inside the top for a while. They'd unfolded them later, perfect and rounded, and pulled their hats on at the same time to shade the sun from both sides. Jacob still did the same thing with all his new caps. Even now.

That day at the baseball game was a good day. His dad paid attention to him for once. But it never happened again. And Jacob never told his mother how he really felt about his dad. What was the point? People had a way of placing dead people on pedestals. And his mother had immortalized Daniel Waterson.

Jacob only saw a man who was miserable, and acted like he didn't want to be with them. It didn't bother Jacob anymore. Sure, it did when he was a kid, but he was an adult now, a college freshman and he'd moved passed it a long time ago. Jacob had concluded other people weren't as lucky. Some of his friends had parents who drank or were drug addicts and ruined their lives. At least his dad, although Jacob never said it aloud, had died before he did any real damage.

He still felt that way sometimes, like his dad had done him a favor. But most of the time, Jacob didn't think about him. And then sometimes, even though it pissed him off, he actually missed him.

He'd be back at that baseball game with his dad, rooting for their favorite players, screaming at the top of their lungs when someone hit a homerun, laughing until their sides hurt. Jacob had even sprayed his soda, but his dad just wiped his face with his shirt and they high fived. He still remembered what his dad said. "Good job, Jake, way to spit."

Jacob squeezed between the bags of sheets and towels on the thin, hard mattress where he'd sleep this year. He sniffed twice, the fan on the desk blew against the side of his face making his eyes water. He wouldn't cry. Not for some guy who took him to one lousy baseball game in his whole life, someone who screamed at his mom, someone who drank too much. No, he wouldn't give him the satisfaction. Jacob pulled out a navy blue hand towel from a white plastic bag and wiped his eyes, the paper tag scratching against his face. He glanced around the dorm room. His roommate had already unpacked. Everything put away. He wondered if Mark's dad had helped him move in. There were no parents in the room when Jacob arrived. Just Mark. If he'd driven himself, did his dad help pack the car? Did he buy the car for Mark?

"You know, you're taller than your dad by two inches," his mother had said in the car on their way. "And you walk like him. You both kind of saunter along." His mom smiled as she merged onto the interstate. "You remind me of him when he was in college. You know that's when we started dating, right?"

"Yeah, you've told me that story, Mom." Jacob glanced out the passenger window, more interested in the different types of cactus than hearing the same old thing.

"Probably more times than you wanted to hear. I'm sorry, honey, but I want you to know about your dad."

"It's been a long time," Jacob said. "I'm starting to forget what he looked like." He hoped that would change the subject.

"Well, you got your mop of hair from him, that's for sure." His mom scratched his head, but he pulled away. "Yours is bleached out from the sun, but just as thick."

Whenever his mom talked about his dad, Jacob felt sorry for her. She lived in a dream world. But Jacob knew the truth. His dad's mother, Grandma Jean, told him something that proved it.

"Your dad was a bad seed," she said. "He did some terrible things when he was alive," she said, on her third glass of chardonnay, the two of them alone on the front porch at the family cottage in Michigan. She seemed frail by then, the death of her younger son having taken a toll on her appearance. The deep lines on her face made her look far beyond her sixty years.

Jacob always felt a little frightened of her. She seemed angry all the time, especially when they were alone, and she was harsh with him, criticizing his clothes or his wild curls.

"Your mother needs to cut that awful hair."

When everyone else was around, she'd paint her plastic smile on and talk in a saccharine voice. But even so, Jacob believed her, he only wished she didn't think he was the same way.

"Don't be like him, Jake, be a good boy."

"What terrible things?" Jacob had wanted to know. Even at ten years old, he wasn't afraid of reality. But his grandmother waved him off.

"He did something horrible when he was a teenager, unforgivable, that's why God took him, you know."

She didn't say anymore, but Jacob could see how ashamed she was of her son, that whatever he'd done had been unspeakable. Jacob stopped feeling guilty, right then, about not loving his dad. But, he let his mom pretend Daniel Waterson was a good man. She'd lost so much. When his dad died, at first, Jacob would climb in her bed when he got home from school and watch cartoons while she slept.

He stood up and shoved a bag of clothes out of his way, kicking it toward the closet. Mark's bed was covered in simple white sheets, a solid black comforter, and a single pillow with a red pillowcase. Einstein stared down from a poster tacked above the bed, his tongue hung out, his white hair a mess. The quote read, *"The difference between stupidity and genius is that genius has its limits."*

34

Jacob didn't laugh, but he thought his roommate might think it was funny. He seemed like the studious type with engineering textbooks already lining his desk shelf. Mechanical pencils poked out from a coffee mug with the caption, *Stay Calm And Caffeine On*. His clothes took up exactly half the closet space, all hung in a neat row on wire hangers. Little else appeared other than atop the dresser with a plastic zip-lock bag full of sunflower seeds and a giant-sized container of hand lotion.

Weird.

Jacob hoped Mark wasn't going to be some nightmare roommate like he'd heard about from his friend's siblings. It appeared obvious that Mark was the brainy type, which meant at least he'd be a quiet roommate. Jacob saw no sign of music, no speakers to plug a cell phone into, no TV, no radio. He pulled open the drawer on the right side of Mark's desk. A bottle of tequila rolled forward and clanked against a few shot glasses. Jacob closed the drawer as careful as possible to keep from breaking the glass.

Well, maybe Mark was cooler than Jacob first thought. Just a neat freak, that's all. He found a notepad on his own desk and wrote a quick message that he'd be out for a while and placed it on Mark's desk. Might as well try to be friends. After all, nobody likes to drink alone.

Jacob glanced at his watch, a gift from Henry at graduation. He needed to change and meet his orientation group in the lobby on the main floor. They were going out for pizza. Still wet from the water balloon fight, Jake needed a dry shirt, since his group nailed every field event and won the competition.

Jacob glanced around at the mess of bags and boxes. He grabbed his duffle bag, unzipped the top and pulled out a clean, folded t-shirt. He'd unpack later. He had all weekend until classes started. Right now, he needed to get downstairs. He slipped the shirt over his head, his room key and student ID, both hung from his lanyard. He locked the door behind him and hurried down the three flights of stairs to the lobby.

"Waiting on two more," the group leader said, as Jacob approached. Just then, Jacob's cell phone vibrated in his back pocket.

He guessed it was probably his mom. But he saw Henry's number instead. "Hello?" He motioned to the group leader that he was going outside to talk.

"Hi, buddy," Henry said. "How's life in Flagstaff?"

"Good," Jacob said. "Don't have much time, though. We're going for pizza." The sun had dropped behind the pine trees beyond the buildings.

"That's great. Who's going?"

"My orientation group." Jacob glanced through the glass doors to where the dozen or so students had gathered. They were all laughing about something and he wanted to get back inside. "There was a competition today, and we're the new dorm champions."

"Good for you, Jake. I'm glad. See, it's easy to make friends if you open yourself up to new possibilities."

Jacob knew he'd open himself up to the possibility of partying with his roommate. But he kept that to himself. "Yeah, like you said the other night, I just have to find a good balance."

"Well, Jake, I've got something I need to talk to you about."

"Yeah?" Jake kept an eye on the group. It looked as if they were still waiting on other people.

"I noticed one of your friends in our yard last night."

Oh, crap.

Jacob wondered if Henry had seen Brady, his buddy from volleyball who'd chosen community college and living at home. But Jacob knew it wasn't really a choice since Brady's grades were too low for even a state university. Brady had hidden some leftover beer in their side-yard last night. He'd sent a text to warn Jacob he'd taken off when he heard someone open the side door. Jacob had called him right away.

"Sorry man," Brady said. "I needed to hide the rest of the beer from the other night." Brady had gotten in trouble with his parents. He promised to get the beer out of there when Henry was gone. But, Brady could be an idiot. So Jacob knew they were caught.

Jacob heard Henry breathing on the other end, waiting for a response.

"Yeah?" Jacob said.

"I scared him off by opening the side door to the garage. I glanced over the fence and saw Brady driving away. You know anything about that?"

"No."

"You sure?"

"No, really. I don't know what he was doing there."

"I bet he texted you, Jake. Come on. I found the beer in the shrubs near the trash cans."

"What?" Jacob tried to think fast what to say.

But Henry stayed quiet. Jacob knew he wanted him to fess up.

Jacob saw another kid join the group. He needed to get going.

"Okay, yeah, he texted me," Jake said. "The truth is, he hid the bottles there because his parents told him to get home right away. They'd found some tequila in his closet and were really mad. He didn't want them to find the beer in his trunk, so he stopped at our house on the way home and dumped it on our side yard."

"Where'd he get the beer?"

"A guy bought it for us the other night."

"What guy?" Henry sounded stern.

Jake felt his heart race a little.

"Just some guy going into the convenience store." Jake knew he needed to be honest with Henry. Tell him the whole truth. "We paid him ten bucks extra to buy us beer."

"So you drank some?"

"Yeah, I had one or two. We all did. Brady kept the rest."

"What about the driver?"

"We were at Brady's house, so we all walked home. Brady drove down to the convenience store when we bought the beer, but we didn't drink any of it until we got to his place, I swear."

Jacob saw the last person join the group. They were headed for the doors now. When they came outside, the leader motioned to Jacob to join them. Jacob held up two fingers to let him know he would be finished soon.

"Henry?"

"Okay, Jake. I believe you. But, you can do better than Brady for a friend. Think about that as you're meeting new people up there."

"Right," Jacob said. "I will."

"I'm not going to tell your mom about this."

And Jacob knew he wouldn't. Henry had promised the same thing before. He'd walked into the family room once when Jacob had a girl over that he'd met at a party. They were making out, the girl's top somewhere on the floor and Jacob had just dropped his pants.

Henry made him go for a run with him the next morning, but he never told Jacob's mom what they talked about on the run. Instead, Henry placed a box of condoms inside Jacob's desk drawer with a note that said, "If you're going to do it, use a condom."

"Thanks, Henry."

"Don't be stupid up there, Jake. You have a lot riding on the line. If you drink, at least don't do it in the dorms. You've heard about binge drinking, right?"

"Yeah, I don't do that. I only have a beer now and then." But, Jacob knew that was a lie. He'd already binged several times his senior year, smoked some pot, and even drank a bottle of vodka with a few buddies on the beach one night. He knew better than to drive. He wasn't that stupid.

"Like I said, don't be stupid, son."

Henry had never called him son before. Jacob wasn't sure if he'd heard him right.

"I won't."

"You can talk to me. You, know that. Right?" Henry's voice sounded earnest, or even a bit worried, which Jacob had never heard before. He knew his stepdad as a straightforward guy who never showed emotion. He was a surgeon after all, and could be stoic and even a little too quiet sometimes. But Jacob liked that about him.

"I know," Jake said, and he meant it. He knew he could talk to Henry about most anything.

"You call me anytime," Henry said. "Okay?"

"Okay." Jacob turned around so the group couldn't see his face.

"I care about you, son," Henry said.

Jacob heard it for sure that time.

"I know."

Quiet followed for a moment or two. But Jacob waited.

"I love you, Jake."

Jake's heart pounded even harder. Henry had never said that before, either.

"I love you, too, Dad."

Jacob realized he not only said it back, but he meant it. He loved Henry, like a dad. Henry was there for him, watched him play volleyball, taught him how to fix up a car, researched college programs with him, pushed him to study harder, even helped him with the SATs. They'd go for runs and talk about life.

"Well, I'm sure the other champions are waiting for you, so you'd better go," Henry said, his voice more even again. "Be safe and have fun."

Jacob hung up and joined the others. As they migrated to the pizza place, Jacob trailed behind the group. He kept thinking about Henry. This man who wasn't even his real dad, loved him, cared about him, called him to talk about drinking, finding better friends. Jacob took in a deep breath of the cool evening air. He decided right then, he wanted to make Henry proud. He wanted to make his dad proud.

Chapter 8
Alex

Alex swallowed the pain medicine with a gulp of water straight from the faucet. His temples throbbed from his jog home. All the way he'd felt like a fugitive, a deserter, an outlaw on the run. He'd told Carlos he was sick and escaped through the front entrance of the restaurant to avoid a confrontation with that woman, with Margaret, who he'd seen in the alleyway. His heart raced as he sprinted from uptown Sedona to the highway toward the ranch where he worked as a caretaker. Alex hoped he'd lost her, that she didn't follow him somehow.

What the hell is Margaret doing in Sedona?

Inside the tiny bathroom of the pool house where Alex lived on the Tyler's property, he splashed cold water on his face, careful not to snag the stitches on his forehead. Still wearing an apron from the restaurant, Alex grabbed a towel from the back of the door. His bandana, soaked with sweat, sat in the basin, a soggy gauze bandage stuck to the fabric.

He noticed right away that the curtains were open on the sliding door. He'd turned the lamp on when he came inside, but he couldn't tell if the slider was locked. Alex crossed the terra cotta tiles and jiggled the latch on the glass door, then drew the drapes closed. He walked toward the other entrance in the room, a heavy wooden door that led to the barn. He opened the rustic door a jar and peered outside onto the gravel driveway that connected a dusty service road along the east side of the property to the front gate. Everything seemed fine. Alex seldom used the pickup truck parked under the portico other than to transport supplies. Beyond the truck, he could see the barn door shut tight.

Alex still needed to bring Maxwell and Lady, still grazing in the paddock, inside the stables before he could sleep. He stepped back into the room and closed the door, secured the lock and grabbed a drugstore bag from the makeshift kitchen counter. The caretaker before Alex had installed some reclaimed cabinets and a small under-the-counter refrigerator that sometimes didn't stay cold, plus a small sink like the type from a wet bar. Alex kept a hibachi grill outside on the gravel next to the front door since he had no stove or oven. Most days he ate a hot meal at the restaurant during his shift.

Alex dug inside the bag of first aid supplies he'd received at the hospital, and then dumped the contents onto the worn, beige tiled countertop. He tore open a box of gauze, folded one of the squares in half, and taped the strip over the cut on his forehead. Without noticing the ladder back chair, Alex almost tripped before he collapsed onto the futon in the middle of the room.

I need to calm down.

But how could he? What if she recognized him? She would've said something, or walked toward him. But she didn't.

Maybe she thought I just looked like him, like Daniel, like me.

The ceiling fan rotated on low as Alex saw the stars shining through the skylight recessed into the vaulted ceiling. He kept telling himself maybe she decided she was wrong. Maybe he looked so different, she thought her eyes had played a trick on her.

Is she on vacation?

The Margaret he knew hated the desert. That's exactly why he came there.

The day he'd left, walked away from his life, he wondered which way to go—south to Florida, maybe the Keys? Or Texas or even Montana? He had no time to plan, so he'd simply started walking. Toward home, like all the others, covered in dust, all of them survivors from the attacks on the World Trade Center.

Somewhere in northeastern New Jersey, Alex hitched a ride from a trucker. He was standing outside a diner when the trucker approached him. "Tell me where you're from, I'll drive you as far as I can." Alex had shown his thumb to the trucker, earlier, but got no response from him on the highway. The trucker told Alex he'd turned back when he realized Alex might be trying to get home. The wingtips and blue suit covered in dust were unusual attire for a

41

hitchhiker. "Sorry I passed you back there," the driver said. "Where're you headed?"

Alex realized later, much later, the trucker's question served as a trigger to somewhere deep inside his soul, a sort of split-second decision, and everything changed. He was free. He could go anywhere he wanted. He didn't have to go back to Cleveland. Ever.

He'd often entertained fantasies of escaping his life. Sudden whims on a rough day, daydreaming about quitting his tedious insurance job, moving somewhere warmer like near the ocean, maybe even get a divorce and start over. It never occurred to him to disappear, to walk away without contacting anyone. But at that moment, as the truck driver asked him where he was headed, Alex knew without a doubt he never wanted to go back to Cleveland again, never wanted to see his parents or his brother or Margaret, none of them, ever again. Not even his son, Jacob.

Alex tried to think of a place, of what to say to the driver, where he wanted to go, like standing before a giant board at the airport, a list of outbound flights. He had a choice now.

The trucker interrupted Alex's daydream. "I'm headed to Arizona, to Tucson," the man said.

"Perfect." Alex told the trucker he'd take a bus from there.

"Where? California?" He got Alex thinking.

"Southern California," Alex said, the picture of mild winters and miles of ocean in his mind, Mexico right there, just in case. And like he'd flipped a coin, the choice was made. "I've got a wife and kid in San Diego."

Alex heard the words come out of his mouth, and wondered about how easy he invented that story. He almost believed his lie. But then, Alex had always been able to deceive people, ever since childhood, and he'd gotten away with it, most of the time. Were his days of convincing others of a fictional version of himself coming to an end? Had Margaret known all along he was alive and had tracked him to Sedona?

Inside the cab of the driver's semi, Alex continued his story. "My wife is freaking out," Alex said. "I decided to walk to a train station away from Manhattan, because she wanted me as far from the city as possible."

Alex lied again when the driver offered his cell phone to call home. "I spoke to her by payphone and she's staying at her parents house until I get back. She knows I'm safe."

The driver nodded, as though he knew how women could be. "I'll get you back, buddy. Don't worry. We'll drive straight through."

Strange, this man who helped Alex, drove him across the country—Alex couldn't even remember his name now.

The truck driver had only tried to help. Overnight, everyone had become stellar citizens, assisting their neighbors, giving aid to ease their fears, and the shock of the horrific tragedy that played out before them second by second on every news channel across the globe.

The world was different now. The rules had changed and somehow, Alex chose to escape, to leave everything he'd ever known, and walk away. They'd never know. He should have been in the building. His family would mourn for a time, then move on. He could walk away and never have to endure the look of shame in his mother's eyes ever again, the disappointment in Maggie's, the irritation of his father—the superiority of his brother, Michael.

No, he could leave. They'd be better off without him. The only one he'd miss was Jacob. But, even Jake would be fine. Michael would see to it. Nobody would look for him. Maggie would never come after him. They didn't care. They never did.

Chapter 9
Margaret

"I'm staying a few extra days," Margaret said, as she tucked a wild strand of strawberry blonde hair behind her ear, the coarseness of a few grey hairs stuck to her fingers reminding her to make an appointment for highlights.

Why did she keep having random thoughts? Margaret's mind had drifted all morning. She found it difficult to stay focused now and sound natural on the phone with Henry.

"It's so nice here," she said, and it was true. The grounds of the resort were gorgeous. Birds were chirping and the morning sun felt wonderful against her skin. The waiter brought orange juice and coffee to Margaret's table. The patio had filled up fast with other guests. "The weather is great. You were right. I need a break."

"I'm glad you're having a good time," Henry said, the composed rhythm of his voice comforted Margaret after a long, wakeful night. "But, I feel bad about not being there to help with Jake."

"Don't worry. He was eager to be rid of me." Margaret hoped she didn't sound anxious. "I spoke to him a few minutes ago, in fact, I think I woke him, he couldn't talk long. He needed to get to an orientation event."

The waiter appeared with an omelet and fresh fruit. Margaret whispered, "Thank you," as he set the plate in front of her.

"What?" Henry said.

"Just the waiter bringing my breakfast." Margaret stirred cream into her coffee, balancing the cell phone between her left ear and shoulder.

"Ah, all we've here are stale English muffins."

Margaret imagined Henry sitting at their over-sized kitchen table, crafted from iron and wood, the sliding glass door wide open, the cool ocean breeze floating in from the deck. She pictured him dressed in his running shorts and a worn t-shirt from the stack she'd folded before leaving. He often waited to shave until after his run. He'd use his fingertips to smooth his short brown hair before tying his shoes for the jog down the winding, hilly street to Pacific Coast Highway.

Even messy, Henry always seemed in order. She knew he'd grab a breakfast sandwich of egg whites with turkey bacon and a decaf at their favorite coffee shop. He'd scan the local paper, then run back up the steep knoll to work off the eggs before he isolated himself inside his study off the living room, to review patient reports and respond to email. Even on the weekends, Henry's days were a methodical exercise in self-discipline.

"Sorry I didn't get to the store before leaving," Margaret said. "But just think, we won't have a hungry teenager around, eating all the food, at least not for the next few months." Margaret felt her eyes burn again with tears.

"True. But, it's awfully quiet around here. I miss Jake. And I miss you, too, sweetheart."

A young couple sat down at a table nearby, so Margaret rotated the other way and hushed her voice. "Will you be okay if I stay longer?" A part of her wanted Henry to say he needed her home, so she could stop this foolishness.

"I'm fine." Henry cleared his throat. "In fact, I've got some work to do this weekend preparing for the conference. Remember, I'm flying to Boston tomorrow."

"That's why I thought I'd stay longer. I'm not sure I'm ready to be in the house alone all week."

"Take whatever time you need. This is a big deal, sending Jake off."

"Thanks, Henry."

"I'll call you before I leave."

"Okay...and sorry I missed you last night. The signal isn't good here." Margaret closed her eyes, regretting the lie. "I love you."

"Love you, too," Henry said. "Work on those tan lines."

Henry's attempt at flirting, Margaret could tell, even though he sounded glib. He'd noticed her deep tan while they showered together the night before she headed to Flagstaff. He surprised her in the shower, when she thought he'd fallen asleep. She'd stayed up late to fold and pack the last of Jake's clothes from the dryer. She decided on a quick shower before bed. The shower was anything but quick, once Henry joined her. He soaped her entire body, and rinsed her hair with her favorite shampoo. Lifting her against the tiles, he made love to her under the rush of the showerhead. She'd dug her fingernails into his shoulders as he kissed her neck and moved inside her.

"Hmmm," she said, letting him know she remembered.

Anyone else wouldn't have thought his voice sexy. They might think he sounded business-like, unemotional maybe, or even sardonic, but Margaret understood Henry, and his clumsiness with words. His body language showed her exactly how he felt.

Margaret smiled, as he breathed heavy on the other end. She knew he didn't know what to say now. He often got himself into trouble when he tried to be cleaver. He'd share a humorous anecdote, only to have his audience stand before him, their eyebrows raised, in anticipation of the punch line, but thanks to Henry, they'd missed it completely. He'd try to explain the joke, realize he'd blown the delivery and everyone would laugh before he could get it straight.

Margaret loved that about Henry. A brilliant surgeon, Henry's quirks made him endearing and more approachable. Yet, patients sometimes complained. With Margaret's help, his bedside manner had improved, and he didn't try to be funny anymore. He kept it simple, straightforward and often paused so patients could absorb the information.

Henry waited to be rescued on the other end, so Margaret chuckled and let him down easy. "Alright, Henry, bye now."

Margaret took a bite of pineapple, realized her stomach felt sour from the coffee, so she pushed the plate away. She felt a bit calmer after talking to Henry, although, still a bundle of nerves.

She hadn't been forthright with him. In most cases, she turned to Henry for advice. But this time, she couldn't. She might be wrong. And Henry wasn't one to ignore her problems. He'd be on the next plane to help her. She didn't want to do that to him. Take advantage of his love, a love she'd never experienced before Henry. Sometimes she wondered how his patients saw him as impervious to their needs. He was the most caring man she'd ever known. Henry's calm nature compensated for all the years she'd spent in a volatile relationship with Daniel.

Daniel had had a fragile ego, and oftentimes acted insensitive to her needs. Henry, on the other hand, possessed confidence, which created peacefulness between them, a safe harbor for Margaret. She could talk to Henry about anything. He never stormed off, slammed doors or yelled.

The other night, Margaret had gone into his study after Jacob left the house. Upset, she'd neglected to notice him on the phone with a colleague, but he reached for her hand, and pulled her onto his lap while he told the other doctor he'd call him back.

"What happened?" he'd said, pulling her even closer.

"I'm so sorry," she'd said, tears burning her eyes. "I interrupted your call."

"It's Jacob leaving next week, right?"

"Yes," she'd said. "Watching him drive away with his friends, made me realize he isn't going to be around anymore. He's leaving us, Henry." Margaret collapsed in tears, but Henry just held her and let her cry.

"It'll be okay," he said, his voice comforting. "Jake will come home for holidays, and we can visit him in Arizona."

Margaret feared something might happen to her boy. "What if he gets sick or has an accident, what if he..."

"He'll be fine," Henry said, as he held her hand. "Jake's a good boy, and he'll make the right choices to keep himself safe."

Henry understood her insecurities about Jacob, how she'd devoted herself to keeping him safe, because of what happened to Daniel.

"Margaret, you've done a great job with him. He's a smart young man with good values and a brave heart."

"A brave heart?"

"Yes, sweetheart, you must know he's tried to protect you all these years. He's worried about you and in fact, he came to me a few days ago to have a man-to-man."

Margaret couldn't imagine why Jake would worry about her.

"He asked me to look after you, keep you safe."

"He did?" Margaret wiped away her tears and realized she needed to let him go. "He should be thinking about school and cute girls, not me."

Henry kissed her then. Everything would be fine. Jacob would take good care of himself. She could loosen her reigns.

She and Henry went for a walk along the beach later, kissed again in the moonlight, made plans, now that they'd have more time. Life with Henry felt calm. He always kept her best interests at heart.

I love you, Henry. But, I have to do this...

She hoped he'd understand, once she came home, after proving if what she'd seen was true, if Daniel was alive.

Margaret shifted again and straightened her dress. She felt terrible, but she couldn't tell Henry right now. It all seemed too ridiculous. What if that man was Daniel? What would it mean for her and Henry?

Awake half the night, Margaret had tossed and turned over the same questions. Was she married to two men? Why would Daniel be in Sedona? What did it all mean?

If she found Danny alive, Margaret had decided she'd call Henry right away. There must be some reasonable explanation. Once she tracked him down, she hoped he wasn't Daniel. Just like when that man had mistaken Margaret for his daughter. She'd feel foolish for a time, and then it would be over.

Margaret shook her head. How outlandish to think Daniel could have survived and now lived in Sedona, working in the kitchen at a restaurant. And knowing Henry, he'd want to help, but she couldn't let him cancel his trip and run to Arizona on some wild goose chase.

"You're the love of my life," Henry told her when he'd proposed. "I want to make time for you, learn about who you are, know your whole life story. And I want you to know mine as well, because isn't that what marriage is all about? To feel understood, for someone to know your story?"

Margaret had said, "Yes," and then yes again to his proposal.

She tapped her fingers on the tabletop, her cell phone nearby.

I should go home, be with Henry.

But, that morning, when she lay awake in bed, her eyes fixed on the ceiling, her stomach tied in knots, she knew what she had to do.

But, right now, she needed to eat, so Margaret pulled her plate closer again and tasted the eggs, still warm, the melted Jack cheese and fresh basil savory. She finished the food and then sipped some orange juice.

Margaret reviewed two addresses she'd jotted down from the White Pages for Daniel Waterson in Sedona. She planned to hike back to her car and then track down the residences. She'd also checked online for the hours at the Mexican restaurant, open for lunch and dinner, so she'd stop by later if need be. She finished her orange juice, knowing the charade might be a waste of time, but she'd check around town anyway, if only to satisfy her curiosity.

The young couple leaned in for a kiss, both smiled afterward. The first time she and Danny kissed, they were naïve to think they knew each other, or themselves for that matter. They'd married young and it didn't take long before the puzzle of problems took shape. She couldn't blame it all on Daniel. They both changed, grew in different directions. When she became a mother, Margaret focused her attention on the baby. She knew Daniel struggled at his dad's company, and he resented his brother's portfolio of clients. He'd often come home in a foul mood.

"If you're not happy," she'd said. Daniel slouched in his chair with the TV blaring. "You should quit."

"Right, the mortgage will pay itself, the doctor will treat Jake for free."

"Don't be so melodramatic. Let's make a plan toward you finding a new job. I could go back to work, too."

But Daniel rolled his eyes, took a swig of beer, and turned his attention to Monday Night Football. She'd tried to understand what he didn't like about the insurance business, but he ignored her, and said she wouldn't understand.

"Try me," she'd said, over dinner on a different night.

"Let's just say, being compared to my brother my whole life is getting old."

"Have you talked to your dad?"

But Daniel laughed at her, "Yeah, right."

He'd left the table without finishing dinner. He flipped the TV on in the other room and raised the volume to drown Margaret out when she asked another question.

She'd never understood Danny's dispute with his father or his brother. He never complained about his mom, but he also never spent much time with Jean either, often avoiding her altogether. Margaret couldn't figure it out. She admired how the Watersons vacationed together at the family cottage in northern Michigan, celebrated with lavish holidays, and invited all their friends. Margaret's parents still had dinner with Daniel's father, Dutch, now and then, and they'd enjoyed a pleasant friendship with his mother, Jean, before she passed.

But for Daniel, he'd grown more irritated by his family each year, until Margaret found herself defending them, often annoyed with Danny's childish behavior. He pulled away even more, added Margaret to his hate list, dismissive one minute, shouting the next. Their marriage had sunk to the lowest level in the days leading up to his death, and she'd even asked him to go to a counselor with her.

"Are you kidding?" Daniel said.

"I'm very serious," Margaret said, trying to ignore his rude tone.

They were on a walk one Saturday afternoon in June, a few months before he died. She'd insisted they get outside together before Jake came home from a play-date. They were up late the night before, in a huge argument, and Margaret had cried herself to sleep.

"We fight all the time," she'd said, as they strolled through their neighborhood in Cleveland Heights. "I want to fix our marriage."

But they never went for counseling. Margaret mentioned it now and then, but they'd end up in a fight, instead. Afterward, Daniel would be sweet for a while, so she'd forget.

Now, all these years later, as she noticed the young couple hold hands at the next table, she wished she'd made the appointment, found out why they couldn't get along. Then maybe she wouldn't be chasing ghosts. She might have accepted his death easier, gone on with her life, not held on for so long.

Go home, Margaret. Go home.

The couple at the next table leaned in for another smooch. The woman giggled when they almost spilled a glass of water between them.

Margaret turned her chair in the direction of the fountain, blotted her lips with a napkin, and rested her elbow on the edge of the wooden table. She inhaled the light scents of creosote, sagebrush, and the warm earthiness of red rocks mixed with the heady floral mix in the courtyard. Without warning, she sneezed twice. She sniffed, her eyes filled with tears, allergens this time.

She had bottled water in her purse from the room, but Margaret reached for a glass of water on the table and drank it in one long gulp. She blotted her lips again, sat straight in her seat with another round of second thoughts. She should get her bags and go home.

Chapter 10
Alex

The truck driver stayed quiet most of the trip, leaving Alex alone. The older man seemed to understand Alex didn't want to share his experience. Thousands of miles of highway passed under the wheels of the semi as they crossed under overpasses, the railings draped in American flags. Other flags hung half-mast on tall poles in front of rural town halls, and lay plastered against the roofs of farmer's barns. Red, white and blue fabric fastened to wooden dowels lined the lawns of homes and city sidewalks. Patriotism bled out from every corner of the country.

When they stopped at motels, the driver insisted on paying for Alex's room, but the driver slept in the extended cab of his truck. He never pressured Alex to spend time with him.

"I appreciate what you're doing," Alex told him at a motor lodge alongside the highway the first night.

"What you've been through," the driver said, handing Alex the room key. "What happened to you and all those people, it's an honor to help."

Alex used a different name on the trip, not Daniel, not Alex. He made calls to a random number in California from the motel room, to make the driver think he touched base with his fictitious San Diego family. All the airports were shut down -- no trains were running, yet. The world remained traumatized. Wall Street stayed shutdown for days. With commerce on hold, the global economy stalled.

"You're probably in a state of shock," the driver had said, about a hundred miles into the journey.

"Maybe."

The driver didn't push.

When they stopped at Wal-Mart the next day, Alex used the restroom, and then waited by the truck until the driver came out of the store.

He handed Alex a bag of clothes and toiletries. "Had to guess your size, but this should get you through until you get home."

Alex thanked him, but he'd already decided to grow a beard by then, so he didn't need the razor. Once they arrived in Tucson, the driver stopped at the bus station and Alex shook his hand. Alex couldn't remember what the man looked like now.

He sat in the bus station for a long while and then walked down the street to a bar. That's where he met Lucky. And Lucky was happy to help, for a price.

"I can get you a new name. That's no problem," Lucky said, "You bring the cash and I'll get you hooked up."

Alex had money in his wallet from when he visited the ATM at the airport the morning he left Cleveland. He had less than five hundred dollars, but if he needed to, he'd hock his watch and wedding ring. Lucky told Alex where he could find a pawnshop.

He slept at the bus station that night and the next day, waited two hours for Lucky to show up at the bar. His new name, Alex Gershom, came from a random list Alex didn't ask questions about. Daniel Waterson was as good as dead.

Those first months, he worked as a construction laborer. He'd wait for contractors stopping in front of a church to hire day laborers. Most of the men who loitered around the parking lot were illegal immigrants. Nobody ever asked Alex where he came from, or what he was doing there, even though his lighter hair and skin made him stand out. He worked hard and stuck to himself. After a while, jobsite superintendents often picked Alex first out of the crowd of men. He even stayed on jobs for months at a time. A strong and willing apprentice, bosses liked him and were happy to pay cash.

His Midwest skin darkened under the southwest sun, and he developed muscles from the heavy labor he never knew he had.

Alex worked the trades for a few years in Tucson and then later, in Phoenix, until one day, he made his way further north to Sedona.

A fence installer hired Alex to dig postholes at a local estate. On his third day there, the owner of the property, Bill Tyler, approached Alex. "You're a good worker," Bill said. "You seem to put in longer hours than the other men." Alex thanked him for the compliment but continued to dig holes while they talked, eager to make some money so he could settle in Sedona.

Alex felt sheltered, hidden away, nestled into the red rock hillsides of Sedona and Verde Valley. The canyons were filled with High Chaparral brush, Pinon Pines, Junipers and Old Sycamores that grew along creek beds.

One thing he missed in Southern Arizona, trees and forests like in Ohio. Although, alive with plenty of vegetation, the desert surrounding Tuscan looked plain to Alex, the nearest forests further away. He'd found the Saguaro cacti mysterious, some more than 70 feet tall and 150 years old. The wide, prickly arms often resembled crucifixes and lanky cowboys, or giant hands, with middle fingers pointed toward heaven.

Alex hiked at the top of Mount Lemmon, north of Tucson, considered renting an old cabin up there, tucked away from the world, where the roads often closed during the winter. But work was scarce. Phoenix had felt like an overpopulated fishbowl to Alex, always looking over his shoulder, worried he might be recognized by a Midwest transplant.

He'd heard about Sedona and its close proximity to the forests near Flagstaff. The terrain north of the Verde Valley had plenty of trails and parks for hiking. The people seemed friendly, and they didn't ask a lot of questions, so life seemed more secluded.

Later that day at the Tyler ranch, Bill came back out to the edge of the property where Alex worked planting posts. "You know anything about horses?" he said. Bill wore shiny, black cowboy boots, clean jeans and a crisp white shirt, starched the same way Alex had worn his shirts back in Cleveland. He'd never wear a starched shirt again, and wouldn't miss it, either.

"I know a bit," Alex lied.

"I talked to your boss," Bill said, "Says you just arrived from down south, might need a place to stay."

"I'm at a motel for now, not too far." Alex wiped the sweat from his brow on the sleeve of his denim shirt.

"Well, I need a caretaker, someone I can trust to keep this place in order while my wife and I are in California. You interested?"

Alex liked the way he got right to the point. He shook hands with Mr. Tyler and started work at the Tyler Ranch the next day. He expected to live in the barn or a bunkhouse, but the Tyler's insisted he use the pool house, since Bill didn't have a bunkhouse on the property. The place seemed more like a hobby ranch, or a gentleman's ranch as some called it, with five acres and two horses, an estate-sized main residence and of course the pool house. Alex would have plenty to do.

Alex tried to act confident around the livestock out in the paddock while Mr. Tyler explained his duties. "I'll do my best, Mr. Tyler."

"Call me, Bill," he said. "All the numbers and the schedules are in the barn above the desk. Call me if you have any questions."

The next day, Bill and Sue Tyler left early for the airport. Alex didn't see them again for three months. By then, he'd reorganized the barn, added a tack room, and another shed outside with an overhang for the grooming station.

Alex learned by trial and error how to care for the gelding, Maxwell, and the mare, Lady, having said he knew how. At first, he'd read books from the library about horse husbandry. But it wasn't until he called the equine veterinarian, that everything began to fall into place.

"Why don't you come by the office and I'll go over everything." The vet returned Alex's call after he'd left a message asking for the health backgrounds in order to provide proper care. A weak cover, Alex knew the vet smelled his fear, but he told Alex what he needed to know. By then, Lady had kicked him the face. Alex played tricks to get Lady and Maxwell to cooperate, used apples and carrots to lure them inside the barn. Maxwell didn't trust Alex at first and Lady completely ignored him. It took hours to get anything done.

A quick study, Alex relied on his ability to adapt and learn in his new life. He'd graduated from the Ohio State with honors then worked his way up at his father's insurance company. But the Tyler's didn't know that, so he learned all he could to run their property right. In fact, once he got the hang of it, he found he had extra time on his hands to work in town at the restaurant. The Tyler's were fine, as long he finished his work at their ranch first.

Between two jobs, Alex had little time for anything else. He used the forest service trails adjacent to the property to exercise Maxwell and Lady, but seldom went for hikes like he'd thought he would when he'd first moved to Sedona. And he hadn't skied near Flagstaff either. In fact, he'd only driven the seventeen miles once, to pick up supplies for the building projects he needed to complete the first year. He hadn't been back since, not in five years. But, Alex liked his busy work life. He had callused hands and chapped lips most of the time. And until the accident, Alex didn't have time to think about his past, to worry if he'd made the right choice. Work became his solace, his way of letting go of the ghosts, the bad memories of his life before he walked away.

Alex often read books late into the evening after his shifts at the restaurant. He enjoyed being alone, studying the constellations, with the radio on low. He didn't have a TV and saw no use for one. If he wanted to watch a baseball game, he'd hike to a sports bar in town or join Carlos and his dad at their house to watch the Diamondbacks on their big-screen.

He'd spend a few hours a week at the library, scan books about desert plants, livestock, and personal interests such as history, the solar system, even engine mechanics. Sometimes, he thought about using a computer, see about his family, but he never did. Better to leave the past alone.

Alex bent forward on the futon, reached for a thick volume on Norse Mythology he'd checked out before he bumped his head. He always kept a few books stacked on the storage chest he used as a coffee table. Alex flipped through to where he'd folded down the page, closed the book and placed it back on the chest. Still wound up from his run home, Alex couldn't concentrate and in fact, he had blurry vision and his mind felt clouded.

He stood, too fast, and blood rushed to his head as he tipped sideways, but he caught himself on the table near the sink. He took a deep breath, made his way to the fridge, and pulled out a beer and a stale bagel, then unscrewed the top of the beer using the fabric of his apron. He ran a splash of beer over the top of the bagel and tossed it inside the microwave for a few seconds to soften the edges. Though hot, he could bite into it now. He set the bagel on the counter with the bottle of beer, untied the knot on his apron, and tossed it over the back of a chair at the table. He took another bite of the bagel with a gulp of beer, and then opened the cabinet above the counter where he kept his clothes.

He remembered Maxwell and Lady again.

Alex left the clothes on the counter with the bagel and beer, grabbed his keys and hit the lights. He locked the door behind him, something he never did, but he felt jumpy and didn't need any more surprises like Sonia. The fresh, night air felt good as he crossed under the portico to the barn. He'd finish his chores fast since he couldn't wait to sleep.

He strode through the barn out to the paddock. And made a clicking noise from inside his cheek to rouse Maxwell and Lady into coming in. His boots kicked up dust on his way to the field. Maxwell and Lady were at the far end of the wide irrigated pasture.

"Bedtime," Alex yelled, and clapped his hands. "Come on, Maxwell," he shouted. "You, too, Lady. Let's go."

When they continued to ignore him, Alex headed to the water trough, filled it full for the next day, and then wrapped the hose and hung it out of the way. Finally, he heard Maxwell behind him.

It took some time to clean Maxwell's hooves. When Alex finished, he headed out in the paddock with a lariat for Lady.

"Always playing hard to get," Alex said, and then guided her to the covered area near the barn.

As he groomed Lady, Maxwell already inside the stable, Alex thought about Margaret behind the restaurant. The way she always crossed her arms when she felt nervous. From what he saw

57

in the dim light, she didn't drop her arms until she ran away. Her golden locks took flight in the breeze when she turned the corner at the end of the alleyway.

He wondered now, if she'd recognized him, but only wanted to confirm he'd left her, and hadn't died. Chapter closed. God, he hoped so. Maybe she'd go back to Cleveland. Let him be. She had to know their marriage was over when he left for New York. He did.

Alex walked around the backside of Lady, humming a tune as he passed by to brush her other side.

Did Margaret somehow know he survived the disaster? He'd been certain the records would show he signed in before the plane hit the building. He later learned the plane crashed into the 93rd through 98th floors of the World Trade Center's north tower with the force of nearly half a million pounds of explosives. Right where Alex had a meeting scheduled. But how would she know he was still alive? Had someone seen him and told her? Had she been tracking him all those years?

Every trace of Alex remained behind in the tower when the building imploded. He'd asked the receptionist to keep his briefcase and carry-on, while he went down to the street level for coffee.

"I can get you a cup of coffee, sir," she'd said, her shear white blouse revealed the outline of her lace bra. He still remembered her grin.

"No, thanks," Alex had said. "I need some air." The gentleman Alex was scheduled to meet had a conference call go long. "I'll be back in twenty minutes." The receptionist signed him in, on her desktop. He watched her and then glanced at her bra again.

Alex only had his wallet when he exited the first floor lobby. He'd left his cell phone behind in his briefcase.

After he paid for his coffee, Alex stepped back out onto the sidewalk, and within seconds, the first plane hit. Stunned, he followed others running up the street.

Alex stopped several blocks away as black smoke billowed out from the top of the north tower. Fifteen minutes later, he heard the revving of another plane's engines, an awful grinding noise he'd never forget. He watched as the second plane hit the south tower. He tripped and fell when he turned to run again, but he found his way to his feet, and stumbled further away.

In the chaos, he stopped to catch his breath at a corner. He stood there, eyes fixed on the inferno in the sky. Sirens blared all around him. And then the south tower collapsed. The sound of steel and glass exploding made Alex run again. He felt disoriented, confused about which way to go, frantic people ran past, screaming and crying, until someone snatched his arm, and pulled him along to escape the cloud of debris. Both buildings had fallen by then, and the giant haze of wreckage chased after them.

"I was supposed to be inside," he said, over and over, as he broke away from whoever had dragged him along. Alex would never forget the giant wall of heavy grey, airless fog that pulled them apart.

In Phoenix, years later, Alex collapsed inside a service station bathroom and covered his head, when a sudden dust storm hit the area. The giant brown cloud, called a haboob, Alex learned later, was a thick veil of sand, a type of atmospheric current that happened in arid regions around the world. But Alex didn't know that yet, locked inside the bathroom for hours, fearing for his life.

Kicking the dust beneath his boots, Alex lifted Lady's front leg to check the hoof. He never allowed himself to remember that day in lower Manhattan, or how he'd felt at the gas station. He'd try to ignore it when his hands trembled after an explosion or even sometimes when a door slammed behind him.

But now, he remembered the planes smash into the towers all over again. Seeing Margaret in the alleyway had somehow brought him back to that day. The memories flooded inside his mind now, and he wished he could shut them down.

He used a hoof pick to clear Lady's front hooves, trying to focus on the task at hand. But to no avail, Alex could hear the buildings roaring down as if he were there again. Panic began to rise in his chest, so he stepped away from Lady for a moment to catch his breath. His heart raced, one foot ahead of the toxic smoke, how he'd begun to feel weak, and covered his mouth and nose with his necktie. He'd battled block after block, exhausted, dropped to his knees several times, when he spotted others escaping inside a lobby. He followed them, marble floors so shiny compared to the streets outside. He'd leaned against a wall. An enormous chandelier hung overhead. And he remembered being worried the building would come down soon, like the others, and they'd all be crushed under the chandelier. But, he'd glanced around at the others as they clung to the granite walls, their cries silent. He focused on the entry doors for a long while frightened the dark cloud of dust would break through the windows.

Odd what he remembered now. A little girl holding tight to a woman's leg, her face covered with dust, terror in her blue eyes. The dust on his own hands, so thick it covered his wedding ring. A single, black umbrella left against the front desk, no doorman in sight.

The strange thing was, when the nightmares came, the receptionist from the tower always appeared, wearing the same white blouse. Not so often anymore, but for several years he'd not slept well, and wondered about the receptionist, if she'd suffered. She haunted him sometimes, like he should have saved her.

Seeing Margaret, he wondered now, why he never dreamed about her? Like a needle on a scratched album, his mind played the same dream over and over. He remembered the receptionist in flames, but forgot Margaret, his own wife. As he stood outside the barn, holding Lady by the reigns, Margaret haunted him, now. Her eyes had glistened with tears in the moonlight behind the restaurant.

"I know it was her," Alex said, as he guided Lady inside the stable. Maxwell settled in his stall. He whinnied as Alex closed the gate on Lady's stall, and then checked the water levels, tossed fresh hay around the stables, hit the lights, and secured the barn door.

Alex made his way past the pool house, all quiet, but he became aware of every other sound. The cool September breeze danced across the darkened desert floor, parched branches crackled underneath tiny desert creatures dashing for cover. He cut through the backyard of the Tyler's house, tested the gates, jiggled the door handles, and made sure they were secure. He was the only security Bill and Sue Tyler needed.

Alex never stayed away from the ranch, unless the owners were in town and wanted more privacy, which didn't happen often, maybe three or four times a year. Bill gave him a rifle to keep unwanted wildlife off the property. The coyotes only needed a single warning shot before they scrambled toward the hills. Otherwise, quiet prevailed.

As Alex rounded the corner from the back of the house to check the mailbox, he noticed movement near the front gate, someone on the road at the edge of the driveway. Even though the wooden gates were closed, he could see a figure on the other side of the gate. He stopped short, hugged the side of the house, the stucco wall pricking his back through his cotton shirt.

He watched as the hooded stranger rattled the gate, though the person could hop the post and rail fence along the front of the property with ease, if they wanted. Instead, they turned and walked away toward town. Alex crept down the driveway. He could still see the image of someone headed away from the property on the far side of the road. He waited, and then checked the mailbox. Empty as usual. He made his way back toward the pool house.

Was that Margaret?

Alex hurried along the service path toward the back of the property and stopped short of his place. The door open ajar, he saw a light from inside. He knew he'd left it dark and locked. He stepped forward, pushed the door open a few inches, and peered inside. The hinges creaked as he entered. But the place was empty. He checked the bathroom, nothing—nobody. Alex realized his fists were clenched, ready for an attack, prepared to protect the property. He ran across to the barn, but saw nobody. He glanced toward the paddock. All quiet. So, Alex went back inside his place, closed and secured the front entry, checked the sliding glass door again, and shut the drapes even tighter. Then he saw the note on the table.

Alex wiped his brow with the apron he'd left on the chair, and grabbed the letter. Sonia. She'd been inside his place, picked the lock somehow, because he never gave her a key. Alex read the note then ripped it up and tossed it in the trashcan, but the first line stuck in his head — *"Alex, I came by to check on you. Take care of you, because I love you."*

He sat down on the futon, rested his head against the cushion, his heart thumped against his temples. Alex flipped off the switch on the lamp next to him, and then fell asleep where upright. He didn't wake again until nearly dawn, his head throbbing. The pain relievers had worn off, and his body dripped with sweat. Losing his balance several times on the way to the bathroom, Alex downed another dose of pills. He collapsed back onto the futon, horizontal this time, foggy and confused.

Images of Sonia faded away, but visions of Margaret lingered. Hazy photographs floated through his mind, like a slideshow of long ago days, forgotten, left behind. He struggled to relax, but the room whirled around him, as he tried to focus on the wooden blades of the rotating fan above him. A metallic paste covered his tongue, his stomach sour from the taste. As he drifted off, the receptionist in the white blouse appeared. She offered him coffee. But the office walls crumbled around her, the floor cracked into large fissures like a frozen lake shattering, and as if the ice had collapsed, the surface gave way beneath her feet. All Alex heard then were her screams.

Chapter 11
Margaret

Margaret needed the waiter, so she could sign for breakfast then go upstairs and retrieve her bag from the room. She'd not even unpacked yet. That guy was just some worker at a Mexican restaurant.

Plus, Margaret needed to drop this plight. She'd checked phonebooks in hotel rooms for years, had scanned the White Pages online, typed in Daniel Waterson, to see if there were any listings with Danny's same age. She'd even called a few of the numbers before, but a strange voice would answer and she'd hang up. This was all just more of the same.

Besides, Danny would never work in a hot kitchen in the middle of the desert.

He hated the desert.

They both agreed. Too dry, and hot, and desolate. Even though the closest they'd ever been was a convention in Las Vegas.

"It's so vast and empty," Margaret announced glancing out the window of the plane.

Danny leaned over from the center seat, squished Margaret against the window, smelling of scotch from several tiny bottles he'd drank. "And they say we're overpopulated." Danny pressed his nose against the window like a toddler. "I don't think so." His laugh sounded obnoxious, and then he tried to kiss her, but she shoved him off. He left a sloppy line of drool across the front of her new turquoise silk tunic.

Once they landed, within minutes, they hate Vegas. The crowds of people, the wall of heat when they'd stepped outside. They stayed inside the air-conditioned casino or in the water at the pool the whole time. And every night, Daniel passed out before they could make love. He'd start with a Bloody Mary for breakfast and drink all day. A wonder he could even conduct the little amount of business he'd managed to do, in between betting on horses and drinking scotch with other insurance reps in the lobby bar.

Margaret gave up the first day, and spent most of the weekend by herself, dropping coins into slots and shopping at the indoor mall next to their hotel.

On the flight home, Margaret said, "I don't want to go back."

Daniel agreed. "All it did was make me dehydrated."

Margaret glanced over at Daniel who'd taken the window seat this time, slumped and rumpled in the resort wear she'd bought him at the mall, and knew the desert hadn't parched his system as much as the scotch.

The whole weekend ended up a disaster. Daniel lost five hundred dollars at the blackjack tables. Margaret had a terrible case of heat rash, the welts so awful she'd gone to a walk-in clinic on a sketchy side street. She'd taken a cab by herself. She'd left Daniel to roam the booths inside the convention center to brag to Dutch later.

Margaret smoothed her hair now, adjusted the silver clip that held back some strands at the top of her crown, and then tapped her fingers on the list of addresses.

She couldn't shake it. The man she'd seen, the kitchen worker, the way he'd stood and cocked his head, the brooding, so familiar, like Danny. She had to figure it out. Then she'd go home, and forget this ever happened.

Margaret straightened the front of her pale-blue linen dress. The gardens surrounding the tables had fresh blooms, butterflies dipped and landed on the flower petals.

Strangely, the desert had begun to grow on her. Sedona was nothing like Las Vegas. Before she'd had dinner last night, she wandered the shops and art galleries in uptown Sedona, knowing she wanted to bring Henry back there. It seemed a good spot for him to unwind from his busy schedule at the hospital. And as far as now, why should she leave? The man couldn't be Danny anyway, and once proven, she'd relax and enjoy the resort. She wanted to explore the area, maybe find some places to hike if she came back with Henry. And she'd looked forward to a little time at the spa, maybe a massage or a facial.

Margaret sipped the last of her coffee, blotted her lips on the cloth napkin again, then placed it over her breakfast plate, and signaled the waiter for the bill.

The night before, the Mexican restaurant had been packed, far busier than breakfast here in the sunshine. The dining room in town had tables crammed together with customers overflowing onto the patio outside the front entry. Here the tables were scattered around the garden, with plenty of room to relax and enjoy a leisurely meal. Once the sun went down in town, Margaret had felt uneasy being alone, but now, at the resort, she felt quite comfortable and safe. The darkened alleyway behind the restaurant had set her back on her heels, and she'd felt anxious sneaking around like some nut. Obviously, not a good spy, she'd had a difficult time seeing anything clearly anyway. And she knew that man just happened to look similar to Danny, that's all. But, nonetheless, she wondered if all this anxiety might provide the clarity she needed to move on from his death, once and for all.

She watched a hummingbird hover near several pink and white hibiscus blooms.

Whatever she felt, she told herself she wanted to look the man straight in the eyes, hear his voice. Danny had a particular vernacular, a tone she would know anywhere, and the night before, she hadn't gotten close enough to hear him for sure.

Margaret didn't care if she made a fool of herself. Nobody here knew her, and she wasn't so sure anymore if she would bring Henry back, anyway. Not after all the strange events since she'd arrived. She glanced around at the offbeat characters waiting on tables, working at the front desk. Just a bunch of hippies, like Laguna Beach with its Birkenstock-wearing artists, retired surfer-types with wrinkled, lizard-like skin, the vegans and the health nuts.   Yet, Sedona seemed more authentic, a colony of true naturalists, who embraced an earthy lifestyle.

But still, for Margaret, Sedona had proven to be less ethereal as described in the brochures.   Instead, it seemed more like a ghost town to her.   Margaret wasn't sure about it being a spiritual oasis.   Was this really where spirits came to dwell?

Margaret almost laughed.   What would the sisters from her parochial school say to such a ridiculous question?   Margaret knew where people went when they died, and this place, however otherworldly, with it's red rocks stretching upward to the brilliant blue sky, hardly felt like heaven to her.

Margaret had decided she didn't want to attend the 10th anniversary for 9/11.   And Dutch agreed with her on the phone.

"You have a new life now," Dutch said.   "It's best you keep moving forward.   Michael and I will pay respects for all of us."

Margaret felt grateful he understood.

She'd traveled only once to visit the sight after the rebuilding project began.   Margaret remembered the notes and photos plastered to the sidewall of the fire station near Ground Zero.   And also the filthy vagrant stumbling down the sidewalk, screaming profanity, a sort of speech about terrorism, she'd let Dutch whisk her away into a cab where they both collapsed in tears.   Jean, Daniel's mother, had stayed at the hotel on the Upper East Side.

"You both go on," Jean said, outside the hotel on Lexington Avenue as the bellhop hailed a cab.   "I'll wait here for you." Margaret had noticed Jean's pallor when they arrived, her usual rosy cheeks, pale and sagging.   "I need to lie down for a while." She waved them on.   "I'll be fine."

Dutch told Margaret, once inside the cab, he worried about Jean.   "She's so frail now since losing Danny."

Margaret glanced out the back window of the taxi to make sure her mother-in-law went back inside the hotel.   She could see Jean, petite and thin, her hair tidy from her appointment at the salon in Cleveland the day before, but needing help inside on the arm of the bellhop.   For a moment, Margaret wished she'd stayed behind, too. Her heart raced out of control the closer they inched toward lower Manhattan.

"I'm not sure she could handle another setback," Dutch said, his voice measured. Margaret touched his arm and Dutch glanced at her. His smile so sad, she saw the surrender in his eyes.

The shock of the scene as they pulled up near St. Paul's Chapel, filled Margaret with dread, a moment she'd never forget. The church remained in fine order, somehow surviving the attacks, but the demolished area, the destruction, almost too much to bear, left her with lasting nightmares. She stayed silent for a long while, beside the historic church, gripping the wrought iron fence surrounding monuments and headstones dating back to the 1700's. Her heart sunk as she stared into the deep abyss, where the towers once stood.

Dutch took her by the arm and they walked the perimeter of the chain-linked fence surrounding Ground Zero to a fire station. Dutch stopped to speak with a firefighter on the sidewalk, while Margaret followed a path along the sidewall of the firehouse where fliers had been pasted on the wall for friends and family members lost in the tragedy. Out of the corner of her eye, Margaret caught sight as two men embraced in a way that only people who have shared in the same disaster can comprehend, like two WWII vets, overwhelmed with emotion, visiting Normandy.

She glanced back at the wall, touching the paper faces smiling back at her from photos of parties, weddings, holidays, all of them lost now, buried in the gigantic graveyard behind where she stood. Margaret held back tears, tried to be strong for Danny, for all of them.

Dutch joined her to read the trail of papers, until the homeless man began his tirade, sending Margaret and Dutch toward Wall Street where Dutch flagged down a taxi. Margaret hoped the trip would serve as closure, but instead, it only brought back the darkness, the tragic sadness still so raw inside their hearts. Dutch comforted Margaret in the cab on the way back to the hotel.

"I'm so sorry," he said. With the windows rolled down, the warm spring air blew in from outside, mingling with the sour odors of worn vinyl and perspiration from previous passengers. "I thought we were ready," he said, holding Margaret as she cried in his arms, "but it's all too much."

Margaret continued to sob. "I'm so angry," she said, her voice quivering. "The people," she tried to explain, her tears staining her father-in-law's blue, oxford shirt, "They've just gone on, like it never happened."

"That's not true," Dutch tried to console Margaret, even when she shook her head to disagree. "They're resilient, that's all," he said. He let Margaret cry, handing her the handkerchief from his pocket. "We have to do the same. We have to fight," Dutch said, as he lifted her chin, his silver blue eyes the same color as Danny's, bloodshot and damp with tears. "We have to find the strength to carry on."

Margaret wasn't able to say anything more to Daniel's parents that afternoon. She'd gone straight up to her room, sat on the marble floor of the shower, and let the hot water run down her body, weeping until she couldn't cry anymore. Later, after she'd slept for a while, the three of them walked a few blocks to an Italian bistro. Jean grabbed Margaret's hand as they went inside, and pulled her close, whispering, "I'm here for you. We'll get through this together." But Margaret wasn't so sure. She sensed it would probably be the other way around. Her prediction had turned out to be correct, as Jean's fragile state eventually sent her to bed. She succumbed to congestive heart failure a few years after Daniel died. But, Margaret always felt Jean had died of a broken heart.

The next day, she and Dutch walked through Central Park, and paused outside the gates to the zoo, where they watched children playing, excited to see the animals, oblivious to the tragedies that had taken place in their city. Margaret and Dutch continued their stroll, but kept to the edges of the park, where they decided to cross over to The Plaza Hotel for afternoon tea.

"I know this was hard, but I'm glad we came," Dutch said. "Daniel deserved for us to witness the scene, where he was laid to rest."

Margaret stirred sugar into her tea, nodding in agreement with Dutch, even though, she hardly felt Daniel was at rest, the sight of the buildings torn apart, workers excavating the land, the city so alive around where he was buried.

"I know how troubled you are," Dutch said. "But Daniel is with God now, and he is at peace."

Margaret tried to have faith in his words, but the way Daniel died had left her feeling unsettled, unsure of what she believed anymore. She sipped her tea, glancing around the lobby, the gilded columns and lavish rugs seemed so civilized. Guests hurried about, bellhops rolled brass luggage carts to the elevators, tourists snapped pictures near the revolving doors, chandeliers sparkled as waiters served finger sandwiches and tea. She'd closed her eyes then, and said a little prayer, for Danny, for Jacob and for Dutch and Jean. She wanted the world to go back in time, to make this not have happened. But, if all she learned from their trip was that they could only go forward, then she'd try to hold onto those moments at The Plaza Hotel, Dutch being a gentleman, people moving about, talking quietly, all of it so elegant and full of grace.

That evening, the three of them flew home to Cleveland. As the plane ascended into the sunset, Margaret held tight to the stuffed bear she'd bought for Jake at FAO Schwartz. Life would go on, there was no choice.

She'd come a long way from that first year after the planes hit, when she fluctuated between frantic and strangely calm. During the first days, she couldn't sleep or eat, trying hard to hang on to her sanity for Jacob.

"Daddy will be home soon, honey, don't you worry." But even Margaret knew her words didn't sound convincing.

Jacob climbed into bed with her a few nights after the attack and said, "Don't worry, Mommy, I'll take care of you if Daddy is dead." Her little boy had tried so hard to be strong, to be the man of the house, to move forward.

And Margaret realized, in that moment, Daniel hadn't escaped the flames, he would remain amongst the missing. After all, they'd heard nothing. He hadn't called, like so many others were able to do with cell phones during the evacuations, and before the buildings came down. Even afterward, survivors called from other parts of the city, to tell their loved ones they were, indeed, safe. They'd escaped or hadn't been in the buildings, after all.

Margaret had hoped and prayed Danny's meeting had finished, that he'd left the building and had gone for coffee and breakfast elsewhere in the city. Surely he'd needed a shot of caffeine, after being so drunk the night before. He must have felt awful with a terrible hangover. She'd held onto that thought as long as she could, he'd gone for coffee, was trying to get out of the city, or maybe his cell phone battery died. After all, he always left his charger behind.

Daniel had a meeting scheduled at offices right where the first plane hit. Dutch had been there before and felt certain of what floor he'd visited. Even though nobody knew yet how many people were able to escape before the building collapsed, Margaret knew Jacob might be right Daniel might never come home. So with her little boy snuggled up next to her, Margaret had begun to absorb the truth, even before Michael came home without Daniel.

"I couldn't find him, Maggie." Michael stared at Margaret from across the kitchen, as the backdoor swung shut behind him.

He walked straight over to where she stood. Margaret held a fresh kitchen towel, his wife, Patty had just handed her from the clean laundry. Patty had helped Margaret a great deal during those early days with meals, keeping the house tidy, even hugging Jacob when Margaret couldn't.

Michael grabbed hold of Margaret as if she were the lifeboat he'd been swimming toward for days. He cried in her arms. Patty moved closer to them, and placed her hand on her husband's back. Michael loosened his hold, turned toward Patty and let go of Margaret, who grasped the counter for support.

Margaret twisted the towel as she felt the full weight of the pain inside her chest, her heart shattering into a thousand tiny pieces. Unlike those mothers on the news, pleading for their abducted child to be released, Margaret knew Danny wouldn't be found alive. He wasn't wandering the city with amnesia or injuries that kept him from speaking. Danny was dead. Margaret stayed near the kitchen sink, staring out the window at the moon.

"I know he's still alive," Michael said.

Margaret shifted and glanced around the kitchen, remembering all the times she and Danny had prepared breakfasts or Saturday afternoon feasts for family and friends. Danny chopped and tossed vegetables into a pan, fresh herbs harvested from their garden. The sizzle would level off to a quiet simmer. The better cook from the start, Daniel could make anything taste delicious, and loved to cook for everyone, dishes he'd often invent as he went along.

Margaret shook her head and faced Michael and Patty.

"I feel it in my gut, Maggie," Michael said.

"No," Margaret said.

Poor Michael. To hear Danny's big brother sound so desperate, devastated Margaret, as if he could make it be true by saying it over and over.

But Margaret became the one who found strength to face reality, to plan a memorial service, to comfort everyone, before collapsing herself, like the towers imploding and crumbling that day, that awful day, the day Daniel died.

With her little boy upstairs in bed, wrapped in his Daddy's favorite Indian's jersey, Margaret looked at her sister-in-law next to Michael, knowing they were waiting for her to say something. Her own parents had just left before Michael came in, Dutch and Jean on their way over now. Margaret pushed away from the sink, folded the towel, once at the seam, and then again in half, and placed it back on the counter.

"Michael," she said, her voice calm and steady, right there in the kitchen where she and Danny had painted creamy yellow walls like sunshine. "Daniel is dead."

She still remembered it like yesterday, the awful look on Michael's face before he turned away and wept in Patty's arms. The kitchen window cracked open, and the cool evening breeze through the sheer café curtains. How she'd noticed the floor needed to be mopped, the recycling bin emptied. The clock on the wall struck the hour in even tones. All of it, the moment frozen in her mind, she'd remember forever.

The dark days came further and further apart. These days, when Margaret fell asleep next to Henry, her dreams seldom included Daniel anymore, and she slept with a peace of mind she'd not felt in years. And she wanted to keep it that way.

71

But now, here in Sedona, the earth under her feet had shifted, awakening feelings she'd buried long ago. She had to follow the cracks in the ground that might lead to Daniel, to see if he was real, or a figment of her imagination.

She felt the vortex of metaphysical energy traveling through her, and push against her heart, in even compressions, one after the other, all of her thoughts converging.

Had the spiritual energies of the red rock formations opened her soul? Had Michael been right? Had he felt it?

Maybe Danny did wander off. Maybe he couldn't remember anything. And maybe he stopped here, in this place, because of the energy—because he was trying to remember. He'd made his home in Northern Arizona, where the red and orange colored sandstone stretched high from the desert floor, where the trees were pine, the landscape brushy, dotted with cacti and shrubbery. Had he landed there after trying to recall his name and where he came from? Could it be possible he didn't remember anything—that he wouldn't recognize his own wife? But even so, didn't she owe it to him to make sure, to help him if he was suffering?

Margaret took in a deep breath of warm air. Her eyes didn't tear up this time, and she didn't sneeze. The lush gardens bloomed with daylilies, geraniums and an abundance of honeysuckle, the sweetness irresistible to the hummingbirds and butterflies that fluttered around the fountain.

Margaret charged the breakfast to her room. She gathered her purse and the list of addresses. She walked past the shuttle parked at the turnaround outside the lobby and began the hike to town, where she'd left her car last night, to find him. Find Daniel.

Chapter 12
Alex

The knocks were repetitive—three raps, a break, three more—but Alex tried to ignore the pounding at his door, he wanted to sleep, then felt the sun beating down from the skylight. He opened his eyes, squinted back at the bright sunshine and pulled his arms from over his head, pins and needles poked at his left hand from the same position for so long. Drenched in sweat again, Alex felt disoriented from the painkillers. Whoever stood outside his door, would not give up.

"Alright, alright, hold on."

The rapping stopped as Alex pulled himself up and sat on the edge of the futon then steadied his legs as he stood. His head throbbed and he felt like he might puke from the awful taste in his mouth. He leaned against the door jam and unlocked the heavy wooden door that always seemed to Alex, out of proportion for the compact space. Designed and built in the same Spanish style, the door matched those in the main house. After all, built as a guesthouse or pool house, nobody considered a space for a caretaker.

The patio outside the sliding door had a view of the pool, but the main house sat off to the left and closer to the front of the property, affording plenty of privacy. Between the pool and the owner's residence, a large fountain and barbeque area served as an outdoor entertainment space when the Tyler's were in town. Otherwise, Alex had the place to himself, but he didn't venture past the pool, other than for caretaking, or to check the main house. He had everything he needed at the back of the property. He kept a pick-up truck under a covered portico a short distance from Alex's front door, closer to the stables. The front gate to the property remained closed and locked, unless he expected a delivery of Bermuda hay, then he'd walk up early in the morning to open the gate, before mucking out the stalls.

Alex pulled the front door a jar, trying to remember the day of the week.

Is it Monday?

Mondays there were deliveries.

He stepped outside, the sun blinding him again. Once he focused, he saw no truck, but around the corner on the dusty gravel driveway he spotted Carlos on foot, headed back toward the gate.

"Hey," Alex cleared his throat. "Carlos," he yelled.

His boss skidded in his tracks, turned around, hands on his hips. Alex glanced down at his own naked feet. "Hold on, let me get my boots." Alex smoothed back stray hairs escaping the braid he hadn't tended since yesterday, and then hopped over a bale of hay toward his door.

When Alex came back outside, Carlos waited a few feet from the stoop, wearing dark sunglasses and a white t-shirt with a large chicken on the front. "You okay?" Carlos said. "Don't look so good."

"Yeah, just overslept from taking those pills." Alex realized he'd striped out of his clothes sometime during the night and only wore boxer shorts now with his boots. His head felt thick, like a bad hangover. "I don't know, man. I'm out of it. What time is it?"

"Ten," Carlos said, and bent over to brush the dust from his sneakers. "Thought I'd drop off the bike on my way to the restaurant. It's in my truck."

Ten?

Alex never slept past six, usually up by five. Took most of the morning, often into early afternoon to finish the currying of the horses and his other chores around the ranch. He kept the pool clean, the lawn cut, the shrubs trimmed, the patios hosed down — whatever needed tending. He headed to the barn each morning and night, cared for Maxwell and Lady, as well as the stables and paddock. Some days were quicker than others, unless the livestock needed exercise, a ride along the trails, or an extra bit of grooming. He'd make himself a sandwich for the walk to town for his second job at the restaurant. With half the morning gone, he'd never get his chores done now.

"You're not coming in today," Carlos said.

But Alex already had a short list in mind, so he'd get there on time.

"You look like hell and you're bleeding again." Carlos pointed to Alex's forehead.

Alex lifted his hand to the gauze bandage. The tape had come undone and he could feel the fresh blood. "I just need a shower and a new bandage...get some work done around here and I'll make it fine."

"Nope," Carlos said. "Absolutely not. Now give me the damn key to the gate, so I can pull my truck around."

Alex went back inside. He pulled a t-shirt over his head, and tossed a set of keys to Carlos from the doorway. Once Carlos headed for his truck, Alex slipped his boots off, pulled on a pair of jeans, and then put his boots back on. He dunked his face under the kitchen faucet, dried his forehead with a kitchen towel, leaving behind bloodstains. Pain ricocheted through his head as he taped sterile gauze over the cut right as Carlos pulled into the carport.

"You didn't need to bring this all the way out here," Alex said, walking toward Carlos. "I could've ridden it home from town."

Carlos tossed the gate keys to Alex as he got out of the truck. "It's not a street bike, dude. You want the cops after you?" Carlos walked around to the rear of the truck then unlatched and lowered the gate on his shiny black Chevy. He climbed inside the bed, tugged up his pants then unhooked the bungee cords that held the dirt bike in place.

Alex didn't want the motorcycle now. He'd changed his mind, not having considered all the potential issues before. He shouldn't have drunk so many beers. He wasn't thinking straight when he told Carlos he wanted the motorcycle before he even rode it. And besides, his boss was right. He couldn't ride on the streets, and to register the bike meant paperwork and identification checks, which Alex tried to avoid.

A few years ago, Carlos mentioned withholding taxes from Alex's wages. Alex panicked knowing he'd be forced to quit, invent an excuse, like ranch work was enough. He had a driver's license, so that wasn't a problem, but Alex preferred to remain off the grid. But for some reason, Carlos never made the changes, and Alex kept showing up for his shifts. He never asked Carlos about it and found his envelope of cash in the same prep-kitchen drawer every week, even though he knew the other employees received checks attached to their timecards.

Alex appreciated his boss making the exception for him, but with the motorcycle, there'd be a bill of sale and transfer of title, so Alex felt uncomfortable now with the deal. But, he couldn't tell Carlos. The man drove all the way out there, and after turning out Maxwell and Lady, Alex knew Carlos was right about that too, he'd be too wiped out to work at the restaurant that night. The less he said now, the better. He'd figure it out later.

Alex glanced at the barn door. He'd never left Maxwell and Lady inside the stables so long before, other than during high temperatures when he used cooling hoses inside the stalls. Only the best for two stable mates, who rarely spent time with their owners, like an old couple at a retirement home with family too busy to visit. Seemed like an expensive eccentricity to Alex, but as long as the Tyler's paid him, Alex wasn't going to complain. There'd be more manure to clean out today and he hoped the two were okay, Maxwell could be temperamental and never did well staying inside for long periods. Lady tended to be unpredictably skittish. He didn't need them weaving from boredom. So, right now, Alex needed Carlos to leave, so he could get his work done.

"Dude, pull that plank down while I get this untied." Carlos pointed at a two by twelve planed cut of timber used for scaffolding.

Alex grabbed the end, pulled it out of the truck bed, and propped it against the back of the gate so Carlos could roll the bike from the truck. They both worked the motorcycle down the plank onto the ground.

Alex's head spun as they lowered the bike, but he kept quiet. Tried to act normal, even though with every movement, his brain pulsated inside his skull. He pushed the motorcycle under the portico and leaned it against a low concrete wall. Carlos rolled up the bungee cords and closed the gate on the truck.

"Gotta get going," Carlos said, "I'll find someone to cover your shift today and you're off tomorrow, but take Monday too, get healed. You need that checked if it keeps bleeding." Carlos tapped his own forehead. "Listen to me, because I know. My kids are always banging themselves up, gettin' stitches. You've probably got a concussion, so stay off your feet for a few more days. Got someone who can help with them smelly horses?"

Alex didn't need Carlos sending some stupid busboy out to help him. "Yeah, I got a guy," Alex lied. If he couldn't take care of Maxwell and Lady, he'd board them with the vet, but he wouldn't do that. Never had before. He could manage.

It's just a cut, for God's sake.

Alex rubbed the back of his neck. A few days off might be good anyway. With that woman snooping around, he needed to lie low for a while.

That woman? That woman is Margaret, your wife.

Alex felt the ground shift under his boots, another dizzy spell.

Carlos shook his head.

"Right," Alex said. "See you Tuesday."

Carlos climbed inside the cab of his truck, dusty now from the service road. He started up the diesel engine, a big whoosh sounded from the V8 system, and then lowered the driver's side window and leaned out on his arm.

"Go see the doctor if you don't improve," he said. "I don't want you back in the kitchen till you're okay...don't need you slicing a finger off with a knife because you're dizzy. Okay, dude?"

"Yeah. Okay. Thanks."

Alex followed the truck on foot as Carlos backed down the long driveway. He gave a nod as Carlos pulled away toward town and waved out the window. As Alex closed the gate, secured the lock, he realized Carlos hadn't given him a bill of sale, after all. Maybe once Alex completed the repairs and found a buyer, Carlos could sign over the title for the new owner right away. If he kept his mouth shut, maybe Carlos wouldn't think of it until then, and Alex wouldn't need to register the motorcycle.

Alex faced the dusty access road back to the barn. Over to the left, a paved turnaround lied in front of the main house with an attached three-car garage for the owners. They kept a Jeep there year round. In addition, Alex had access to the pick-up truck. If he needed to transport Maxwell and Lady, he'd use the trailer kept at the end of the service road on the other side of the barn.

A breeze kicked up. Alex felt lightheaded as he walked past the main house. Carlos might be right—he shouldn't handle knives in his condition. He walked as far as a shady white oak growing wild along the edge of the dirt path. Under the tree, Alex lowered his achy body to the ground. He leaned against the trunk, closed his eyes, and tried to control the wooziness he felt. He'd stay quiet until the pain calmed down. The livestock would have to wait he needed to rest first.

Alex remained under the tree for longer than he planned. A gust of wind rattled the front gate when he awoke. Startled, he got to his feet, and headed past the pool house, wishing he could go inside, collapse on the futon, and sleep the day away, but he continued on to the stables, instead.

Heading under the portico, Alex noticed the top-half of the barn door wide open, with Maxwell hanging his head outside.

"What the hell?" Alex knew he'd closed the Dutch door after he secured the stalls.

Alex squeezed past Maxwell inside the barn, and gave the gelding a few pats to the hindquarters. Maxwell kicked up dust as Alex led him outside to the paddock. With Maxwell in the field, Alex doubled backed to Lady in her stall worried she might get out somehow, too.

"You look fine, girl." A rope held the gate on Maxwell's stall open, tied to the next stall. "Was someone here?" He knew Lady couldn't say, but he felt confused. That door was closed when Carlos came by. Something didn't feel right. He knew someone had been there, he never tied the gates open.

Then he noticed a heavy wool blanket tossed over the desk chair. Alex yanked the bottom drawer open, nothing missing, so he folded the blanket and hung it inside Maxwell's stall, and kept the gate open for now. Lady seemed riled from the confusion now, so Alex turned her out into the paddock. Maxwell grazed in the far corner as Lady stopped short in the middle of the corral and dipped her head several times before chewing on the grass. Alex scratched the back of his head as he glanced around, the gates to the paddock were all closed, and nothing seemed amiss in the grooming area, so he headed inside the barn.

Maybe he did come back last night, to check the schedule and then opened the gate thinking it was early morning. He couldn't be sure. He still felt blurry from the night before.

After a couple of hours mucking out the stables, Alex scrubbed the water troughs and feed buckets, spread fresh sawdust in the stalls, then headed out to check the field and the fences. He scooped manure piles from the grass and fixed a cracked rail on the fence that surrounded the paddock.

Maxwell wandered over from the corral to where Alex cleaned his tools, the gelding often followed Alex around the field when he worked. The older Appaloosa still had some mischief in him. Often, when Alex greeted him, he'd canter away as quick as he'd arrived. Alex ignored Maxwell now, sensing his restlessness and need to play. Instead, Alex grabbed a bucket of feed, shook it as he headed back toward the stable. He hoped Maxwell would lope along behind him, so he could check his points.

"I'm not putting you back in your stall, Max, I need to clean your hooves." Alex shook the bucket again and Maxwell shadowed him over to the grooming area.

Lady, the mare, and every bit her name, hung back in the field, still grazing. She ignored them both, as always. The same breed as Maxwell, Lady had distinctive markings with a snowcapped coat and black stockings. She could graze for days if allowed. Alex took them for rides along the national forest paths that surrounded the ranch. He'd usually ride Maxwell first or bring Lady along holding her by a lariat so she could trot alongside.

He groomed them daily, except during scorching heat or frigid cold. On those days, Alex allowed a layer of dust and mud to build up on their coats, to protect them from the extreme weather. He'd still check them, a ritual before and after they were turned out, for cuts, bites, or tender spots. Never having ridden a horse in his life before he came to Sedona, Alex learned, the hard way, how to mount a horse, address the reins, let his weight sink into the saddle, allow his hips to glide with the natural movements of the horse, and of course, how to give a tight tug on the reins if he wanted to stop. Maxwell dipped his head as he trotted up to where Alex waited under a covered shelter he'd built his first year there.

Alex gave Maxwell a good scratch, comfortable around the horses nowadays, unlike when he'd first started as caretaker.

He'd learned to enjoy the solitude of rides along the desert pathways. But at first, he'd had trouble riding. Thrown from Lady early on, Alex chewed a mouthful of gravel when he landed, cutting his lip. They'd come upon a snake, he and Lady, and she spooked, then reared up and dumped Alex hard. He'd run a mile before he found her grazing near several shade trees.

Since then, he didn't ride Maxwell or Lady into wide-open spaces. Rather, he'd stick to trails near the property. Nevertheless, they'd trot a few miles each time, and sometimes he'd let them canter or even gallop along the straightaways.

He never failed to check their hooves, and used a pick to clean out any manure or rocks.

Today, he wouldn't ride, and neither Maxwell nor Lady had received a good grooming since mid-week, which had never happened before Alex got hurt. He felt weak since he fell off the motorcycle, and hadn't been able to keep up. His head ached all the time now and he had to rest between chores.

Once Alex finished with Maxwell, he called out to Lady, whistled a few times, and then gave up when she ignored him. He grabbed a ripe apple from a box on the tool shelf. She never bothered to glance his way, playing hard to get, as Alex moseyed out into the field, and right on cue, Lady tossed her head to tell Alex she was still hungry and had no intention of cooperating.

"Hey there pretty Lady, look what I got." Alex tossed the apple from one hand to the other, and brought the shiny red fruit to his nose. "Hmmm, smells sweet," he said. "Want some?"

Lady sauntered over to Alex and let him slip a halter with a lead rope over her head. She devoured the apple before they reached the shaded area outside the stables. Alex tied the lead to the post using a clove hitch knot, something he learned from a book about cowboy life. He could tie knots in his sleep nowadays, so he knew he didn't tie that rope in the barn, barely secure, he always used the right knots. Alex placed a hose in the water trough near the shed, and turned the spigot to fill it full. He glanced around again, out beyond the pasture, wary of being watched. He returned to Lady under the shelter, trying to shake the notion that someone might be spying on him.

"Lets see what needs doing, my Lady." Alex used a gentle voice as he passed behind Lady. He'd learned she needed to know his whereabouts and didn't like surprises.

He ran a firm hand down her leg before he raised a hoof to clean the frog, a triangular area that Alex cleaned, so they didn't get thrush. Alex used the hoof pick to clear some debris and moved on to the next hoof. After he'd checked all four, he left Lady in the shade, and took a swig of water from the hose before he rolled it back up near the shower. He'd bathe them another day. They were both in good shape and he didn't want the oils in their coats to diminish since September could get hot. The thermometer read 88 degrees in the shade before he returned to Lady.

"Hot day, my darling," he said. "I'll give you a good brush and then you can get back to your grass. Sound good?"

Alex grabbed a currycomb to loosen the dirt while he continued to talk to Lady. "Want a new style? Something fancy, maybe?"

Lady gazed straight ahead as Alex combed in a circular motion and then used a hard bristle brush to clear the hair of dust. Once he finished with her belly, he used a softer brush, then finally, combed through her tail and mane with his fingers to make sure nothing caught in the dense hair.

"There you go," Alex said. "Still got plenty of light to get more grub in that belly." He patted her on the hindquarters and let her go free of her harness to enjoy the grassy paddock for the rest of the afternoon.

Alex swept and made sure the tools were put away, added fresh hay to the stalls, and then checked the schedule tacked up on the wall inside the stables. Maxwell and Lady were due in a few weeks to visit the farrier for trimming hooves and new horseshoes.

They'd had a visit with the equine veterinarian last month, and they were up-to-date on deworming medication, but the vet mentioned Maxwell's teeth were due to be floated. That would have to wait until he felt better.

Back outside in the paddock, the sun hit Alex hard as he tried to ignore yet another attack of vertigo. He was getting sick of it. And it didn't help that the temperature seemed to rise from the desert floor like heat waves radiating off a lit charcoal grill. The earth tilted and shifted under Alex's boots, the sky faded, darker and darker with each step.

Alex blinked again and again, trying to focus, but the dimmer switch continued to fade the world around him, until Alex fell onto his knees, and crawled toward a patch of shaded ground before the world went dark and silent.

Chapter 13
Margaret

The steering wheel felt hot and the air stale inside the car, despite Margaret only being gone a few minutes. She made no move to turn the key in the ignition. Instead, she sat in silence, and gazed out through the front window, clutching her purse to her chest. A woman stood outside a few houses up on the left, hosing down the walkway leading to the front door of a single story bungalow with a clay tile roof.

Margaret decided the thicket of trees lining the street must be a variety native only to northern Arizona, because she'd never seen them before. The bushy overgrowth resembled tall Junipers. There were random Ponderosa Pines shooting up between the shrubby foliage, almost as an afterthought. The copious vegetation hung over parts of the street obstructing access to pedestrians. As a jogger ran past the lady with the hose, Margaret watched him head around another clump of trees, then ran to the end of the block before he turned left and disappeared.

"What am I doing?" Margaret whispered, gripping her bag even tighter. "I need to go home," she said, "Right now."

The area where she'd parked felt stranger by the minute. This town seemed to be a place where people went to hide, runaway—disappear. Even though she'd been told otherwise, she didn't buy it. Something odd hung in the air, a hint of quiet desperation. Although, Margaret wondered if she might be the one feeling desperate, she'd certainly acted that way.

"Daniel Waterson is a common name," the man had said. "Some spell it with two t's."

Margaret had sat in this stranger's living room on a brown plaid sofa near the front picture window, wondering what in the world she'd been thinking.

"Maybe you got the spelling wrong?" he offered.

She gazed at the wall behind the beige, faux-suede lounge chair, where the man sat, unable to stop staring at three mirrors, cut in zigzag patterns, hung side by side. She wanted to shove them together like puzzle pieces, but stayed put, somewhere between curious and freaked-out. Circus mirrors, like at the carnival when she was a kid, except smaller.

An identical chair sat to the right, a vintage TV tray table with a sixties-style floral bouquet print, separated the two recliners. The retro-style tray teetered atop a set of thin legs, corroded over time, giving it a rusted patina. Aluminum doesn't rust, Margaret knew that, a simple case of oxidation, but her mind kept racing from one peculiar piece of furniture to another. CNN blared from a flat screen TV propped atop a mid-century console television, the old screen half-covered by a vibrant, orange and yellow Native American blanket. A limp, plastic plant hung from a macramé holder in the corner and the room smelled like pet urine, yet she saw no dogs or cats around.

So distracted by the eccentric environment, Margaret had to force herself to pay attention to the man perched on the edge of his recliner, wearing red suspenders, and a navy blue t-shirt with a military emblem on the left pocket, his grey hair buzzed short.

Noise and disorder had always distracted Margaret. In college, Margaret took a part-time position as a mother's helper, running errands and watching children for a woman who had nine kids, all under the age of 12. Whenever Margaret entered their home, she'd fall into a trance from the chaos. Telephones ringing, children crying over each other, cartoons blasting and the mother herself, loud and edgy. She pulled Margaret aside one day, warned her if she continued to stand frozen in place, she'd fire her. Margaret couldn't lose the job. Her parents were only able to cover part of her tuition that semester. So she learned fast to use her calm temperament to draw the children into an activity, like reading them classic children's literature from the public library. She'd bring The Secret Garden, Where the Wild Things Are, or

The Adventures of Tom Sawyer, and the children would actually sit still for a while, mesmerized by the characters, begging her for one more chapter. They'd take nature hikes and collect pinecones and twigs for art projects. She even coaxed them to create an entire fairy world at the edge of their wooded backyard, collecting cast off figurines, dolls, scraps of fabric, and ribbons while the boys made houses out of popsicle sticks and toothpicks, and carved roads between the fairy houses.

Margaret knew she'd been daydreaming too long, the man's eyebrows were raised, something about different spellings.

She cleared her throat. "No, that's the right spelling," Margaret said, and kept her clammy hands folded in her lap. "I'm sorry I bothered you." She rubbed her hands on the skirt of her dress. "Obviously, you're not the Daniel Waterson I'm trying to find." Margaret rose from the sofa, holding her purse against her chest.

Mr. Waterson followed her to the front door.

"Got a son in Florida, but his name's Mark. My wife wanted to name him after me, but I never liked the idea." He held the screen door for Margaret. "I think people should have their own name, don't you?"

"I'm very sorry I bothered you."

"Not every day a pretty lady rings my bell," he said, smiling, his teeth straight and white against his deep tan. "Don't worry, you'll find him."

Margaret stepped out into the sunshine. The clay pots near the front door were empty except for dried, cracked dirt and a few weeds.

"Wife died a few years ago," the man said. "Son doesn't come around much anymore, so I know what it's like to want to find someone you love."

"No, well, he was someone from my past."

"Love is love." The man placed his hand over his heart.

Margaret glanced again at the dirt in the flowerpots before she walked away. "Earth to earth, ashes to ashes, dust to dust." The words from Danny's memorial echoed in her mind as she marched down the street to her SUV parked in front of another house where the branches weren't hanging so low.

Margaret placed her purse on the passenger's seat now, and turned the key in the ignition. Hot air blew out from the vents, but soon began to turn cooler. Tilting the rearview mirror, she dabbed at her eyes, wiping away smudges of mascara. She pulled her sunglasses from the outside pocket of her purse. Fastened her seatbelt, her fingers touching the soft skin along her chest. Daniel had once told her the skin between her breasts felt like satin. She let her fingertips linger for a moment against the velvety smoothness.

Why did he leave me?

Margaret had convinced herself she was good for Daniel. That inside, he really just wanted peace. He'd play sports so loud on the TV, but she knew he did that to drown her out toward the end of their marriage. At first though, he'd come home after work, and she might have arrived before him, started dinner already, music playing lightly on the stereo, and they'd sit together in the kitchen and talk about their days.

"This is nice," he'd say. "We never did this in my family."

She knew what he meant. The Watersons tended to talk all at once, each of them wanting to be the center of attention, especially Dutch and Michael. She didn't mind their banter and lively repertoire, having come from a quiet home, it was fun for her, but she could understand how Daniel felt. Even she grew weary over the years of their speeches and grandstanding. But still, she'd always love them in some way. She only wished Daniel hadn't become so withdrawn, and bitter, and with her, too. Somehow they lost their way in their marriage, and the quiet place they'd found together seemed to disappear once his family came over all the time. But those first years were nice, just the two of them, fixing up their house, going for walks in the evening. Those were the years she tried to remember after he died. That was how she wanted to remember him.

A tear escaped from beneath her sunglasses, but Margaret wiped it away with her free hand as she placed the car in drive, and steered past the lady who now watered plants on her porch. Margaret turned right at the end of the block toward town.

She'd begun the search with the furthest address out. But she'd had enough after only one stop. She wasn't going to another stranger's house looking for a man who was dead.

"Ridiculous," she said, slowing down to stop for a red light. "Have you lost your mind?"

What was I thinking, going inside that man's house?

She took a deep breath trying to hold onto her emotions.

"Chasing after a ghost?" she said, waiting for the light to change.

Real smart.

She glanced right and then left as traffic went by.

"You're searching for a dead man," she said, noticing a young boy in the back seat of a sedan in the next lane. She smiled at him and he turned his head. "That's right, you should look away from the crazy lady." But nobody could hear her with the windows shut.

The light turned green and the car with the boy pulled away. Margaret could still see his curly hair rising above his car seat in the back window, reminding her of Jake at the same age. Jacob, already tall as a toddler, barely fit in his car seat by the age of three.

"Shouldn't he be in school?" People would ask at the grocery store.

Margaret would explain he wasn't old enough for school. They'd comment on his size and smile at Margaret as though she'd achieved something phenomenal by having a tall child.

Watching him trek back to the dorm the other day, so lanky, still growing into his big feet, all grown up and independent, ready to take on the world. Margaret realized Jacob was the phenomenal one, and raising him, indeed, had been her greatest achievement.

Had seeing Jacob walk away sparked this craziness inside her? Had letting him go caused another round of letting Daniel go?

It made sense. Daniel didn't leave her. He died ten years ago. Time to let go, to move on.

Margaret knew one thing. She would go back to the hotel, pack her bag and go home to Henry.

She grabbed her phone, but realized Henry always went for a run around the same time on weekends.

Henry, I need you.

Maybe she shouldn't tell Henry at all. Instead, she'd handle it on her own, see this for what it was—an emotional moment, a journey to letting go. Maybe this part of the country did have some magical hold that could take you over, and force you to face matters you'd thought you'd buried.

If she hurried, she could get home tonight and still have Sunday with Henry before he left.

Margaret made the final turn in town toward the inn. She passed by the Mexican restaurant where this whole mess began. People were gathered outside at the tables under the shady overhang covered in leafy vines. She glanced at her watch— already lunchtime. Traffic slowed at the crosswalk for pedestrians, and just ahead, Margaret saw a car pull out from a parking space as traffic began to move again. She pulled into the spot and shut-off the engine. She sat there for a few seconds then grabbed her keys and purse, and headed to the restaurant.

She'd ask once more and then she'd know for sure. And that would be the end of this, done, finished, moving on.

Margaret picked up her pace, passed by several people on the sidewalk waiting for a table. She pulled the door open to the main dining room.

I promise, Henry. I'm in and then out.

The busboy from last night came out from the kitchen, through the same door where she saw the man who resembled Danny. She waved to the young man, trying to smile as she pulled her sunglasses off. Good, he remembered her. He walked toward her with a large plastic container under his arm, and a towel in his other hand. But he went right past her outside.

"Can I help you?"

Margaret hadn't noticed the pretty, young woman with olive skin and long, wavy, black hair nearby with a clipboard.

"Do you want to put your name on the list," she said. "It's a twenty-minute wait right now."

"Excuse me?" The hostess spoke perfect English, with scarcely an accent, but Margaret didn't understand her at first.

"Oh, right," Margaret said. "I don't need a table, but I'm looking for someone."

"Are you meeting a party here?"

"No. No. What I mean is, I'm looking for someone who works here. Daniel Waterson. Danny?"

By then the busboy came back inside with a full tub of dishes and just before he went by, Margaret stopped him.

"Do you remember me?"

He looked at her for a moment. "Ah, the lady from last night. Si. I know you."

The hostess wrote a man's name down on the list and he went back outside. "So, you've found him, then?" she said, turning back to Margaret and the busboy.

"Well, no, not really," Margaret said.

"She knows Alex," the busboy said.

"Well, I think his name is Danny, but yes, I'm looking for the man I saw last night."

The hostess seemed confused and gave a small wave to one of the cooks peering out from the kitchen. He came out through the swinging door.

"Diego," the cook said, "tables need cleaning."

"I was trying to help the senorita." The busboy hurried away to wipe down the empty tables.

Margaret turned her attention to the cook.

"I'm the owner," he said. "Can I help you with something?"

Margaret moved out of the way of a group of diners trying to leave. "I'm sorry, I can see you're busy. Do you have a Daniel Waterson working for you in the kitchen? I saw a man standing inside that door last night, with an apron on, who looked like him."

"No Daniel working here, sorry."

"He's thin, long hair, I think...tucked under a bandana." The same type of headscarf the cook wore. "He was smoking in the alleyway last night and talking to a girl with black hair."

"Alex?"

"That's the name the busboy said. He looks so much like someone I know."

"Alex is home sick today," the owner said, "He lives outside town at the Tyler ranch. Takes care of the place for them." The cook shook hands with a man passing by, spoke to him in Spanish, but nonetheless, Margaret recognized the greeting, 'Have a good day' from her limited command of the language.

Turning back to Margaret, he smiled, and let the hostess pass by with a man and a woman to one of the clean tables. "He'll be back soon," the owner said, "Bumped his head, so he's off for a few days."

A loud clatter of dishes came from the kitchen and the cook went through the swinging door before Margaret could ask more questions.

"Do you know where he lives?" Margaret asked the hostess when she came back.

"He takes care of Bill and Sue Tyler's place, but I don't know the address."

A large group entered, and spoke to the hostess as she smiled at Margaret. "I'm sure they're listed." She grinned again, her brown eyes warm and engaging, which made Margaret feel better about asking.

"Thank you," Margaret said. "Bill and Sue Tyler, right?"

The hostess nodded, and then turned her attention to the group waiting to add their name to the list.

Margaret slipped around the crowd, and put her sunglasses on as she went outside. The sun sat high in the sky. She hurried to her car, and used her cell phone to search for the name.

She found William and Susan Tyler with an address and phone number. Margaret hit dial and the call rolled over to voicemail. She didn't leave a message. Instead, she entered the address into the GPS system and flipped the air conditioner switch to high as she pulled away from the curb.

Margaret turned right at the next corner as directed. Two more turns and then a straight shot down a two-lane highway. The house would be on the right side. She couldn't think of anything other than Danny. Her heart raced as she drove out of town. The ranches and estates appeared to be acres apart. She slowed when she came upon a dramatic, arched gate at the entrance to an estate with a gorgeous Spanish-style home set back from the road. The GPS startled her when it announced she'd reached her destination.

Chapter 14
Alex

The tree branches rustled in the mild breeze, but Alex kept his eyes closed when he first awoke, trying to keep the pain inside his skull at bay. He rotated onto his back, the ground rough and gritty against his skin. Feeling dazed and disoriented, he squinted at the sky through the leaves.

"Where's the gate?" Alex said, his voice scratchy. He could have sworn he was near the front of the property. "Wait, where am I?" He pushed himself upright, bleary-eyed, and glanced straight ahead into the paddock. He noticed Lady near the back fence and heard Maxwell nearby, a familiar playful snort as hooves struck the ground. Alex glanced left to see Maxwell at the water trough.

"You're near the stables," a woman said from somewhere behind him, or maybe he'd just imagined it. The world spun in figure eights around him and he couldn't focus. "You fell. Your head is bleeding," she said.

Alex flinched and pulled away as someone touched his forehead. A woman with wavy hair stood beside him. Alex reached up to trace the familiar honey-colored locks. His fingers brushed the silky skin near her lips. She resembled Margaret, the same indigo eyes, but with lashes darker than he remembered. Alex began to slump, he felt lightheaded again, his vision blurry.

"Oh, no you don't," she said. Her arms supported him from behind. "I'll never get you back up again."

She smelled like a sugary combination of vanilla and some type of intoxicating scent of a flower. He turned his head, but she had already reached underneath his arms to pull him on to his feet. Somehow, he stood, but he felt unable to walk on his own.

"Hold on to me," the woman said. "Put your arm around my shoulders."

"You look like someone I used to know," Alex said, and wondered if she really was Margaret. The world began to spin again as he caught sight of Maxwell outside the covered area. "Max, don't worry, man." Alex tripped on something, but didn't fall. The woman held tight to him, and directed him toward the entry to the stables. "I'm fine," Alex said, but felt like he might still be asleep. "Am I dreaming?"

Why is Maggie here?

Then, like an alarm, a loud buzzer began to reverberate inside his skull. "What the hell?" he shouted.

"Just a bit further and I can help you lie down and call for help."

"What?" Alex struggled to hear over the noise inside his head. "Don't call anyone."

The light began to dim again and Alex felt he might go down before they reached the barn. He leaned against her, and somehow knew she'd take care of him. "Just get me to my house, it's through the barn." Alex could see the stalls as the woman led him to the door.

Alex shouted over the incessant loud buzz. "Do you hear that noise?" He noticed his place across the portico. "Make sure to shut the barn door." Alex leaned heavier against her. Her small frame felt like it might give way to his height, but somehow he knew she'd do what he said. "Close the top half, too." He listened for the familiar click of the latch. Then they moved under the portico, the smell of hay and motor oil hung in the air. "That small house, there." Alex eyed the woman, and almost stumbled again.

"Come on, Danny, you can make it, we're almost there."

The ground shifted again and again, like the earthquake he remembered south of Tucson when he still thought he might go to Mexico.

Margaret?

Her grip tightened against his side.

Why is she here?

93

Then he felt the futon beneath his body, a pillow under his head, his boots removed and a cool cloth placed under his neck. The buzzer sound began to dim, but through it all, each time he glanced her way, he couldn't help but notice how long Margaret's hair had grown.

"Your wife is pretty."

Daniel stood near the elevator as the receptionist sat behind her desk, her pallid face rose above the tall countertop surrounding the workspace where she answered phones and greeted clients and associates. "Do you miss her when you travel?"

"I did."

"You did? You mean, you do?"

"No," Alex said, walking a few steps back toward her desk. She wore the same white blouse—her nails painted red. Margaret always wore a light pink color. "I mean...I used to miss her, but not now."

Ding-ding. The elevator doors opened. Alex turned around. Inside the elevator, the passengers were covered in ashes, silent—their eyes vacant, bloodshot. "Are you coming?" one of them asked.

But Alex didn't respond. He gazed back at the receptionist. Her hair in flames now. Her screams silent, the same hollow expression as the elevator people.

Someone from the elevator, who sounded like Alex's mother, spoke. "I bet she misses you." Alex shuddered, trying to twist around, but he couldn't move his body.

The floor collapsed beneath him. Alex fell through the air, as massive chunks of steel zoomed by. He felt a woman move behind him. She reached around to hold him secure against her body as they floated down and then out over water. Their feet skimmed the top of the rapid currents of a river, and they moved in unison with several flocks of birds that seemed to lead the way. When they reached the sea, they gained speed and passed the Seagulls, Barn Swallows, Sparrows, Cardinals, Red-winged Blackbirds, Orioles, Orchard and Baltimore varieties, all the species in the bird book Alex's father gave him for his eighth birthday. Alex fixed his sights on the birds heading in a different direction now, as he and the woman continued on, until land lay beneath them again, and she let him down in the middle of a field. The tall grass smelled of fresh rain as she lay down by his side and held his hand.

"You're safe, Danny."

So peaceful the moment—his mind drifted, quiet at last.

When he came to again, the woman had vanished. Shivering atop a frozen lake, Alex could see nothing beyond the heavily flocked trees that encircled the frigid pond. Only the full moon illuminated the ice beneath him. He tried to rise up, the slick surface impossible to stand on. Then somehow, upright all at once, he felt the cracking below his feet and watched as the ice splintered in all directions around him. Far from the shore, he realized he would go under soon, the ice becoming thinner beneath him. Hundreds of murky eyes from bodies lining the depths of the lake, gazed up at Alex, their arms reaching upward as he struggled. The ice broke apart under his weight. He sunk deep into the water. The shocking cold pulled at his torso as the hands reached up from below and grabbed his legs. Alex gulped the bitter cold water. His screams for help, unheard.

He felt a warm hand on his shoulder, another against the skin on his face.

"You're okay."

Alex gasped for air. "I'm freezing."

"Chills from the fever."

Alex held on to the woman who looked like Margaret. "What's happening? Why are you here?" He tried to shove her away, but he felt too weak.

"I found you outside near the barn. You were lying on the ground. Your head was bleeding."

Had he been asleep? Or had the nightmare taken over his consciousness?

"You were screaming." She let him go and moved to the other end of the futon. Had she been crying? Pieces of Alex's world whirled back into his mind, coming together in one shocking realization.

Margaret. Right there, in the flesh. She wore a pale blue summer dress, her hair pulled up in a clip at her crown. Long tendrils floated down past her shoulders, the color lighter. Her cheeks appeared flushed, like they did when she felt nervous. Her eyes glowed with tears.

Alex felt like he was gazing into his past, at the woman he'd run away from, the life he'd turned his back on. Margaret sat there, beautiful, as lovely as the day he'd left, maybe even lovelier.

That final night, at the house in Cleveland, Margaret went up to bed after everyone left. Alex climbed the stairs, careful, so the staircase didn't creak. He found the pocket watch he'd stolen from his brother's jacket during the party, hidden in his sock drawer. He packed his bag and slipped the watch into an inside pocket on the suit he planned to wear.

On his way out, he stopped at the foot of the bed where Margaret slept. She lay on her side, one arm draped across his pillow. Filtered streetlight trickled in through the window from across the room. Margaret looked like an angel. Before he could change his mind, he left the room.

The next morning, Alex boarded a flight out of Cleveland.

He'd never forgive Margaret. *Never.*

Margaret stared at him now. She appeared shaken. She didn't talk. Maybe she'd discovered him by accident. Didn't know he was alive, hadn't been on his trail after all. He tried to read her eyes, but she just sat there like she wasn't sure if it was really he she was seeing.

"How long was I asleep?" Alex said, aware of the full weight of the moment.

His wife, Margaret, who probably believed he died ten years ago, sat a few feet from him. She didn't respond to his question. Darkness filled the skylight. The lamp on the side table added a gloomy sheen to the strange ambiance in the room. A blanket from the storage chest covered his legs.

They were both motionless for a long moment, silent, observing each other. Her skin appeared luminous, suntanned, her hands folded in her lap, one leg tucked under the futon. Several strands of hair had come loose from her clip. And then, he noticed a simple gold band with several diamonds on her ring finger, not the same ring he'd given her at their wedding. He glanced up at her face. Tears brimmed at the edges of her blue eyes. She looked so vulnerable. Alex almost wanted to pull her close.

"Do you know who I am?" Margaret's voice fell into a whisper.

Once when they were at a party in college, before they really knew each other, Margaret was across the room with a few other girls. They were all giggling and Margaret spilled her drink on one of the girls, staining the front of the girl's blouse with beer. Margaret pulled her sweatshirt over her head to help dry up the mess. She looked pretty with her hair disheveled, and her t-shirt tugged up halfway. Alex noticed the creaminess of her exposed skin. He'd never before noticed her in that way, not since high school anyway, even though they'd been part of the same group all year. He spent the rest of the night trying to get to know her, and when the moment felt right, he kissed her and she looked surprised, but she kissed him back. And they were a couple.

Margaret's eyes seemed filled with concern, the same way she looked the night they'd fought before he left. The same woman he'd married and traveled with through Canada on their honeymoon, their old Toyota barely making it back to Cleveland. The same girl he fell for that night in college, her familiar honey-kissed complexion shimmering in the low light, the same skin he felt when they laid together in his dorm room bed, where they first fell in love. The same Margaret he preferred to remember now, the one he thought would never hurt him. He wanted to say, "Yes, I know you. You're my wife, the woman I love."

"Danny?" She moved forward, and touched his arm. "Do you remember me?"

This time he didn't flinch when she touched him.

"Should I?"

She pulled her hand away and straightened her back, tucked the strands of hair from her face, all of her movements seemed in slow motion. He felt the room spin, his heart race. Was this real? Was she really there?

Alex closed his eyes for a moment and rubbed his forehead. He could feel the smaller gauze bandage taped to his wound. She changed the dressing. He opened his eyes, praying this figment of his imagination, this impossible moment, would be over. But she sat beside him, tears running down her face. By instinct, he moved toward her and wiped away her sadness with his fingertips, her skin warm under his touch.

She grabbed ahold of his hand; her mouth hung open a bit, as if to find the words. He remained cool, like he didn't know her, as if nothing about her seemed familiar.

"I'm Margaret."

Alex stayed motionless.

"You're wife."

Alex stared at her while a thousand thoughts ran through his mind—I'll go to Mexico or maybe Oregon. He smirked and raised an eyebrow. "I'm not married." Alex stood up and moved across the room, near the door. "I don't know who you are or what you think you're doing."

"Danny, it's me, Margaret."

"I'm not Danny. My name is Alex."

Alex waited by the door, holding his ground. He watched Margaret glance around the room, and straighten her dress.

"I think you better go now," he said.

She held onto the futon with both hands as though she might get up, but instead, she pulled her hands to her face and began to sob. "You don't understand," she said between cries, "Let me try to explain."

Alex didn't want to hear, so he opened the door wide. The cool air hit his face. He stepped outside, hoping she would follow. But she stayed.

His feet bare against the gravel, he hurried toward the stables, the door closed leading to the stalls. He opened it. Both Lady and Maxwell were safe inside the box stalls, so he closed the door and turned back toward his place. He could hear Margaret weeping inside, so he headed for the pool area, his temples still sore but no longer throbbing. The brisk air did nothing to lower the heat in his body. He dove straight into the deep end of the pool, and touched the bottom with his fingertips before pushing off and swimming to the surface. He could feel his temperature cool in the chilly water as he floated on his back for a while, like he did as a kid in the middle of the pond behind his house. When he'd become too tired to swim across in one lap, he'd rest on his back, and then swim some more, his best friend, Brian, always trailed behind.

"Danny, wait up," Brian would yell.

By the time they were teenagers, they swam across with no problem, but Danny always beat Brian to the other side. Once, walking back from their swim across, they spotted Margaret on her front porch. Danny's heart raced. Her hair glistened in the summer sun as she bounced down the front steps toward a car full of girls at the curb. Just before she slipped inside the backseat, she glanced at Danny and Brian and smiled. The boys argued about it all the way home.

"She looked right at me, Dan." Brian shoved him into an overgrown shrub along the sidewalk and they'd wrestled for a bit, before they pulled apart, and then laughed at the thought of any girl paying them attention.

Neither of them went to dances or dated. They didn't get invited to parties. They hung out in each other's basements on the weekends, went to sci-fi movies with a few other quirky types like themselves, or the video game store at the mall.

Danny and Brian were not the cool kids. But neither of them were dreadful looking by any means or even brainless. They were just those boys who ate their lunches outside, sat along the sides of the classroom if there wasn't a seating chart, didn't play sports or join clubs, got decent grades, but not good enough to win any awards. They were the guys who never stood out, wore boring brown cords and shirts in non-descript colors, in the winter covered up with heavy jackets, and hooded sweatshirts in the spring. But even so, like any of the other boys, they'd slow down in front of the cute girl's houses, hoping for a glimpse inside their windows, into their worlds or maybe even into their lives.

"She was looking at me," Danny had told Brian. He'd never forget those eyes, the way they sparkled in the summer sun, the way she smiled at him with her mouth closed at first, and then with her white gleam of teeth. No, she'd looked right at him. And he'd never forget it. Not ever.

Alex swam to the shallow end of the pool and sat on the steps. He'd wait a while, hoping she'd left. The pool smoothed out, once again calm. As the moon shone down, the water shimmered like glass.

Brian never knew Danny ended up with Margaret. He wouldn't have believed it if he did. She was out of their league back then. Even now, all these years later, he still thought about Brian, wished things had been different.

Alex remembered the lake, frozen over, Brian standing there right before he slipped through the ice.

They were all drunk that night, Danny, his brother, Michael, Michael's friends, but especially, Brian. He'd been dancing around at the edge of the dock, acting juvenile. At one point Brian jumped onto the ice, lost his footing and fell hard on his back. All the boys laughed at him, except Danny, who couldn't believe Brian was blowing their chance to hang out with older guys—football players. But, Brian just lay there like some idiot, laughing even harder than the other guys. After a while, Michael and his buddies seemed bored with the high-jinx and headed up the gradual slope toward the Waterson's daylight basement.

"Brian," Danny said, trying to keep his voice down. "Come on, let's go." But Brian rolled onto his belly, laughing even harder. "I'm not kidding," Danny said, his voice tense now, no longer worried if anyone heard. "Get off the ice," he warned, knowing it might be thinner where Brian landed. "I'm not coming out there to get you."

Brian tried to get up, but slipped again and landed on his butt this time. "Ah, does Danny want to go play with his new friends?" Brian sounded childish loud enough for the other boys to hear, but when Danny glanced up the hill, the group was at patio door uninterested by them anymore.

If he could, Danny would have punched Brian right in the face. Danny wasn't even sure why they were friends right then. "Get up, asshole," he said, ready to fight. It wasn't like he had to invite Brian. He'd just tried to be a good friend. And now Brian made fun of him?

What a jerk.

"Get your ass off the ice," Danny shouted.

By then, Danny's head was spinning. He felt his brain expand and contract, like a sponge sopping up every last drop of alcohol, making the world seem distorted around him. They'd had shots of tequila after finishing several beers each. The lake seemed to shift, the dock swaying underfoot. He remembered knowing he was drunk, and trying to keep his feet planted so he didn't tumble off himself. His hands were frozen, his gloves in the basement. If Brian didn't get up soon, Danny was going without him. Brian's voice seemed to echo off the lake as he continued to mock Danny.

"Poor little Danny wants to be popular."

But what Danny really wanted was maybe play some poker, have a good time for once, instead of thumbing controls for boring video games, like usual. But it was painfully obvious Brian couldn't even hold his liquor, let alone hang out with seniors. Danny watched Brian recline again, throwing up before his head hit the frozen surface and he passed out.

Danny ran the length of the dock, grabbed a small log from a stack beside the fire pit he'd built with his father the summer before. He dashed back along the slippery boards then hurled the chunk of wood like a shot put toward his drunken friend. The log hit the ice a few feet from Brian, skated through the vomit before landing hard against Brian's torso. He stirred and then rolled back into a seated position. "Hey, what the hell?"

"Get off the ice, Brian."

"Fuck you, Danny."

Danny had enough of Brian's act. "Fine, do whatever you want, I'm going inside." With that, Danny made his way up the hillside, the door still open. Halfway up, he glanced back at Brian. Even in the dim light, he could see Brian was in trouble. Brian stood now, his arms extended to stay balanced, he glanced at Danny, the lights from the basement glowing down on him. His eyes wide and frightened as if something bad was about to happen. Danny knew the ice had probably cracked, but at that moment in his own inebriated state, he didn't care and did something he'd always regret. He turned away, stepped inside and closed the door.

It was Danny's dad who later begged the question. "Where's Brian?"

The details of that night had become murky over the years, but one thing was for certain. Danny knew his friend was in trouble, and he did nothing to save him. Nothing.

"I thought he went home." A more sober Danny felt his heart sink as he lied to Dutch. "The last I saw of him, he was fooling around out on the dock."

They found Brian drowned ten feet away from the opening in the ice. The coroner told his parents, he'd likely passed out from the cold before hypothermia set in and he drowned. That he hadn't suffered long. But, Alex knew different. He knew Brian died knowing his friend turned his back on him and let him drown beneath the frozen pond.

"We need to talk." Alex was startled by Margaret's voice. She stood near him by the pool. Her dress hugged her legs in the breeze. "Let me help you." Margaret reached down to pull him out of the water. "I'm sorry I scared you. I know you don't understand. Please let me explain."

Alex took her hand, letting her help him. He felt cold now, the breeze sending a chill through his body. "I just want you to go," he said.

"Not until we talk," she said. "Then I'll leave, I promise."

She seemed calmer. Her tears were gone, her mood more pensive and restrained. They strolled back to his place, the moon high in the sky. The breeze trickled through the wispy sage and bamboo planted along the edge of the patio. The movements of small desert animals scurrying along the surface of the open land that surrounded the ranch, followed behind them until they went inside, and Alex closed the door on the world for now.

Chapter 15
Margaret

The day seemed warmer already when Margaret stepped from her car into the midday sun. There were miles and miles of open land across the street. Out on the horizon, the desert floor met up with the sky, like a seam in a brilliant quilt, cerulean heavens stitched to the terra cotta soil. As she moved behind her car, she glanced left toward the estate and out beyond to the vast acreage as far as the eye could see, red rock rising from the desert floor in the distance.

The house sprawled, like a large hacienda. A post and rail fence surrounded the property, with an impressive gate near the driveway. Margaret made sure to park beyond the windows of the estate. She left her purse and phone in the car and hit the lock button with her key fob. She hoped nobody heard the sound of the locking mechanism. But as she glanced around, it seemed deserted. If this was where Danny lived, he wasn't home.

The locked gate and the garage doors on the house were closed. She didn't see anything stir, no pets. A path ran alongside the house to the back of the property where she could see the roofline of an outbuilding. She rattled the gate. Then climbed up on a three-foot high concrete and stone post with a lamp on top. Careful to not kick the light fixture, Margaret used the post to climb over the fence.

She landed hard in the reddish dirt on the other side. She got to her feet, brushed the dust from her dress, glanced again toward the front windows, and hoping nobody saw her. She crept across the driveway, past the garage and peeked inside the giant picture window near the front door. She didn't see anyone, but she rang the bell, anyway. After three attempts, she stepped back from the tall, carved doorway and looked inside the window again, used her hand to block the glare from the sun. Seemed nobody was home. And not a single car went by since she scaled the fence.

Margaret noticed a snag in the fabric of her dress, and reached down to pull at the hemline to check for tears.

I know he's here, I can feel it.

Margaret walked back past the front door, where she could see her car parked near some trees. She held tight to her keys as she glanced along the side yard, full of rock gardens and fruit trees, so she headed back toward the garage and knocked at the service entrance. No answer. She continued down the path on the right side of the property. Large shade trees blanketed the side yard where she found a stone pathway behind the house that led to a patio area with a view of the red rocks in the distance. She spotted the pool past a garden of desert flowers with a large cactus in the middle, more than six feet tall. Boxwoods surrounded a huge fountain. Benches and wooden tables lined the patio area where someone had built a covered outdoor kitchen with a barbeque, sink, and refrigerator. Quite a nice spread.

Why would Danny be a caretaker at an estate like this?

She wanted more than anything to find him. She didn't care if someone caught her trespassing. The closer she came to finding him the more she felt determined the man she saw last night was Danny.

Going back to the Mexican restaurant brought it all back.

His profile. She knew his face, the crooked smile, the way he dipped his chin as he tied the apron around his waist. His shoulders were as broad as ever, but his body thinner, like when they were at Ohio State.

Danny had gained weight after they married. He dined out often with clients. He'd become the weekend chef, grilling Italian sausages with peppers and onions from their garden whenever friends were over.

She wondered if he cooked for the owners in this expansive outdoor kitchen. Did he cook for new friends now?

Margaret had no idea, but she wanted to find out.

Chapter 16
Margaret

Margaret worried about Daniel before he disappeared. He'd put on more weight, went through a case of beer every weekend, and had become a heavy smoker. She thought he might be depressed. But he wouldn't get help. Refused counseling. Had become sullen and withdrawn.

She'd hoped the party would help. He'd turned thirty-four, still young, but Margaret felt so concerned she'd made an appointment for him at the Cleveland Clinic. And hoped to convince him to go.

She'd scheduled the appointment after her own visit to their family doctor when she'd found out she was pregnant. Margaret had broken down and told the doctor about Danny's moods and his drinking. The doctor counseled that with a high-risk pregnancy, she needed to avoid stress. And with her history of miscarriages, he referred her to a specialist to handle her care.

Margaret planned to tell Daniel about the pregnancy on his birthday. But he'd been so drunk they'd had their worst fight ever.

She'd heard him come into the master bedroom and pack a bag for his flight the next morning. She pretended to be asleep. Still angry, Margaret didn't want to start another argument. He'd slept on the small sofa in the den like he always did after a fight, and then drove himself to the airport in the morning. She never saw Daniel again.

Things had changed between them and she wasn't sure why. She had hoped to talk with him upon his return from New

York, try to straighten things out, get him to the doctor and then tell him about the baby.

But the buildings came down, and a plane crashed into the Pentagon and another into a field not too far from Cleveland in the Pennsylvania countryside, and she'd felt like the world had turned upside down.

Weeks later, Margaret lost the baby. She'd gone to the store to pick up a few things so she could make a special dinner for Jacob.

By the time she got home, the cramps were horrible and she noticed the blood. She called her mom, who rushed over, but by then, Margaret had collapsed in the kitchen. They transported her by ambulance to the hospital where they told her the sad news. She went into surgery soon after. They'd done all they could, but the surgeon had to perform a hysterectomy to stop the hemorrhaging.

Margaret felt dead inside when she woke up in the recovery room. Her parents moved in with Jacob and her the next day.

Margaret stopped near the pool now, and felt inside her pocket for her cell phone. She'd left it inside the car. She knew she couldn't call her mom right now. What would she say?

Hi, Mom, I think I saw Daniel last night and I'm sneaking around a beautiful estate property where he lives.

She almost laughed out loud at how ludicrous that seemed.

But, nonetheless, Margaret continued past the pool, across another service area where a she noticed a truck parked. Under the carport, a motorcycle sat propped against a post next to the truck. Just beyond, a barn stood tucked against the horizon, the type of barns she'd seen at hobby farms as a girl, not like the huge barns looming beyond crisp-white farmhouses in the Amish Country, or other tall red barns around northeast Ohio with giant chewing tobacco ads painted on the sides.

Living in California now, Margaret had seen those smaller-type stables behind beautiful Spanish and Mediterranean style estate homes in San Juan Capistrano, south of Laguna, where she and Henry lived.

She spotted an enclosed field behind the barn. She wondered if Danny worked as an estate manager rather than just a ranch hand. Someone with substantial wealth definitely owned the place. The small barn, complete with a Dutch door, had been built with quality lumber. A beautiful fence surrounded the grassy area. Everything looked well maintained and expensive. Even the truck parked near the barn had tinted windows and shiny hubcaps.

Maybe the caretaker's quarters were inside the barn. She didn't see any other outbuildings other than a shed and a pool house, but the drapes were drawn when she passed by. A white horse with black markings stood munching grass in the field.

She couldn't picture Danny around livestock. He'd never even wanted a dog. For a moment, Margaret's heart sunk, realizing once again, the idea of Daniel alive seemed impossible.

The Dutch door stood open on top, closed on the bottom. She always liked those doors. Her parents' kitchen had a similar one, on a smaller scale. They'd often leave the top open in the summer. The breeze would filter in while she and her mother rolled out pastry for blackberry pies.

"You'll go on," Margaret's mother had said, when Margaret asked how she'd ever move forward when she arrived home from the hospital. "Once you're healed and feeling better from surgery, you'll take care of Jacob and rebuild your life."

"But Mom, how?" She'd felt in that moment like her life had ended and secretly wished she'd died in the operating room.

"You carry the burden with you," her mother explained from the foot of Margaret's bed. "This type of tragedy never ends, so you carry it with you, live your life, and find a new kind of happiness."

You carry it with you. Margaret had repeated those words a thousand times in the past decade. Sometimes her life felt heavy. Other times, lighter. The sadness remained, though more gentle over the years, like a breeze. When life became a burden, a cruel anchor weighing down her heart, Henry would step in, help her see life was good, and feel less connected to her past and the tragedies she had suffered.

They'd even talked about adopting a baby when they were first married, but when Margaret felt overwhelmed with the move west, they decided to wait. By the time the subject came up again, they both felt the time had passed. They were older now, and it would be hard to adjust to being new parents.

Margaret heard a horse whinnying nearby. She opened the lower door to the stable and noticed a schedule tacked on the wall. Danny's handwriting — not script but careful block lettering, the same hand that kept notes on their finances and entries in the checkbook. Daniel only used cursive when he signed his name. She leaned against the desk, holding her breath and touched the calendar. Her fingers traced the letters, Daniel's notes.

Chapter 17
Margaret

Margaret heard a loud thud somewhere outside, so she ran out into the paddock area. A large spotted horse came straight toward her.

"Whoa, whoa," she yelled, and tried to keep the horse from stepping on Daniel, sprawled out in a heap on the ground beneath an overhang. "Shoo, shoo," she cried, and waved her arms in the air, as the horse trotted out into the grassy area.

She could see the white horse still grazing, and panicked for a moment.

Do they attack?

She'd never been so close to horses before. Cows and chickens on Daniel's grandmother's farm, but never horses. The big one she'd yelled at, stopped short for a moment. Margaret's heart beat fast, but then it walked toward the white horse, and dropped its head to chew on grass.

Relieved, Margaret stood over Daniel, who seemed to be unconscious, his face turned sideways in the dirt, his arms extended out, one leg twisted in an awkward position. Margaret checked his pulse and could feel his heart beat under her fingertips. She noticed blood on his forehead, so she tried to turn him on his side, but dead weight, he rolled back.

Margaret glanced around, and thought maybe she should pour water on him. But then she felt an urge to see his face straight on, so she pushed him harder onto his side, and propped a heavy container behind him, so he couldn't fall backwards and choke if he'd had a heart attack or a stroke. She dragged a half-used bale of hay several yards to wedge it against his shoulders.

She felt for his pulse again and cleared his mouth of debris. Dirt covered his clothes. She couldn't tell where the dust ended and his dark tan began. His leathery skin seemed different from the freckled skin she remembered. But he was Daniel. No doubt at all.

She lowered to her knees near his face to listen for his breath then felt under his nostrils with her fingers. She brushed the hair from his face, his braid longer than her hair. He had a full beard, trimmed in a line along his neck. He smelled of horses, perspiration, and cigarettes. He still smoked, but that was the only familiar thing about him, even his sweat smelled different to Margaret.

She took a good long look. And wondered how she'd even noticed him the night before. Tattoos covered his forearms, a bird of some sort, maybe an eagle, the edges out of proportion, with an awful green color, and reddish wings. The colors bled together. On his other arm, she noticed the snake, wrapped around a sword.

Danny, what in the world?

Margaret turned her head away for a moment, swallowed hard to keep from getting sick. Her heart pounded hard, and she felt the earth shift like she might pass out.

She took in more air, recognized the symptoms of hyperventilating. She needed to slow down. Margaret pulled the skirt of her dress to her face, breathed into the fabric, her fingers numb against the thin fabric.

With her other hand, Margaret turned Daniel's wrist to see another tattoo, a single word, simple script, the same faded green as the ugly bird.

Alive

"What the hell?" Margaret glanced at the horses in the field. "Danny, wake up." She kept her voice low, shook him by the shoulders, patted his cheeks. "Come on, open your eyes."

Margaret spotted a water trough nearby and pushed onto her feet. She sunk the bottom half of her dress into the water. She made her way back to Daniel and wrung her hem over his face. He stirred a bit, so she knelt down, blew into his face, rubbed her palms against his cheeks.

"There you go. Come on. Wake up." She shook his shoulders again. He started to come around more.

In one sudden movement, Daniel pushed himself into a seated position against the scrappy bale of hay, squeezed his eyes open, then rubbed the back of his neck. He looked like hell.

Margaret moved a few feet away, so not to startle him. Daniel called out to the horse she'd shooed away, walking toward the trough now.

Daniel appeared disoriented. He glanced around, and she knew he'd spot her soon.

"You're near the stables," Margaret said, in a gentle voice. "You fell. Your head is bleeding."

She shifted behind him, shoved the hay aside with her leg, to help him upright, move him inside the barn, away from the horses, somewhere safe.

Daniel nearly fell backwards. She repositioned her arms underneath his armpits, reached her hands across his chest. In one fell swoop she pulled him to his feet. He leaned heavy against her. Margaret hoped she could hold him long enough to get him inside.

Daniel wobbled and twisted as they made their way toward the barn. "Just get me to my house. It's through the barn."

He shouted not to call anyone, to close the barn door, the top-half, too.

Margaret kicked the door closed, the top-half slammed shut, as the latch clicked into place. By the time they stumbled across the gravel to the pool house, Margaret was drenched in sweat, mostly Daniel's.

She was exhausted.

But, she managed to shove the heavy door open and lower Danny onto a small sofa in the center of the room. She removed his boots, as he lay down and placed a pillow under his head.

"Are you sure I shouldn't call for help?"

But Daniel slurred his words as he fell unconscious again.

"Oh, my God, Danny, try to stay awake." She slapped his arm to no avail. He was out cold.

She grabbed a hand towel from the sink nearby, smelled the terry cloth, then ran it under cold water, and went back to Daniel and placed it under his neck. Whenever Daniel felt sick, she remembered he liked a cool cloth behind his neck, never his forehead.

Danny always had an opinion about everything and would badger her until she gave up. She'd often told him he should be a lawyer. He could be quite stubborn. Even about simple things like a cool compress.

She pulled off his boots. Bare feet? So odd, unlike the Danny she knew, always so particular about his wardrobe. His socks always matched his suits, wool in the winter, lightweight cotton in the summer. Margaret sat down on the edge of the sofa, actually a futon, she now realized. She glanced around the room, no bed. Was this where he slept? Margaret studied Danny's face, like he might respond, with her hip against his side. She lifted his arm across her lap to examine the tattoo on the inside of his wrist again.

"Alive," she whispered. She traced the word with the tip of her finger. "Yes." A rainfall of tears escaped down Margaret's cheeks onto Daniel's wrist. "You're alive."

Chapter 18
Margaret

Margaret watched Daniel's chest rise and fall as he slept. He snored, off and on, the same way he always did. When they first married, she'd sometimes sleep on the sofa in the den until dawn, and then climb back in bed with him before he awoke.

Back then Margaret wanted her marriage to be perfect. So she let it go, along with other things that bothered her, like his smoking. She spotted an empty carton on the kitchen counter where she'd found the towel. A cheaper brand, but cigarettes, nonetheless.

Danny's darker side had excited her at first, the way he stood apart from the group, acted aloof, and serious-minded, enigmatic in nature, which gave him an air of mystery. But the more he drank, the more he accused her of things she didn't do. After a while, his edginess wasn't sexy anymore.

"What the hell, Maggie?" Daniel had pulled his fist back at a bar, years ago, ready to punch a man who'd sat down next to her. "I can't leave you alone for a minute." He'd been outside smoking when a guy sidled up to Margaret, asked her if he could by her a drink.

Their friends needed to get home to their new baby. "Yeah, let's go," Daniel had said. "Since my wife can't stop flirting."

He'd grumbled all the way to the car and halfway home, Margaret drove along the snowy roads careful to pump the brakes at each turn to the house they'd bought in Cleveland Heights.

All their friends had settled down and started families. She and Daniel had a mortgage, but hadn't changed their lifestyle since they married. In bed that night, the furnace turned down to save money, Margaret snuggled close to Danny, whose eyes were already shut.

"Want to have a baby?" she whispered.

Daniel opened a lid in her direction, rubbed his head. "Huh?"

"I'm ready, Danny. I'm tired of working all the time and staying out late." She rested her head against his chest, stroked his arm with her fingers. "I want a family."

Daniel pushed himself up against the headboard. Margaret fell back onto her own side, landing against a pillow.

"You think that guy at the bar can give you that?"

"What?" Margaret struggled to untangle herself in the blankets.

Daniel turned the light on next to the bed, leaned toward her, his eyes hard. "You flirt with other guys."

Margaret sat up, faced Daniel. "That's not true. He thought I was single."

"Yeah, right." Daniel kicked the blankets off. "Every time..." he said.

"Every time, what?"

"You give other men looks," Daniel said, his face red now, a vein popped out on his forehead. "I see you trying to get their attention."

"I don't do that," she said, as she rotated against the headboard next to Daniel. "What's wrong with you?" she said, and touched his hand. He pulled away. "You're changing the subject." She tried to touch him again, but he swatted her hand away. She paused, swallowed her tears and folded her hands in her lap, her legs stretched out, her light pink nightgown the only thing to keep her warm. She shivered, and wished Danny would apologize, give her the blankets. "Are you scared to have a baby?" Almost as soon as she said it, she cringed, knowing he'd probably blow up.

Daniel shoved off the bed, stormed across the room out the door, and shouted from the top of the steps. "Yeah, I'm scared," he said. "Scared to have a baby with a slut."

Margaret could still remember how hurt she'd felt. Like a knife to her heart, he'd cut her to her core. The blankets on the floor by then, her heart pounding fast, she'd wanted to go after him, slap him across the face. But she'd stopped near the door. She knew his words were from drinking too much, but it didn't keep her from slamming the bedroom door. Their wedding picture crashed against the wood floor, but she left it, stepping around the mess then cried herself to sleep in their bed.

Margaret hated those ugly fights, which always left her confused and embarrassed. Her parents never argued, and if they did have a disagreement, it proved to be over something important and real. They never raised their voices, but instead, discussed their problems like civilized people. Danny often diverted attention away from the subject and then attacked her for something she didn't do.

Over the years, she'd thought about the hundreds of fights they'd had over nothing to do with what she'd wanted to say. So sidetracked, Margaret often couldn't remember what she'd wanted to discuss. If she did recall, she'd let it go. It wasn't worth it.

When she became pregnant with Jacob, she'd made the decision on her own. Margaret skipped her birth control. When they were vacationing with his family at the family cottage in Michigan, she'd forgotten to pack her pills. She didn't tell Daniel. On birth control for so long, Margaret thought a few missed pills wouldn't make a difference.

After Jacob's birth, she'd tried to get pregnant again, but had two miscarriages a few years before she became pregnant again. She'd held off telling Daniel, in case she lost that baby, too. Daniel left for New York the week she entered her second trimester. They'd fought all week, so she felt hesitant to tell him.

When Margaret had coffee with her sister-in-law, Patty, a few days before Danny's birthday, she'd expressed her reservations. "I'll tell him when he's had some rest."

"You need to tell him, soon." Patty sipped her latte and picked at an English muffin Margaret knew she wouldn't eat, as always. That's how she stayed so thin, even after two babies.

"I know," Margaret said. "I just want him to be in a good mood for once. He's been so tense lately. I think he's working too hard."

"Yeah, Michael's keyed up, too. Dutch wants them to pull in new clients." Patty pulled her hair into a ponytail with a band. She wore yoga pants, since she had a class after they were finished at the coffee shop. Younger than Margaret by only one year, and three years younger than Michael, Margaret always felt far older than Patty. She often wondered if living with Daniel had made her an old woman.

"I wish Dutch wouldn't pit them against each other," Margaret said, while she checked her list for Danny's birthday. "It's hard enough their working together in that office."

"Need any help with the party?"

"Nah, I've got it together," Margaret said. "I hope he's surprised."

She'd planned the party for weeks, ordered the perfect cake, from his favorite bakery in Shaker Heights, made lasagna, in the freezer. She'd invited everyone, family and their closest friends. Margaret hoped Danny would see she loved him. He'd pushed her away, stormed around more than ever all month. She'd wanted to believe it regarded work, and clients, but she wasn't sure. She had worried he didn't love her anymore.

"It'll be great," Patty said. "I'm sure Danny's just stressed. Like I said, Michael's been acting crazy, too, snapping at the boys."

"Maybe if Danny can land this client in New York, he'll settle down." She watched Patty pull on her fitted, knit jacket, zip it up, then toss the English muffin in the trashcan behind their table. Patty's thighs were so trim, Margaret figured it might be why Danny complained so often about her not losing the last ten pounds after she had Jacob.

She weighed less now than before she married Danny. Just like her mother, Margaret had thinned out as she aged, partly due to genetics and partly due to a healthier lifestyle. She'd cut out refined white sugar and flour years ago, tried to stick to a low-carb diet. She wondered if her curves had really bothered Danny. Sometimes she missed her fuller breasts and her curvy bottom, but she didn't miss feeling tired all the time and using caffeine and sugar to keep going. She could keep up with Henry on his runs these days, swim in the ocean between jetties, and hike the jagged hillsides around their home, her body strong and toned.

Back in Cleveland, she'd had to drag Danny to go for a walk. Every effort she made to be healthier as a couple, he shot down, cooking heavy meals, sitting in front of the TV. And now, as far as Margaret could see, Danny still seemed unhealthy, yet in the opposite way, his skin rutty, his limbs skinny, he looked strung out.

Margaret touched his wrist again. This man she married so long ago, who drifted away from her, who seemed so sad all the time, and angry. Did he ever love her?

Chapter 19
Margaret

Margaret glanced at the tattoo, inked across the narrow blue veins beneath Danny's skin, the same veins people sliced wide open with a razor blade when they'd had enough of life.

Daniel seemed to breathe easier now. So, Margaret went into the bathroom, found a bar of soap and a towel from the back of the door. She cleaned Danny as best she could, trekking back and forth to the sink to rinse the towel. She noticed the wound on his forehead had stitches, and then remembered the owner at the restaurant said Danny bumped his head.

"Probably re-opened when you fell," she said, Daniel slept, his breathing even. "I bet you were in a fight."

What are you doing? Why are you here?

She scanned the room. The entire studio couldn't have been more than two hundred square feet. A futon, a small table and two chairs sat near the counter. A few cabinets, a tiny fridge and microwave made up the kitchen. The bathroom housed a tight shower stall, no tub, a toilet, a tiny sink and a window with a café curtain. Margaret noticed a radio plugged into the wall on the tile floor across the room. On the same wall as the kitchen and bathroom sat the main entry. Behind the futon, a second entry, a sliding glass door, had a drape pulled shut. Framed desert scenes hung in the center of each of the other two walls. A small stack of books rested on a storage chest, and a lamp on the end table. No clues to how Daniel ended up there not even a photograph. Nothing personal, other than books, and most were volumes about horses and astronomy. It looked like more of an undecorated guesthouse, not a home where someone lived full-time.

She noticed a box of gauze on the counter near the sink and found tape as well. She drank some water from the tap, and used a wet paper towel to blot the dried blood from Danny's cut. She ripped the tape with her teeth and covered the wound with fresh gauze. Daniel stirred and mumbled in his sleep, nothing she could understand. He calmed again under her touch as she stroked the side of his face with her fingertips.

She stood and backed away, letting her tears flow, a chill down her arms, the terracotta tiles beneath her feet cold and hard. This place felt lonely, like a self-imposed cell, with little food, nothing warm or cozy, no life.

Yet, right there, Danny slept on the futon, alive, in a room, no larger than Jacob's dorm. Not even a full kitchen.

"But, you love to cook," she whispered.

Margaret wiped away her tears, went over to the counter, opened the cabinets for anything that might say why he lived in Sedona. There were folded clothes, canned food, a few dishes, bowls and cups.

She found a blanket inside the storage chest, so she covered Daniel. His face felt warm, a fever. The cut might be infected. She checked the prescription medicines on the counter, a strong pain reliever and an antibiotic. She opened the medicine cabinet in the bathroom for aspirin, anything for a fever. Nothing.

Margaret sat at the table for a while, waited for Daniel to wake up, read about constellations, and the atmosphere above the desert. But he stayed in a deep sleep, so she joined him on the futon, sat at the other end, pulled the other half of the blanket over her legs. A fan twirled above, made a quiet whoosh noise as Margaret glanced out the skylight. Danny stretched his feet toward her. She leaned sideways against the cushion, and watched him sleep as she ran her fingers along his calf. His body felt so warm and alive. She wished she had a phone. She should call Jacob or Dutch. Someone should know.

He's alive, Jake. Your dad is alive.

"Danny." She said his name once in a while to wake him. But he didn't, the rhythm of the fan relaxed Margaret as she rested against the cushion.

She awoke later—startled she'd fallen asleep. Danny still slept. She changed the cloth under his neck, folded the blanket down, and set the thermostat cooler. She heard the air-conditioner rumble then she switched the lamp on since the day had shifted to early evening. Margaret stayed close to Danny, afraid to leave him for long, in case he awoke. She found an apple inside the mini-fridge and sat near him again. Margaret touched his chest and stroked his arms with her fingertips, everything about him so familiar. She wondered if he did drugs, he had become so thin. She checked his arms again, but saw no sign of needle marks.

Margaret thought about Henry back in California. She'd dreamed about him while she slept next to Danny.

Henry had walked toward her in the dream. She remembered him talking to her as he moved closer. He wore running clothes.

Margaret could see Henry, high cheekbones, brown eyes, sparse eyebrows and closely trimmed light brown hair. He smiled tight-lipped most of the time, but sometimes when Margaret made him laugh, even his dimples would show. Henry hovered near six feet, average build, trim and fit from years of running. He lifted weights, his arms and shoulders well defined. Margaret loved his long, elegant fingers, surgeon's hands. She oftentimes traced the veins on the back of his hand while they sat together, quiet, watching the waves from their deck. When Henry greeted people, he met their eyes straight on with a firm handshake. She'd thought sometimes, since meeting Henry, how different he acted from Daniel. She wondered if the way Henry spoke, in measured tones, his simple, sophisticated style, so opposite of Daniel, had been the reason she could love again. The reason she loved Henry in particular. He'd made it easy to forget the past.

Just let me figure this out, Henry, and I'll come home.

Margaret noticed Danny's beard and bushy eyebrows. He'd always kept his face clean-shaven before. She laid her head against his chest and he flinched a bit, so she pulled away. Certain

120

he remained asleep; she lowered her head again, to listen for his heartbeat.

"You're alive," she whispered.

Margaret stayed there for a while and when she stood up and crossed the room, she cried again by the wall. She decided to retrieve her phone from her car to call for help. He'd been sleeping for such a long time. Then, she remembered Danny had said not to call anyone. Maybe he'd taken the pain medicine earlier, and that's why he'd been out of it. But she worried. She hadn't seen him fall, didn't know if he'd tripped or collapsed somehow.

Later, after sitting on a chair she'd pulled over from the table, Margaret got up and paced around the room. She needed some air. She felt restless, cooped up for hours now, so she stepped outside onto the stoop.

She watched as the hue of orange began to melt along the horizon from the setting sun. Henry would be out on the deck, watching the sun sink into the ocean, probably worried about her since they hadn't spoken since breakfast. No doubt, he'd left several messages. Just as well her phone remained in the car.

My keys.

"Oh, my God, where are my keys?"

She remembered putting them down on a workbench where she'd found Daniel.

She peered inside to check on Daniel then closed the door and headed to the barn.

In the paddock, the big spotted horse from before stood under the shelter. The white horse drank from the water trough. Margaret spotted her keys on the workbench, but the sky darkened fast now. She moved around the head of the big horse, grabbed her keys, and shoved them inside the pocket on the front of her dress, nervous so near to the animals. The big horse stepped closer to Margaret and she almost screamed. But she controlled herself and covered her mouth.

You're being ridiculous; they're probably more scared of you. Just be calm. Her mind was racing.

Margaret cleared the hair from her face, dropped her hands to her sides, and stepped forward.

"You're Max, right?" Margaret spoke in a gentle voice, trying to control her nerves. She remembered Danny called out to the horse, like a friend. So maybe they were mild-mannered.

She reached out to stroke the horse between the ears when he lowered his head. "Good boy," she said, glad he hadn't tried to bite her. "That's a good horse."

Backing away, Margaret turned toward the barn, but the horse followed her inside. She panicked, as she realized he might get out when she opened the door at the other end. But the horse went into one of the stalls.

She closed the stall door quickly and latched it tight. "Is this where you sleep?" Margaret realized she'd spoken to the horse as if he might answer.

The horse dipped his head to drink from a water trough along the length of the stables. There were three stalls, another with the gate open. Margaret went back out into the field and found the other horse headed toward the grassy area.

"Whoa," Margaret yelled. "This way." She clapped her hands, and once she reached the horse, she patted the side of the horse near the rump to guide the animal under the covered area and then inside the barn.

Some time passed and several attempts made before she managed to direct the animal inside. Once the horse entered the stall, she secured that gate, too. The bigger horse focused on some hay, ignoring them both. But when Margaret backed away, she almost screamed again, startled by the clanking noise from one of the stalls, the one called Max had poked his head through the front grille of the gate. Margaret thought the gate might open. She stumbled backward, her sandals collecting sawdust as she steadied herself against a post. But the gate stayed secured, and she placed a hand to her chest and sighed in relief.

"My God, you scared me, Max." She spoke to the horse as the pretty white one chewed on some hay. "I thank you both for your cooperation," she said, then curtsied and brushed dust from the bodice of her dress.

She leaned against the post and rested her palms against her cheeks, her skin warm and tacky. The air felt cooler now, but her game of tag with the white horse had left her sweaty.

Margaret sighed, keeping an eye on both stalls worried the horses might get out somehow. She glanced around the barn, up to the rafters. Tin covered lights shone from the beams overhead, so she pulled the string on one of the lamps and left the other one on. Jacob always liked a light on when little. Maybe horses did, too.

She glanced back at the stalls, wondered how long they slept, and if they slept standing. She really knew nothing about horses. But they seemed content.

She made sure the door clicked shut when she headed back to the small house where Daniel lay asleep. But Margaret stopped short of the truck, when she noticed someone near Danny's door. She ducked alongside the passenger's door of the pickup truck. A boy stood knocking on the stoop. Margaret wasn't sure what to do. And then, realizing how stupid she was acting, Margaret stepped out from the shadows. She had every right to be there, to be with Daniel.

"Can I help you?" Margaret said.

When she moved closer, she realized the person wasn't a boy after all. A young woman, dressed in a hoodie and jeans, like something Jacob would wear, turned to face Margaret.

"Who are you?" the girl said, both hands inside the pockets on her jacket.

She had a snarly face, quite homely. Margaret tried not to stare, but the girl's thin upper lip exposed incisors that looked like fangs. Her other teeth were crooked, and even in the dim light Margaret could see a yellowish cast. The girl had an awful hump on the bridge of her nose, pockmarks covered both cheeks and her pale skin appeared almost sea green against the black hood. Wine-colored half-moons sagged beneath her bloodshot eyes. Several piercings lined both earlobes and a small silver ring poked out the side of her left nostril.

Like a character from a Tim Burton film, Margaret wondered if Edward Scissorhands might show up next. The girl looked downright freakish.

Why would Danny know such an odd person? Maybe he was into drugs after all.

Margaret stepped forward to close the gap between them. She was ugly, but Margaret wasn't afraid of her.

"Are you looking for Daniel?"

"No," the girl spat. "I'm looking for Alex. Are you the owner?"

That name again. Alex.

"No, I'm here with Danny," Margaret said. "I mean Alex." She didn't want to explain the situation to a total stranger.

"Where is he?" the girl said. Something foul about her made Margaret's skin crawl.

"He's sleeping right now," Margaret said. "He's ill, so he needs to rest."

"I know all about his stitches," the girl said. "That's why I'm here, to check on him. He's my boyfriend." She sounded brash, impertinent.

Margaret had enough by then. The girl seemed like trouble. Margaret felt certain Danny wouldn't want her around, or would he?

"And you are?" the girl said, her lips coated in dark red lipstick, her jet-black hair escaped the edges of her hood.

Margaret remembered, now. The alleyway. The young woman Danny had argued with last night.

"I'm his wife." Margaret couldn't help herself. She didn't care what that girl thought.

"I'm talking to Alex." With that, the girl turned around to open the door.

Margaret grabbed her by the arm, pulled her off the step.

"Let go of me." The girl struggled then took a swing at Margaret. "Bitch, let me go."

But, Margaret held tight to her arm, swung her around and tossed her onto the ground.

"What the...?"

"Go home. I'll tell him you were here." Margaret fled inside, locked the heavy door, and leaned against it as she tried to catch her breath.

What in the world? Margaret didn't consider herself a violent person, nor had she ever been so aggressive. She'd grown up in a quiet home, raised her son to be responsible. She and Henry went for walks if they needed to work out an issue.

This was crazy. In the space a twenty-four hours, she'd wrangled horses, shoved a girl, lied to her husband, neglected to call her son, driven all over Sedona, gone inside a stranger's home, and then trespassed at another.

But, that's how it always felt with Danny. Maybe not so out of control, but chaotic at times with big, loud fights, and his wild behavior.

She remembered now, frozen against the door, Danny asleep on the futon.

"You're even more insane," she said, hoping he'd hear. "Who the hell are you?" she shouted now. "What are you doing here?"

Margaret pushed away from the door, marched around the room, and slammed cabinets, to wake Daniel.

"You left us for people like her?" She wanted to have a fight. "What's wrong with you, Danny?" The fight she should've had all those years ago. "You're living in this weird little town in the middle of nowhere. It doesn't make sense." Margaret slammed another cabinet, "Wake-up." But Daniel didn't move.

Exhausted, her hands trembled and she felt faint again. She sat down on the cool terra cotta tiles below the sink at the counter, leaned her head against the dark wood cabinets and closed her eyes. She could hear Danny snoring, each time he took in air, his tongue caught on the back of his throat, like gargling after brushing his teeth.

"God, Danny," she opened her eyes then. "I'm so mad at you."

Margaret's eyes burned with tears. She cried for all the lost years with him, and without him. "Why Danny?" she whispered. "Why?"

Chapter 20
Alex

Alex held his ground near the door as Margaret stood in the middle of the room. He watched her press her palms against her dress to smooth the wrinkles before she tucked a few locks of hair behind her ear, and then fiddled with an earring as if she were stalling for time.

He'd seen her do this before. Once, when they were at a furniture store in Cleveland, she'd wanted a new bedroom set and paused the same way. She then presented her argument as to why, in addition to the bed, they should also purchase the two nightstands and dresser. He remembered the way she wore her hair that day, tied up in a knot atop her head dressed in her faded jeans and sweatshirt. Jacob snoozed in the stroller at her side. He liked to have the final word, even though he knew she'd order the furniture anyway. But for a moment, he felt like the boss.

Margaret cleared her throat now and squared her shoulders. Alex noticed her eyes sparkle in the low light, the same way as their wedding day. She'd been vulnerable and shaky at the candlelight service. Her hands trembled, as she held tight to the note cards with her vows. Alex had taken her hands in his, helped her feel calm. He knew she hated speaking in front of a crowd. And now, he wanted to move toward her, touch her hands in the same way, so she wouldn't be afraid. But he stayed by the door, waited for her to speak.

At the church on their wedding night, her voice sounded soft, filled with hope. "I knew the first time we kissed that I loved you." Margaret smiled when she said the words. "But I waited for you to say it first, and when you did, my whole world changed." She'd paused to gain composure and then continued. "Danny loves me," she said, her face glowed in the candlelight. "He loves me, I thought, and I knew everything would be okay."

Alex wondered if she would sound angry now, instead, like the night before he left, how she'd screamed at him and then stopped herself. "I don't want to fight with you anymore," she'd said. "I'm going to bed." Those were the last words he'd heard from her before he left. He'd sat on the bottom step in the dark and listened as she opened and closed the door to Jacob's room upstairs, before quietly shutting their bedroom door. He pictured her earlier that evening, in his brother's arms inside the kitchen and it made him sick to think of it. Alex didn't care what she said now. He didn't owe her a thing.

"How are you feeling?" she said now.

Margaret spoke in a gentle voice as she stood across from him in his tiny home in the desert. Still so pretty, thinner maybe, a longer, leaner version of Maggie stood before him, more tan than he'd seen her before, just like him. Was she living nearby, watching him? Had the desert sun turned her buttery skin to a deeper shade, or did he remember her differently?

"You were out for quite some time," she said. "Should we call someone, a doctor? Are you alright?" She stepped forward then, closed the gap between them. But he moved away toward the sink, grabbed a coffee mug and filled it full of water. He turned to face her as he tipped the cup until empty.

"I'm fine," Alex said, and turned to place the cup in the sink, then grabbed the plastic vile of painkillers. "I think I took too many of these pills, I'm better now." Alex dropped the medicine on the counter and faced Margaret again, this time he leaned against the counter with his arms crossed, his shirt still damp from the pool. "Listen, lady, I'm not sure what's going on or why you're here. Is this some sort of joke? Did Carlos put you up to this?" Alex laughed then, a little louder than he intended. "That's it, Carlos did this." Alex shook his head.

He laughed some more as Margaret sighed. Alex pretended not to notice. His braid had come undone, so he pulled the rubber band from the end to free the long, soggy strands, knowing

Margaret must be appalled by his appearance. She knew him as Daniel Waterson—businessman, husband, father, who once resembled the other clean-cut guys on their manicured, tree-lined block. Now he was just some dirty cowboy with tattoos.

That's right, this is who I am now.

Alex paused to let her take it all in. He wasn't the person he used to be. The changes he'd made in his appearance were only part of who he'd become. He had a new life now, a new identity, a new way of thinking.

He continued to act as if he didn't know her. "Carlos said he might send someone out to help with chores," Alex said. "Are you a new waitress?"

See, I don't remember you. Go ahead, cry, do whatever you want, I left you and I'm never coming back.

Alex pulled open a cabinet near the end of the counter, closer to Margaret, grabbed a fresh shirt and jeans. He shook his head, and slammed the cabinet shut. He could smell her perfume again.

"Did he tell you to say we were married?" Alex didn't give Margaret a chance to speak. Instead, he shoved by her into the bathroom to change out of his wet clothes. "You're a good actress." Alex raised his voice from inside the cramped bathroom. "I'll have to get him back."

Alex finished, hung his pants and shirt over the shower door, then came out with a wide smile, expected to see Margaret right there, but she'd moved to the futon and held her chin the other way, toward the wall across the room.

"Well, anyway..." Alex cleared his throat and stepped around a rugged wooden column supporting a crossbeam that ran the length of the vaulted ceiling. He stopped shy of the storage trunk between them. Margaret turned to meet his eyes, but he ignored her. "Thanks for bringing Max and Lady inside." Alex patted his empty pockets, and kept his voice light. "I don't have cash on me, but I'll pay you on my next shift."

"I'm not a waitress, Danny."

"I told you, I'm Alex." He placed his open hand against his chest. "Didn't Carlos tell you my name?"

128

"Carlos didn't send me. I assume that's your boss at the restaurant. I talked to him today and he told me you were a caretaker out here, so I came to see for myself." Margaret pulled herself forward, held her knees.

"Now you've lost me again." Alex looked her straight in the eyes. "Seriously, do we know each other? Because I'm drawing a blank."

"Yes, we know each other."

Alex crossed his arms again. "Sometimes I drink too much. Did we meet at a bar?" But he didn't drink much at all these days. Hadn't hung out at the bars in town for years, his work kept him too busy and preferred to stay sharp. Alcohol could make a person talk too much, and he'd learned the hard way. His tongue tended to slip when he let himself get sloshy. No, Alex made sure to be careful and now he wished he hadn't taken those damn pills. Did he talk in his sleep? Alex wasn't sure what she knew or what game she might be playing. "The tavern?" he said. "Did I meet you there?"

"No." Margaret sat back again, and tucked one leg under, as if she couldn't get comfortable, the deep incline wedged her against the cushion. "Can you sit down, please?"

"I'm fine right here. Just tell me what the hell this is about."

Margaret gave Alex the same frustrated look she'd given him a thousand times. "Please, this is very important and I think you should sit down to hear it." She patted the cushion on the futon.

"There's no way I got you pregnant. I always use a condom, no matter how drunk I am."

Margaret's jaw dropped, her blue eyes popped wide open. He'd hit a nerve and it felt good.

"Just sit, please," she said.

Alex moved around the storage chest and sat at the other end of the futon, his arms stretched out on his legs, his head turned in Margaret's direction.

"Go ahead."

She pulled her leg tighter underneath herself as she faced him. "I don't look familiar to you at all?"

"Nope."

"I know you. Your name is Daniel Waterson and you're from Cleveland, Ohio. You went to Ohio State, that's where we met," she said. Her cheeks flushed, as she implored him. "Actually, we grew up in the same neighborhood, but we never hung out until college." Margaret watched him for a long while.

But Alex just shook his head. "I don't think so," he said. "I'm from Tucson. I've never been to Ohio. They grow corn there, right? Or is that Iowa?"

Margaret took in a deep breath and let it out. "Stop joking, Danny." She scooted closer to him. "I know you know me," she insisted. "I can tell."

Alex moved away to stand up again. Margaret grabbed his arm. He jerked it away, which knocked him off balance. He fell back onto the futon, almost landed on Margaret. But she caught his shoulder to steady him.

"Damn," he said, pulling away. "My name is Alex and whoever you are and whatever your problem is, I don't really care."

Once more, Alex tried to get up, but Margaret clutched his arm with such force, it shocked him. She drew him flush against her side, wouldn't let go.

"Okay," she said. "You're name is Alex." She breathed heavy from the altercation, and Alex felt her breath on his face. It smelled sugary like sweet fruit. "Now let me talk."

"I've heard enough." Alex wanted to get up, but his head felt like it might split open, not like earlier in the day, but enough to keep him still for now. "You're crazy."

"I know it seems that way." She touched his arm, but this time, he didn't pull away.

The dive into the pool, and now her fingers on his skin made him dizzy.

"Let me start over," she said. "I'm saying too much too fast."

She smelled so good. Alex glanced down at her hand on his forearm.

"Let me ask you this," she said. "In Tucson, do you have family?"

"No."

"Did you grow up there?"

"I don't know." Alex kept his eyes away from Margaret's gaze.

"Do you remember your childhood?"

"Listen, lady..."

Margaret stroked Alex's arm. "You don't remember, do you?"

"I had an accident," he said as he stared straight ahead. "I can't remember much about anything. They found me by the side of the road, hit and run."

"That's what I'm trying to tell you," Margaret said, her voice gentle. "Did they say you have amnesia?"

"No." Alex kept himself steady, careful to sound firm.

"But surely someone took you to a hospital?"

"Yeah, but I had my wallet, and my license said I'm Alex Gershom."

Margaret rubbed Alex's arm. "But you're not Alex Gershom," she said in a whisper, her touch even softer against his skin.

He leaned his head back against the futon and closed his eyes. "Listen," he said. "I came to Sedona from Tucson after I got hit. I couldn't remember anything, so I moved on, that's all. I don't know anything about Ohio or who it is you think I am."

Alex opened his eyes to see if Margaret heard what he said. She had leaned closer, her face inches from his. She stroked his cheek, and he wanted to pull away, but somehow he couldn't. He let her stroke his lips with the tips of her fingers. She leaned in for a tender kiss, her breath even sweeter upon his lips.

He pulled his head away. "I don't know you," Alex said.

"It's okay," her voice soft. "You don't have to remember me right now."

She caressed his face again, even more affectionate this time. Then she kissed his cheeks and his forehead near his cut. He shut his eyes again, light-headed. She brushed his eyelids with her lips before she kissed him on the mouth again, longer this time. He kept his eyes closed, tried to ignore her. But heat flowed through his veins, warmed him up from the pool.

Margaret kissed the side of his neck, below his ear, her familiar touch along his shoulders and chest made his head spin. She slipped an arm behind his neck. He felt her face even closer, so he kissed her, out of instinct. But then he kissed her again with more intensity this time, and held her against him. Her perfume smelled intoxicating, not the same scent he remembered, spicier, exotic. Alex couldn't hold back. He wanted her. He didn't care what happened, not right now, not when she slipped her sundress off and lowered herself on top of him, or when he kissed her again, and ran his hands along her curves.

She whispered into his ear. "It's okay," she said. "My name is Margaret, but you can call me Maggie."

Maggie.

He repeated her name over and over in his mind. She was always Maggie to him. Always. The futon felt narrow like the twin bed in his dorm room when they first fell in love, when he held her close, her skin soft and warm, before she betrayed him, before he went away, before the buildings tumbled down, before all of it.

Chapter 21
Margaret

Margaret woke before dawn, the room quiet and still other than Danny's even, rhythmic breaths. She rested against his chest, his arm wrapped around her as a barrier to the hard tile surface beneath the narrow futon. She felt the chill of the desert air dance across her naked flesh. The temperature had dropped during the night.

Margaret had offered herself to Danny, not so much out of desire, but rather to comfort him, to jog his memory about when they were together, help him find his way back. She'd stayed awake long after he fell asleep, listened to his heartbeat against his chest, as she ran her fingers along his skin. He smelled of chlorine from the pool and the earthy scent she remembered from when he slept. She'd been afraid to close her eyes. Frightened he'd vanish again. She finally gave in and fell into a deep sleep.

Margaret dreamt of Henry again, this time she awoke startled as if her guilt jolted her awake.

She'd caught her breath, kept her body motionless against Danny, when she remembered where she was and why.

She'd found Danny. Alive.

She hoped now he would remember—his physical response to her seemed encouraging. They'd talked for a while before Danny murmured something incoherent then succumbed to sleep.

After they made love, she settled into his arms, and told Danny that he'd been missing for ten years. He stayed quiet as she told him about his family in Cleveland, how shocked she'd been to see him at the restaurant.

"You have a son."

He still said nothing.

"His name is Jacob."

Margaret waited for Danny to respond, to say anything. But, at least he didn't storm out this time. He seemed to listen to everything she told him.

"Jake started college this week," she'd said. "That's why I'm here. He's at Northern Arizona University in Flagstaff. He's a great kid and he looks so much like you."

"I'm sorry," Danny said, at last. "If what you're telling me is true, I don't remember any of it."

"You don't have to remember right now. I just want to tell you about him, about us. Maybe it will start to come back to you." Margaret willed herself to stay calm. "You know, trigger your memory somehow."

"I have no memory from before the accident."

She told him about his parents, and his older brother.

"But, Danny," she said in a near whisper, "I'm sorry to say, your mother, Jean, passed away several years ago. She wasn't well after losing you. She loved you so much and took it hard when you were never found."

She stopped then, feeling she'd said enough for now. Several minutes passed before Danny spoke.

"So you thought I was dead," he said. "That I died at the World Trade Center. I've read about that day, about the planes crashing into the buildings. But I've never been there. Don't you think I'd remember being there?"

"Maybe the trauma of what happened made you lose your memory. That can happen to people." Margaret had thought maybe he had begun to believe her, that he'd lost his memory before the hit and run, before he ended up in Arizona.

"But why would I be in New York?"

Margaret glanced at the stars through the skylight, hoped she could make him understand. "You had a meeting that morning at the Trade Center. They checked the computer records and you signed-in right before the first plane hit."

"Meeting? What kind of meeting?"

"A new client for the firm," Margaret said, and then she realized he had no idea he what he'd done for a living. "You worked for your dad in insurance."

Danny seemed to consider what she'd said, so she waited.

"But I don't even own a suit," he said. "I don't know the first thing about insurance. In fact, I don't even have insurance. I'm a prep cook and I tend this property. What you're saying makes no sense to me."

"Well," Margaret said. "You hated it. You hated your job and you were miserable selling insurance. I was really worried about you. In fact, you've always loved to cook, so working in a kitchen makes sense. It's one of your natural skills. Now, the horses, that's another thing entirely and not you at all."

Margaret laughed. The light moment felt good.

"Sorry," she said. "I shouldn't laugh, I know you visited your grandmother's farm as a kid, but I never once heard you say you liked the animals."

She could hear Danny breathing heavier and thought maybe he'd fallen asleep or even passed out like he did earlier. Margaret glanced up at him, but she could see his eyes shining in the darkened room.

"Do you remember the farm?" she asked.

"Like I said, I don't remember anything. But if this is all true, maybe that's why I like working with livestock."

Danny took in a deep breath and let it out slowly. Margaret lay her head back down and could hear his heart beat faster. She'd said enough. He seemed agitated again and she decided to change the subject.

"The horses are beautiful."

"I like taking care of them," he said. "But mostly, I like the quiet."

His tone left Margaret feeling sad, he sounded so detached. She had no idea how she'd convince him of the truth. He'd sounded so hard and distant.

"I wouldn't lie to you, Danny." Margaret put her hand on his chest, leaned in tighter. "I hope you can see that I'm not some crazy woman trying to manipulate you. Everything I said is true.

I'll help you remember. We can go as slow as you want. I promise."

Danny mumbled things she couldn't understand, so she stroked his forehead with her fingertips until he fell asleep.

She lay there now, wondered about his reaction. How monotone he'd sounded, he'd had few questions, seemed uninterested about having a son. All of a sudden, in his arms, her clothes tossed on the floor, Margaret felt self-conscious, like maybe to Danny, she was just some woman who made a pass, seduced him.

Then she thought of Henry.

I'm married to Henry now.

Everything seemed so confusing. But in the moment, last night, it felt right. She'd somehow thought the only way to convince Danny. Prove they'd once been together and were married.

Margaret wondered about the time, so she slipped free of Danny's arm—careful not to wake him. Her dress hung draped over the storage chest nearby. She held it against her body as she stood up, and crept across the room to the bathroom. Inside, she washed her face with warm water. Margaret pulled her dress on over her head, examined her face in the mirror. She cried, soundless, tears welled up, spilling onto her cheeks. She'd cried more in the last forty-eight hours than she had in ten years.

What have I done?

Margaret knew she'd only followed her heart the night before. But she couldn't help but think of how hurt Henry would be if he found out what she'd done. She didn't want to make that kind of mistake with him. She loved him too much.

Henry, I'm so sorry.

Margaret shook her head, the tears still streamed down her face. Her desire to hold Danny, to show him the love they once shared, was so intense, she didn't think. She'd acted on instinct, convinced that had been the only way to prove to Danny, Alex was not his name.

But now, as she stood there, she had to admit the real truth about last night. She'd loved every minute, his hands on her body—the taste of his skin. He never called out her name, never showed any sign he recognized her in any way. But she still craved every moment he held her, grabbed her hips, and devoured her lips. Henry never crossed her mind. The desire had taken her over. There, in the middle of the desert, where nobody would know, she'd needed to make Daniel want her.

Last night, after the shock of finding Danny alive, Margaret felt a passion toward him she'd not felt in years. Alone with him, after finding him near the barn, she'd felt drawn to him, in a physical way. She'd wanted him to wake up so she could hold him, prove to him, she was beautiful and desirable. He'd stopped looking at her that way so long ago and she realized now, the pain from his rejection was the reason she'd not been able to let go. He'd shoved her aside after they were married, pushed her away when she tried to love him.

But, last night, she felt certain Danny desired her, found her attractive, and couldn't resist her. She'd proven it to herself, but at what cost? Henry told her she was beautiful all the time, showed her, too. And Danny didn't remember her, even after they made love. And probably never would.

Margaret pulled the clip from her hair, and ran her fingers through her locks. She placed her hands on both sides of the sink, braced herself as she leaned closer to the mirror. "He doesn't remember you."

She stepped away. Dried her face, determined to stop the tears. Margaret smoothed her hair again, wiped away a smudge of mascara, raised her arms, stretched her neck and blew out a deep breath. She rolled her shoulders back, stood tall and glanced into the mirror again.

"He didn't feel a thing and you need to face the fact, he stopped loving you a long time ago." She sniffed away her tears and hung the towel back on the hook. She pulled the curtains aside, the sun would rise soon and she could say what she needed to say to Danny and then leave. She let the curtains drop and used a tissue to wipe her eyes.

Get it together. You're not that girl from back then. You're a woman who is married to a wonderful man. You found Danny. Jacob will know his father now. That's what's important. All the rest doesn't matter.

Margaret breathed in deep again, raised her arms above her head again for a tall stretch, her neck stiff from the same position all night. She lowered her arms, straightened her dress, and opened the door to face Danny.

She found her sandals near the futon, her panties on the floor. She shoved them deep inside the pocket in her dress. Then she noticed, though still gloomy in the room, even as morning eased its way through the skylight, Danny was gone. He wasn't on the futon and for a split second, Margaret felt like maybe it had all been a dream.

But when she twisted round, she saw the front door a jar and his boots were gone from where she'd left them. She pulled out her underwear and slipped them on.

She made sure her keys were on the counter and marched outside.

Birds chirped, and the sun rose along the horizon as a gentle breeze stirred the leaves in the trees on the property.

Margaret glanced around. The top-half of the barn door hung open. She wrapped her arms around her waist to keep warm as she passed by the truck under the carport. She noticed the motorcycle again, and several hoses wrapped and hung on the posts nearby. Danny behind the wheel of a truck struck her as odd as him with horses. He wouldn't even buy an SUV when they were together. A diehard sedan man, Danny always had an eye for a shiny Cadillac or Mercedes. Margaret always thought his cars were impractical for the snow, but he liked a flashy ride and always drove the best, even if they couldn't afford it. Dutch joked about how Danny drove the most expensive car at their office. He and Michael drove company cars, Chevrolets. But, Danny opted to take the company car allowance in cash, bought himself luxury cars every two years, supplemented with their savings.

And now he drives a truck and a motorcycle?

How could amnesia make someone change so much? Wouldn't his personality be the same? And why would he choose slutty women?

Margaret realized she'd neglected to mention the young woman with black hair.

What's her name?

Margaret had no idea, didn't really care, anyway.

But she needed get to the bottom of what was going on—Danny living in Arizona, his job at the restaurant, a caretaker? None of it made sense. Danny was playing a game. She could feel it.

I know he remembers me.

The way he'd held her, she felt him being the Danny she knew. Then his new façade emerged again, and it all felt contrived. During their marriage, Danny often avoided intimacy after a fight. His defenses down, his love would pour out. But when they were together last night, Margaret saw him, she saw Danny. This so-called Alex character, she didn't buy it. Not one bit.

Margaret pulled the bottom door on the barn open, let it slam against the exterior wall, and didn't bother to close it. The horses were gone, so she continued to the paddock, collected dust inside her sandals just like last night.

The sunrise blinded Margaret for a moment as she glanced out to the grassy area, but she spotted the white-capped horse at the far end of the field. She didn't see the other horse, but she heard a voice and then the sound of hooves against the dirt. She glanced toward the red hillsides, and noticed Danny on the back of the larger horse.

"Danny!" she shouted. "Come back."

But he didn't respond. Instead, he slapped the horse hard on its rump and took off at a full gallop, away from the ranch, until Margaret couldn't see them anymore.

"He's crazy."

She trudged back through the barn, slammed the door shut, went across to Danny's house, and slammed that door, too. Then she screamed. And she screamed again. And again and again, until so tired she nearly collapsed. She leaned against the kitchen counter and grabbed her keys.

She'd leave, go back to her hotel, get her bag and go home.

Home. Henry.

She said both words in her head over and over.

I'll call Dutch and Michael. This is their problem. Not mine. I know he knows who I am. I know it. That's why he left.

"Why?" Margaret said. She gripped the keys so tight they cut into the palm of her hand. "Damn it," she yelled and then dropped the keys back on the counter, flipped the faucet to cold, and let the water run over her hand until the puncture wounds didn't hurt. She wrapped a paper towel around her hand and tried to pull herself together.

"Think." She turned around, faced the room, left the paper towel behind with tiny bloodstains, and walked over to where they'd made love. The blanket she'd draped over Danny lay in a heap on the floor. She folded it and moved around to the storage chest. She lifted the heavy lid to place the thick wool blanket inside.

Margaret noticed a wooden box tucked to one side, with a few shirts folded on top. She set the blanket on the futon and shoved the shirts aside. One had a silkscreen of a skull. Margaret shook her head, then tossed the t-shirt with the others, grabbed the box and set it on the folded blanket. She unhooked the latch to the carved box, revealed a stack of papers folded with a paperclip, let the lid to the storage chest bang shut, sat down atop the trunk, and placed the smaller box on the futon.

She pulled out a sanded piece of wood, with 'Mexico' carved into it, a key chain, belt buckle, bandana. She found more papers, which she unfolded and read, the first, a birth certificate with the name Alexander Paul Gershom listed. Born two years before Danny. A social security card stated the same name. She also found a stack of receipts attached, for various items.

Danny always kept receipts for everything, known to return items more than a year later, insisting on a refund.

Beneath other folded papers toward the bottom, was a wallet. His wallet. The wallet she gave him for his birthday the day before he left for New York. It still looked brand new, like he'd never used it. When she pulled it out, underneath, she noticed a pocket watch. The heirloom timepiece Dutch gave to Michael. The watch had disappeared, Michael certain he'd left it behind the night of the party, tore the place apart to search under sofa cushions, in Jacob's room, in case he'd thought the wallet a toy. But Michael never found it.

Margaret felt bad about the antique watch, and thought it might have been tossed with the trash when she'd cleaned up the next day. Her nerves frayed from the reports of the twin tower disaster, she kept busy bagging up remaining paper plates and cups while the news played.

Michael let it go after Margaret explained what she thought happened. But she'd known it meant the world to him, and his father had treasured the piece for years before he passed it along to his eldest son.

Danny had sat solemn-faced at dinner when Dutch presented Michael with the gift. Toasts had gone all around before the steaks arrived. They were celebrating the growth of the company, and the fact Michael had a hand in the growth. Daniel, new to the firm at the time, made Margaret annoyed when he didn't congratulate his brother. He remained pensive the entire night. Margaret found herself gushing over the watch to make up for Danny's rude behavior.

But why would Danny take Michael's watch? Does he remember? Or did he have it on him somehow?

Margaret decided she wasn't going anywhere until she spoke to Danny. She had too many questions, now. She'd wait until he came back and ask him to explain, if he could. She placed the watch next to the papers on the futon and opened the wallet, expected it to be empty since it felt so light.

But, she found a license inside, with the same name, Alexander Paul Gershom. The picture showed Danny with shorter hair, not the crazy long hair he had now. She removed the license from behind the clear plastic cover. And there it was, another license tucked behind. She felt her breath catch in her chest. An Ohio license, Danny's license, with their old address stamped across the front, a BMV picture of the Danny she remembered.

Her hands began to shake and she felt sick. She dropped the wallet, ran toward the sink, but she didn't make it. Margaret vomited on the terra cotta tiles, bile burned at her throat from her empty stomach, and her body convulsed with dry heaves. She reached for the counter to steady herself, and tried to breathe. She grabbed the paper towel she'd left behind and wiped her face, then gulped water from her hands at the sink. She turned around to face the box across the room, the wallet on the floor near the storage chest. Her heart pounded inside her temples and she felt light-headed.

He lied. He left us. He left me.

Proof. Danny knew his true identity whether an amnesiac or not. He knew where he'd lived in Ohio and his true name. Margaret dropped the paper towel over the vomit and shifted to the box.

She picked up the wallet and slipped both of the licenses back inside the sleeve. She felt inside behind where the credit cards should be, there were none, but she felt something behind the empty slots and pulled out three small photos.

Two of them, Margaret recognized, since she'd placed them inside the wallet herself, before wrapping the gift for Danny's birthday. One captured Jacob in Kindergarten, and the other, a wedding photo of them cutting the cake. But there was another picture she hadn't put there, one from long ago, a shot of her at a park near Lake Erie, hair in a ponytail, her smile wide, making a peace sign. She'd forgotten all about that day.

Danny had snapped the picture the summer right after Danny met her parents. Her mom and dad seemed happy, so Margaret felt she and Danny were really a couple.

She wondered now if he'd slipped the picture into his wallet before going to New York. If he planned to leave her, why would he take that picture? Why would he take the watch?

Margaret felt numb. She sat there for a long while before she placed the three pictures back inside the wallet and then packed up the box and returned it to the chest, the blanket on top.

She found her keys, left the door wide open and headed up the path toward the front of the property, climbed back over the fence, unlocked her car and got inside.

The leather seat felt warm and the air stuffy from the heat through the sunroof the day before. She turned the key, adjusted the mirrors, checked for her purse, placed the gearshift in drive, pulled forward, and then turned the wheel to perform a three-point turn before she drove away.

Margaret never looked back.

Chapter 22
Alex

Alex didn't look back even though he could hear Margaret's voice chase after him along the desert floor as he drove Maxwell on. He'd trotted away right before Margaret reached the fence along the back of the corral. He thrust his lower legs sharp against the charger's sides now.

"Yaw, yaw," he shouted. "Yaw, Max, yaw."

Alex held tight to the reins and leaned downward as Maxwell took off in a full gait, galloping swiftly along the dirt path further and further away from the ranch until Alex could no longer hear her voice. He steered Maxwell off course and headed out into the open toward the brilliant blood-orange hills, the first ribbons of sunrise had begun to streak the sky along the eastern horizon.

Hooves pounded against the desert floor, adrenaline pumped through Alex's body, his own muscles in sync with his sturdy mount. Alex felt transported to a place of fearlessness, as if flying, soaring above the earth. Maxwell, born to run, spent his days trotting round the corral. Yet out here, along the vast, open terrain instinct set in, driving Maxwell to his most primitive state of being.

"You're free, Max," Alex shouted. "Run like the wind."

With each forward motion, Alex felt the cool air drum against his face, his hair wild in the wind, as they approached the foothills. Alex pulled back on the reins, but Maxwell continued to run, so Alex tugged harder until Maxwell began to slowdown.

"Whoa, boy," Alex said. "Whoa, whoa." Alex drew Maxwell into a jog, circling, as Maxwell almost reared up.

Once Maxwell held a firm halt, Alex gripped the saddle horn and dismounted, brushing against the damp coat as he slid from the saddle.

"Good job, Max." Alex had never run him so fast. "You're like a getaway car," Alex said. Maxwell snorted, breathing heavy, and shook his head up and down, pulled against the reins, restless from the ride.

Alex tightened his hold while he stroked the crest of Maxwell's neck where the mane grew. Once Maxwell calmed down, Alex eased his hold on the bridle, but not enough for Maxwell to bend and graze. Alex didn't want him tangled in the reins or grass caught in the bit. They'd fled the paddock without a lasso, so Alex knew he needed to be mindful as he rested against a bulky set of red rocks. His shirt now stained with sweat besides his being winded, too, like Maxwell. Alex tapped the bandage on his forehead with his free hand, still secure and dry despite the brisk ride. He smacked his lips, his dry tongue screamed for water. But he'd have to wait to gulp from the hose, like he often did after rides.

"Let's just rest a spell, Max."

The cut seemed to be healing and Alex realized he wasn't as light-headed today. He shut his eyes now and listened to the gentle melodies of birds nesting nearby, the quiet breeze rustled against the leaves of ancient cottonwood trees and lofty willows.

"Hell I'm gonna do?" Alex spoke aloud, and yanked on the reins when Maxwell tried to pull away.

Oregon. Eastern Oregon.

The population tended to be lower in those parts. And Alex knew a guy there—someone who'd worked the trades with him in Phoenix. Maybe he could find work up there, and lie low for a while.

He opened his eyes again, resting against the red rock cliffs, shaded by a canopy of trees. He gazed out along the open windswept desert. Wooded grasslands sounded appealing and the high desert of eastern Oregon seemed more verdant than northern Arizona, at least from the pictures he'd seen. Up to now, the dry arid climate of the Verde Valley had served its purpose. Alex discovered he could tolerate a solitary existence. In fact, he'd thrived in his life unencumbered by the tangles of relationships. His closest friend, Carlos, his boss, would never really be a best friend. And as far as women, Alex only got involved for one reason, the need to dominate. A pressure would build up inside, unyielding until released.

Alex took a deep breath picturing Margaret straddled low across his hips on the futon. Her long, wavy, golden hair pulled to one side, falling against her breast, as she pressed her fingers into his belly to balance herself. Her hips and waist rotated in a natural rhythm as her eyes glistened in the dim room, her lids fluttered as she shifted atop him. The feeling of control evaporated when Alex lost himself to her gentle, sensual movements.

Alex blew out, and rubbed the sweat from his neck.

He'd go to Oregon. Soon.

In fact, the more he thought about it, the more it made sense. He just needed to get back to the ranch, settle some business, and get Margaret out of there. She seemed to believe him, so he'd say he needed time. Maybe she'd back off, retreat to her hotel or wherever it was she'd been staying, so he could pack and leave.

"What'd think, Max?" But Maxwell stared straight ahead at the rocks.

Alex leaned the back of his head against the sandstone. No use heading back until he and Maxwell were rested. Maybe she'd be gone by then. Margaret talked so long into the night Alex had pretended to fall asleep. But, some of what she said had intrigued him.

He'd always assumed she and Michael ended up together. But, she married someone else and Michael and Patty were still together and even had another kid. Had they broken things off when they thought he died? He wasn't sure now. And he didn't really care. Whatever they'd done together would catch up to them someday. Maybe he'd be the one to snitch, inform Patty and Margaret's fancy new husband. The doctor.

He didn't for one minute buy Margaret's sweet, innocent tale. She never suffered when he disappeared. He was convinced she'd put on an act for family and friends, to look good. And the

145

baby she lost? That child was probably Michael's, too. Just like Jacob.

Sure, the baby could have been his, since they'd never stopped having sex. That's why he'd stayed so long, even though his mother had thought Jacob was Michael's son. But he knew Jake could just as likely be his. Margaret had never turned him down. He always thought she used him to cover her tracks. Or being kinky, she liked doing both.

Look at her now, up to her same old tricks. Cheating on her new husband. What a slut.

Alex pulled himself up, brushed the red dust from his jeans while he held the bridle. Maggie was driving him crazy. He'd left her years ago and had seldom thought of her since.

Back in college, she wasn't the same girl she'd been in high school. She hadn't known him in Cleveland when they lived in the same neighborhood. But in Columbus, at Ohio State, they'd hung out with the same group. A dozen or so castoffs from leafy, enchanted neighborhoods of Shaker Heights who'd headed south to be more independent than the kids who stayed in town and attended Case Western or Kent. They called themselves rebels, drank too much on the weekends, then staggered into the library on Sunday afternoon to hunch over their textbooks, exchange notes from classes, and drink coffee.

Still hanging around the same group, who remained their closest friends after graduation, he'd asked Maggie to marry him the day before they graduated. He was relieved when she said yes, because he thought she'd meet someone else when they started working.

Over time, when Alex realized Margaret wasn't the woman he thought she was, he developed an appetite for brief, one-night stands, which gave him a strange sense of satisfaction. Almost as a way to get back at Margaret for the way other men were drawn to her. He'd always felt a bit anxious with Margaret, like he wasn't good enough. The affairs helped him relax, made him feel more confident, especially when the women were attractive.

But he wasn't like that anymore. He didn't need to prove himself like in those days. He'd fallen hard for a gorgeous, young Mexican woman in Tucson. But she wouldn't see him again after

146

they'd made love. When he pressed her for a reason, she told Alex her father would never approve of their age difference. But nonetheless, he realized a woman could love him. Afterwards, he had no interest in love anymore. He moved on to women whom he found attractive, but held little interest for him.

Alex drew Maxwell around by the bridle and prepared the saddle for his mount. He settled atop Maxwell, made a clicking noise, set out at an easy pace toward the estate. The sun higher in the sky now, the bands of red and orange had faded to scattered white billows of clouds.

Chapter 23
Alex

Alex steered Maxwell back toward the barn, careful to direct him away from stray cacti, as if weaving through traffic on his commute back in Cleveland.

In the final months before Alex left, he drifted to a dark place inside his mind. He thought about death all the time, how it might feel to die. He didn't want to commit suicide, but he experienced cryptic fantasies about death just the same.

Sometimes on the interstate at Dead Man's Curve near downtown, he'd imagined a semi-truck slamming him from behind, his car sent projectile into Lake Erie.

Lately, since his head injury, he'd had similar illusions, as if all the work he'd done to get his head straight had flown out when he hit the ground. He'd allowed his life to expand too far, to dream of bigger things, and in doing so his mind had tripped out of control again. He needed to get away, find a new place. Too many people knew him in Sedona, now. He felt crowded, limited, and it had turned him again.

Back in Cleveland when it got really crazy, and he needed to calm down, he'd drive to Voinovich Bicentennial Park near Browns Stadium to watch the currents in Lake Erie.

But if the clouds were heavy, the weight of the pressure system could flip the switch in his mind and the intense fantasies would return. By the time he'd finished his sandwich, the cloud coverage would sometimes be so thick it resembled a grey, mildewed blanket over the city. Then he'd wonder what it would be like to jump from the top bleachers of the stadium, land against the sidewalk below.

Oftentimes, on flights into Cleveland, the pilot would perform a wide turn over the lake before descending beneath the grey veil of clouds. Alex, who was still Daniel back then, would feel the problems in his life press against his temples. He'd shut his eyes and will the plane to crash upon landing.

The problem was, he couldn't escape his past in Cleveland. All roads led back to the same point, to the pond at the edge of his childhood yard, at the bottom of the twisty, brick pathway behind the house his parents had still lived in, to the night when Brian sunk under the ice and drowned.

And until last week, when he slammed his head against the desert floor, and the nightmares returned, and somehow Margaret appeared out of nowhere, his life had been manageable, and the guilt that haunted him after Brian's tragic death was dead and buried in Ohio.

But now, the demons were resurrected, and danced upon the stage of his fragile psyche. The pain from his injury only served to remind him of the constant grief and blame he'd left behind. His mother starred in every scene, and he couldn't rid her from his mind now, even though she was dead. Her stricken look, the cast of sorrow in her eyes for her evil son. He knew she stopped loving him the day he told her the truth.

And yet, when he learned his mother had died, Alex didn't cry. He wouldn't grieve for her. Nor would he feel relieved. He felt nothing, like always, ever since the day his mother betrayed him. If he didn't get away now, the same darkness would move in and plague him forever.

"Everyone will hate you," his mother had said.

He'd gone into his parents' bedroom, desperate, out of his mind from the horror of losing his best friend. He could have saved him.

"Your father will be so ashamed."

His mother closed the door to the bedroom, faced him.

Young Danny focused on the sea green, floral wallpaper on the wall behind her. To this day, the color could make his hands clammy, his stomach turn.

149

"Don't you tell another living soul," his mother said, her voice hushed and stern. He'd wanted to escape the room when the walls began to close in around him. But his mother blocked the door. "What you've done is awful," she said. "Unforgivable." She ran her fingers along the pearls at the nape of her neck. "God will punish you."

His mother's face because grim, no longer beautiful to him. The spell broken, she was not his mother.

"You'll have to live with what you've done."

The harshness of what she'd said slammed the door on his childhood, forever.

He remembered the window across the room open a few inches from the night before. His father liked the room cold when he slept. The chill floated in from the backyard and lifted the sheer curtains to reveal the frigid winter pond at the edge of the snow-covered yard. Out on the weathered dock, still covered in yellow police tape, Danny saw Brian beckon to him to come outside. Bare trees surrounded the modest lake and the prickly black raspberry canes shot out along the frozen edges. The breeze settled, and the curtains fell against the windowsill then fluttered open again, and Brian had disappeared.

"I'm going to forget you ever told me," she said.

For the first time in his young life, his mother's voice had sounded spiteful. As if she'd spat the words across the room, yet her voice barely above a whisper, he could smell her heavy perfume on the cool winter breeze from the window.

He stayed frozen in place while she straightened her blouse and left the door ajar. He listened to each of her footsteps upon the creaky staircase until she reached the bottom.

Then he breathed again.

Nobody could help him. He was alone.

His mother never forgot as she said she would. She tortured him in all sorts of ways for having to keep his secret.

"Why, Jean?" he'd said, years later, taken to calling his mother by her given name as an adult, since he no longer felt like her son. "You constantly badger me about the same things," he complained, seated next her in a weathered wicker chair on the front porch of their family's lakeside cottage in Michigan.

The others were still inside getting ready for their stroll to town for dinner. A constant inaudible hum of voices floated out from the screen door. The search was on for a misplaced sandal and then for the iron to touch-up a wrinkled shirt.

"Must you keep on about those two?" He hoped she'd stop with the insinuations for once.

They'd been having a decent conversation for once, a discussion about the sunset, the brilliant shimmers of light cast across the water, when his mother had to mention Michael and Margaret going for a sail earlier. Fine with him. He wanted Maggie to enjoy the beautiful day. After all, he'd been late driving up alone, since he had a meeting in Detroit. He made the four-hour drive north that afternoon. Everyone else arrived the day before.

The pleasantries ended when his mother found it necessary to interject one of her bogus observations about the supposed love affair going on between his brother and his wife.

"The warm sunshine was the perfect romantic backdrop for a boat ride." Jean's tone had sounded wicked and cold.

And then, of course, she denied any innuendo. "I have no idea what you're talking about."

They both knew what she meant. She'd suggested the two were having an affair before, nothing new.

"You want me to think my wife is with Michael," he said. "It's disgusting and I'm sick of hearing it."

His mother kept her eyes fixed on the lake across the street. "I thought you'd want to know," she said, and then unfolded her handkerchief, twisted it between her fingers. "But that's right, you like to pretend you don't see things."

Another long weekend of insults ahead, he hated going to Michigan, the cottage, his mother, and the useless conversations.

"You told me to never tell anyone," he said. "For God's sake, I was only a kid." He sat forward in the chair, rubbed his temples. "You're the one who hides things, Jean."

His mother gave him a chilly glance. "If I remember right," she said, her voice detached. "I merely pointed out how many people would be hurt by your selfish actions."

He'd felt a tight pressure inside his skull, as if transported back to his parent' bedroom, the green walls closing in all over again, like a heavy vise around his head. Exasperated, he'd dropped his hands and leaned back in the chair again. With gritted teeth, he took in a deep breath then closed his mouth, and released the lungful of air out through his nose, like a bull ready to charge.

He straitened up again. "But, Jean," he said, trying to defend himself. "I didn't do anything."

"Precisely." His mother dabbed at her red lipstick with the corner of her handkerchief and then pressed it inside her palm.

"Like I said, I was kid." He slumped back into the chair, and knew it was useless. He'd never gain her sympathy.

The screen door flew open, the hinges screeched into the night air, before it slammed shut.

"Careful, Dutch," Jean said. "I called the repairman to fix that thing, so go easy on it, please."

Dutch examined the screen flap, torn open in the top corner like a triangle-shaped flag. "Definitely on its last leg," he said, as he turned to face them both. "Get him to take a look at the electrical outlet in the laundry room while you're at it. Plugged the iron in and it wouldn't heat up." Dutch straightened his pink oxford shirt, tucked it tighter inside his Bermuda shorts.

"Oh for goodness sake," Jean said, and squeezed her hanky inside her palm. "That old iron has been broken for years."

"Well, Christ, Jeanie," Dutch said. As he ran a hand through his silver hair, the scent of spicy pomade filled the air. "Why the hell haven't we tossed the damn thing?" Dutch always said 'we' when irritated with Jean, as if she only had a few things to do in life and why couldn't she have everything perfect for him all the time?

His secretaries did. At the office, his dad's executive assistant and the other office workers would drop whatever if Dutch needed something. He knew his dad felt entitled as the owner of the firm. He'd said so, many times, in meetings. He'd complain when his coffee cup stayed empty, or if 'the gals' neglected to provide the requisite Danish platter, or at the very least, a plate of donuts on the walnut credenza inside the conference room. Some type of urgent situation had preceded the only time the gals forgot. Even then, Dutch would mention it later to his assistant. Remind her to always have a supply on hand.

It wasn't enough that his dad acted pompous that night on the porch, but when Michael stepped outside the cottage, wearing nearly the same outfit as their dad, plaid shorts, pastel oxford, dress loafers with no socks, he couldn't help but roll his eyes at his older brother. If Maggie was, indeed, having an affair with Michael, well then, she'd fallen into the idiot category, too.

"Great minds," Dutch said, with a hardy rap to Michael's shoulder.

Again, he'd rolled his eyes. His father and his brother let out the same obnoxious laugh. Copious amounts of men's cologne filled the air, blending with their barbershop pomade, Michael's dark, brown hair slicked back like Dutch.

He hated how his father and brother took up all the oxygen in every space they occupied. The oversized porch felt crowded with the two of them, so he'd moved onto the front lawn, and stuffed his hands deep inside the pockets of his cargo shorts. He tried to ignore the ridiculous spectacle behind him on the porch, stared out at the water, as the sun dipped toward the western end of the lake.

When he'd glanced back at his family, the sudden rush of being an outsider flooded his soul. He didn't belong. And he didn't want to. After being on the road all week, even signing a new client, nobody bothered to asked him about his meetings since he'd arrived. Not even Margaret. She'd barely glanced up from reading a book when he found her upstairs, sprawled out on the bed in the room he'd stayed in since childhood. Michael always had the larger that faced the lake, while he and Maggie squeezed into the room over the alleyway.

"Is that what you're wearing, Danny?" she'd said, after he changed out of his suit. "This new restaurant is pretty nice."

Out on the lawn, he'd glanced down at his worn shorts and flip-flops sinking into the lawn, then again at his family. His mother's face pinched as she leaned against the balustrade now, her hair smooth and tidy, as if the wayward strands didn't dare stray, not even in a driving wind. She crossed her arms, her expression gave away the utter shame she felt toward him.

Screw you, Mom.

He'd turned back toward the lake, sick of his life.

His mother's resentment and bitterness toward him had filtered throughout the entire family, like a disease without inoculation. Every symptom toward him, each cough, and insult became a reminder that he wasn't part of their world, their need to be perfect, to be admired, to feel superior. A sickness he wanted nothing to do with. He always felt like they resented him for being different. And his mother led the pack.

Alex pulled on the reigns now to slow Maxwell. After they'd crossed a ravine, and when Maxwell had climbed the slight embankment on the other side, he broke into a trot. Alex didn't want him injured on the rough areas of the terrain. He'd let Maxwell run again, once they were back on the trails. Alex reached down and gave his friend a good pat—their final ride together. And Alex wanted to enjoy every minute.

Chapter 24
Alex

Miles of desert stretched out before them. Still a ways before they reached the edge of the property, especially if Maxwell kept loping along at the same pace.

They'd picked up the trail again, so Alex tapped his heals against Maxwell's sides, urging a quicker gait, but not a full gallop like before, somewhere between. Maxwell responded. Alex imagined he needed water, just like him.

That night in northern Michigan, he'd been miserable and drank several beers at the restaurant. The walk back to the cottage had done nothing to clear his head. He'd fought with Margaret inside their cramped room, a quick, whisper war, since she wouldn't fight him, then he passed out on the pine floor where he slept until morning.

From that weekend forward, he tried to avoid his mother altogether.

But, when Margaret gave birth to Jacob, Jean had come to the hospital and in front of everyone, went on about how Jacob resembled Michael as a baby.

"Well, look at that," she'd said, standing next to Margaret's bedside, Jacob swaddled in her daughter-in-law's arms. "Why, he's the spitting image of Michael."

She kept it up, too. At every family gathering, she'd point out any similarities between the two. And after a while, Alex couldn't help but notice she might be right. Early on, Jacob seemed more coordinated than other boys his age, a natural athlete like his Uncle Mike.

The night before Alex went to New York, he witnessed something between Maggie and Michael that he'd never seen before. Maggie had given Alex a surprise birthday party and invited all their friends and family. He actually felt kind of happy for once. He'd been touched that Maggie had gone to so much trouble.

Toward the end of the evening, Alex stepped out to the backyard with a bag of trash. When he came back from the side yard onto the patio, he noticed Michael and Margaret in the kitchen window near the sink.

Alex stopped to light a cigarette. They seemed to be in a deep conversation, the window closed, he couldn't hear what they were saying.

He watched as his wife wiped away tears from her face as she glanced up at Michael. They were standing close, too close. They seemed too familiar with each other. Michael's hand grazed Margaret's cheek, neither flinched, and then she leaned in closer. Alex had several drinks during the course of the party, and by no means, in shape to judge the situation, but saw the comfortable intimacy between them. Michael pulled her even closer, held her in his arms.

What the hell?

Alex nearly bolted inside to break them apart, but he held his ground. He couldn't take his eyes off them. Everything seemed to move in slow motion. Michael smoothed the hair from Maggie's face as she glanced up at him again, gazing into his eyes, and then he kissed her.

It still made Alex's blood boil to think of it, even now all these years later. It was something about the way his brother had acted so entitled, shameless even. As if he didn't care who found out.

At the time, he'd felt like throwing up. But instead, his pack of cigarettes slid from his hand onto the concrete patio, as he froze trying to comprehend what he just saw.

Then Maggie pulled away from Michael.

And Alex felt relieved. Maybe she wasn't interested after all. Maybe Michael had taken advantage of an emotional moment, and forced himself on her. But she didn't slap him. Instead, she moved back into his arms and kissed him again.

Alex felt his heart break.

He still couldn't move, paralyzed in the moment. And then Maggie rested her head against Michael's chest, and reached up and kissed him on the cheek.

They pulled apart and disappeared from the window, like the ending to a romantic comedy. Yet, to Alex it had been a tragedy, the saddest show he'd ever seen.

Everything changed. Alex finally believed his mother.

He bolted for the door, heard his brother inside the living room. Vociferous as always, Michael was talking about something Alex couldn't remember now. He'd spotted Maggie on the staircase, headed up, alone.

He'd started after her, but dipped inside the den instead. To this day, he knew that if he'd gone after her right then, he might have killed her.

His adrenaline pumped so hard in that moment, he'd closed the door to the den, paced back and forth, then punched a leather ottoman stacked with coats over and over, grabbed the pile and threw them against the wall landing on the sofa. There were other coats sprawled across his chair, and he noticed one in particular on top, Michael's jacket. He sat down hard in his chair and tossed the other coats across the room toward the sofa. He'd wanted to throw his brother's into the fireplace and watch it burn. But he went through the pockets instead.

He felt his grandfather's pocket watch inside the lapel and pulled it out and stuffed it inside his jeans.

When he rejoined the party, someone gave him a fresh beer, the last thing he remembered about the night. He knew he'd screamed at Maggie later, and broke a lamp. But nothing else happened.

He'd gone upstairs to pack during the night, almost as a reason to check on Margaret. He'd woken in a heap in the den, the top half of his body hung off the sofa. Blood had rushed to his head. He noticed a cut on his hand from the broken lamp, but panicked, thinking it might be Maggie's blood. He couldn't remember what happened for sure, the house so quiet, it felt eerie.

He'd climbed the stairs fearful he'd beaten her, or maybe even killed her. He'd gone straight past Jacob's door and found Maggie asleep in bed, no blood. Her breathing the same even pattern it always was when she slept. He watched her. The light streamed in from the streetlamp, her hair spread out on the pillow. Beautiful Maggie, like an angel.

Right then, he knew he wanted to leave her. Not only because she'd hurt him, but he felt dangerous. Like he might be capable of doing something to hurt her. The rage he'd felt the night before felt insane. And he didn't want to harm her, not really. He still loved her. But, he couldn't be around her anymore. He needed to get away from all of them. He knew life with them had come to an end. Right there at the foot of the bed. He knew.

All those years, he pitied them, his family, his wife, if he even thought about them.

When his family crossed his mind, he'd imagine Michael telling the same tired stories, sneaking kisses from Margaret when Patty wasn't looking. Or maybe they'd divorced and Michael married Maggie and they were living happily ever after. But even so, he felt sorry for Michael, working for their dad until Dutch retired and then taking over the business, commuting to the office under those awful grey clouds.

No. Michael could keep it all, even Maggie.

Alex only remembered bits of the fight he'd had with Margaret that night. He called her a slut. She cried and left the room. He didn't remember how he ended up on the sofa. But he was glad he'd somehow controlled himself. Except for breaking the lamp, and maybe slamming some doors.

He almost missed his flight the next morning. Woken in a start, raced to the airport. But when the plane ascended, his head cleared the sky a brilliant blue, like a sign, as they landed in New York. Out from under the clouds, he could think again. He planned to quit after he signed one final account for Dutch. Then he'd move away, for good. He almost felt relieved.

Maggie could do whatever she wanted. She could have the house. But he wasn't paying child support. He'd have a paternity test. As the plane landed that day, for once he didn't want to crash. He wanted to live.

Chapter 25
Alex

Still high in the saddle above the red clay soil, Alex pictured Maggie yelling for him to come back. He hoped she'd left, but also knew she could be determined. He'd get rid of her somehow. The sun had warmed the atmosphere and Alex took in some fresh desert air. He wondered if the stars were as bright in Oregon, if he'd be able to see his favorite constellations.

He tried to think of anything except Maggie now. Because the closer he got to the barn, the more he remembered how Maggie felt in his arms last night. God, her skin was like satin. Sex hadn't felt that good for him in a long time.

In fact, the last few times he was with Sonia, he'd had to force himself to be with her. She talked too much during sex and if he caught sight of her face, he'd lose desire. He'd started to notice a strange smell on her, maybe the weed she smoked, but even her skin had taken on a foul odor. He'd gotten out of there fast, the last time, told her he had to work, a lie. She'd gone to the restaurant that night and bothered Carlos.

Alex would never be with her again.

But last night with Maggie felt real, not only a physical act, it felt loving, if he'd admit it. Could that be okay? Maybe Margaret would go home, leave the past where it belonged. Because no matter if Maggie did love him, she'd also been with Michael, and what was done was done. He hoped she'd leave it alone. Move on. But God, how beautiful she'd been last night. He wouldn't forget. Not ever.

When Maggie rested her chin on his chest, he could see the regret in her eyes.

"You were in a bad way the day you left for New York," she said, her voice sleepy.

He knew she'd wanted a response, but he'd stayed focused on the constellations beyond the skylight.

"It was your birthday," Margaret said. "You drank too much, and after everyone left, you yelled at me, and carried on about things I didn't understand."

Alex listened to his wife's lies.

"You were keyed-up about work," she said.

"Did you get married again?" Alex had said, changing the subject.

She became quiet then and shifted her head back onto the pillow and glanced up at the stars like Alex.

Did you marry Michael? Say it. He'd wanted the truth.

After all, she wore a new ring, fancier than the one he'd given her, a sign she'd married his brother.

"I did get married again, yes."

"If you're married, why are you here?" Alex stretched his legs out from being tangled together with Margaret's. Even though the room felt chilly, his thighs remained drenched with sweat. The futon seemed narrower than ever.

"As I said before, I took Jacob, our son, to college in Flagstaff and then came to Sedona to relax for a few days before heading back to California." Margaret shifted again, facing him. "I never expected to spot you in the hallway at that restaurant. I knew it was you, the second I saw you, even though you've changed so much."

"Changed?"

"You're different," she said, reaching up to touch his hair.

He knew he should flinch, like a stranger might, but her touch felt too good.

"Your hair is long now and you're thinner." Then she traced her fingers along his arm, sending warm embers through his veins. "And you didn't have these tattoos before." She paused for what felt like a long time, making him nervous.

He wanted out of there, but felt too weak to move. Not sure if his injury or the shock of seeing Maggie again caused the room to shift, but he felt so dizzy, the world spun almost as fast as the blades on the ceiling fan.

"I saw you again in the alleyway, with that woman." Margaret touched his hand. "I thought my eyes may have played a trick on me, so I walked around back to see for myself," she said. "But then I got scared, so I went back in the morning and your boss told me where you were living."

Carlos told her where I live?

Alex couldn't believe it. But he stayed still. He had to know. "What does your husband think about this?"

"I haven't told him."

"Doesn't sound like a very good marriage."

She became quiet. Alex thought he heard her crying, then she sat-up with her back to him on the edge of the futon.

She'd tell him now. So he waited.

Alex caught her profile in the moonlight, the curve of her back. He wanted to run a finger down her spine to see if she'd arch again, like she'd done when she lowered herself atop him. But he didn't touch her, too risky. She had never been as sensuous when they made love before.

She stretched her arms into the air above her head. He could see the curve of her waist meeting her hip. The years had been kind to Maggie. She'd developed into a beautiful woman, not the girlish one he'd known, but a woman who knew how to satisfy a man. She'd learned how to use her body to get what she wanted, too. He waited for her to stand up, but instead, she leaned down and pulled the blanket from the floor and covered them both as she settled against him, again.

"It's a good marriage," she said. "Henry is a wonderful man. I don't know what I'm going to tell him. I'm just trying to focus on this moment, right now." Maggie wrapped her arm across Alex's chest and held him tight.

Henry? Who's Henry? Alex kept his right arm above his head, his left arm folded over his chest, as he tried to process what she'd just told him.

Maggie grabbed his hand and brought it to her lips, kissing his fingers. "You're alive," she whispered. "That's all that matters."

Alex felt so confused, certain she married his brother. All he could think about was Maggie kissing Michael. Her arms around his neck, she'd lingered for a moment, a kiss of passion. Why had she married someone else?

"I met Henry several years after being alone with Jacob," Maggie had whispered in the night. "I was still in love with you."

Lying next to her, Alex took a deep breath, but remained silent.

"I kept everything the same for so long," she said. "To keep you with us, so I could stay with you. I kept the house and your things for years," she explained. "But slowly, I began to move on. That's when I met Henry. He's great with Jacob and he helped me heal. I don't think I realized how far gone I was until I met him. We took it slow. Henry never pressured us to let go of you. We even have pictures of you in our house in Laguna Beach."

"But you said, Cleveland."

"Henry took a new job in California," Margaret said. "So we moved after we got married."

That's why she's so tan. And her hair is lighter, bleached from the sun.

"Do you ever go back to Ohio?"

"Yes, my parents still live there and we see your family, too. They've been very good to me and Jacob." She remained quiet for a few moments. "Your dad lives in a retirement community now. Your brother took over the company when he retired. Oh, and Patty had another baby, a boy. I mean, Patty, your brother's wife, so they have three sons now, younger than Jacob."

"I don't remember them." Alex kept his voice even.

"Maybe you'll start to remember now that you're hearing about them," she said. "Your brother's name is Michael and your dad goes by Dutch. Does that sound familiar?"

"No."

"Michael and Patty bought a new house when their boys got bigger. They were only a few miles from us before. I sold our house when Henry asked me to marry him. It was really hard. But, maybe I can take you to see it one day. And your dad and brother."

"I don't like to travel." Alex took in another deep breath and tried to move away from Margaret a bit, but he had nowhere to go as she pulled him closer.

"I'm sorry," she said. "This is overwhelming you." She loosened her grip and rolled onto her back. "We'll take things slow," she said. "Whatever you need."

Enough time passed that he thought Maggie had fallen asleep. So he closed his eyes and felt himself drifting, the room still spun even with his eyes shut.

"Jacob's going to be so happy," Maggie said, startling Alex. She sniffled, like maybe more tears. "He's a wonderful young man, Danny," her voice soft, almost a whisper. He pictured the little boy he'd left behind. It seemed impossible he was in college now. "You'd be so proud."

Alex squirmed against the back of the futon. Sometimes Alex missed the boy. But he wasn't his responsibility, and as always, Maggie sounded delusional. After all those years, she still believed her own lies. He felt feverish again. He wished she'd leave.

Maggie patted his arm. "I called you Danny, again," she said. "I'm sorry, Alex, but that's who you are to me."

She tucked her arm along his side, and then rested her head against his upper arm, as if they were still married, and not just on paper. As if she'd never cheated with Michael.

As his fever spiked, he felt sweat beading up on his neck and forehead. He felt trapped, like an animal after going for the bait.

"It's a lot to take in," she said. "I just want you to know your family is okay. They love you very much. Your brother went to New York to try to find you. Your parents were strong for Jacob and me. But over time, your mom's health failed when you never came home."

"I told you," Alex said. "I don't remember them." He wanted to shove her onto the floor. "What do you want me to say?"

"You don't have to say anything," she said, her voice soft and gentle, sounding almost condescending which irritated him even more. "But you should know, we tried to find you. Your mom was heartbroken. She was never the same after you weren't found."

Heartbroken? More like relieved. The evil son gone, dead and buried in the rubble, like he deserved.

Alex could smell Margaret's breath against his shoulder, more sweet than sour even at the end of the day. He didn't remember that about her.

"I'm so sorry," Maggie said, and moved closer to him. "Your dad really misses her. That's why he lives at a retirement home, so he can be around other people. But, he still golfs and goes to the theatre. But you don't remember that, I know."

Alex remained quiet. He couldn't breathe, his chest felt heavy, as if something giant pressed against his sternum.

"Are you okay?" Margaret seemed to be studying him when he opened his eyes, her face inches from his. He nudged her away with his shoulder, but she didn't move, she stayed by his side.

"I don't feel well," he said, the truth. "This bump on my head is making me sick."

"You should rest now," she said. "We can talk more in the morning.

Alex tried to get comfortable as Maggie stroked the side of his face with her fingers.

"You don't have to do that," Alex said, still agitated.

"It's okay," Maggie said. "You always liked it when I did this to help you relax." She trailed her fingers along his neck. "Your fever is high again."

"Just so you know, I'm still not sure who you really are, and all this talk, this stuff you're saying about some family I supposedly have in Ohio, it's not resonating, and in fact, it's making me very uncomfortable." Alex moved her hand away. "I wish you'd stop now. I want to sleep. I wish you'd go, but it's the middle of the night and I don't want to walk you to the gate. I'm too dizzy. So, please, just stop talking." He hoped that would do it.

Margaret shifted away from him a bit. She stayed silent, except for her breaths as they both laid there together, the fan turning above each small breeze against Alex's face a relief from the heat inside his body.

"All I can tell you," Alex said, his voice calm and steady, "Is that I've never questioned why I don't recall my life before the accident, so I assumed I had no family or my mind wanted to forget somehow. You seem like a nice person and I appreciate you taking care of Maxwell and Lady and helping me when I collapsed, but I just don't know if I believe your story." Alex didn't speak for a moment, and hoped she'd get the message. He wasn't going to remember. "I'm sorry," he continued. "I can't even remember your name right now. I know that's not polite to admit after what we just did, but I still have no recollection of knowing you, at all."

"You didn't feel anything when we made love?"

"It felt good," Alex said. "But not what you're asking, no."

"It's Margaret, by the way," she said, her voice soft and filled with sorrow. "My name is Margaret, but you can call me, Maggie."

"Nothing," Alex repeated in a flat tone. "I remember nothing."

Both were silent then. The news about his mother had jolted him. The pressure in his chest felt better now, but he hadn't expected his mother to be dead. After all, she had been younger than his father.

My mother? Dead?

Alex repeated the words—surprised the news even bothered him. He hated his mother. But he mourned for her somehow, for the Mom she'd been before Brian fell through the ice, before she turned her back on him. He closed his eyes and concentrated on his breathing while Maggie seemed to drift off to sleep.

Her body curved into his. Different from Sonia and the other women he'd been with over the years, Maggie felt softer, her body warm against his. Sonia had a great body, but she never fit into his arms like Maggie did. Like they were puzzle pieces hooked together. Even now.

The body sweats got worse for a while and Alex couldn't sleep. He shoved the blanket from his legs onto Maggie, but held her tight, his arm wrapped under her shoulders. He didn't want her to fall, now. He lay in the dark, and listened to her sleep, her head rested in the crook of his arm, the same way he'd held her when they were younger, when he still loved her.

Through the skylight, Alex could see one of those nights where the sky opened up and the stars shone vivid, the constellations seeming within reach. He wished he could get to his telescope on the patio to see the dim glowing of the Milky Way Galaxy, a galaxy he knew to be only one of many billions of other galaxies.

He gazed at the stars until he couldn't keep his eyes open any longer.

He awoke later, but kept his eyes shut when he heard Maggie whimper in his arms. She must be dreaming, but then she spoke, so low, he strained to hear her.

"I was going to tell you when you got back from New York," she said.

Alex pretended to be asleep.

"We were going to have another baby," she whispered. "But I had a miscarriage." He heard her soft cries, felt her body tremble against him. "I lost you, and then I lost our baby."

Maggie lifted her head to wipe away her tears and then settled back and seemed to fall asleep again.

She'd been pregnant again? He'd had no idea. Why hadn't she told him? Had that been what she talked about with Michael in the kitchen? Had they conceived yet another child together? Why keep lying?

He held her, confused about everything. Was she telling the truth? Had the child been his after all? She felt petite in his arms, had acted tender toward him. Had his mother said it so many times that he'd somehow believed her and pushed Maggie into his brother's arms? Was Maggie somehow innocent in all of this? Part of him wanted to believe she still loved him, always did.

He did believe her story about finding him in Sedona by accident. He'd seen the way she wrapped her arms around herself in the alleyway, how she'd run away when exposed. Maybe the kisses in the kitchen were their first. Maybe she'd found out about his affairs and went to Michael for comfort. But he couldn't ask. So, he'd never know. And that was fine. He didn't care anymore. He'd left Ohio for more reasons than Margaret kissing his brother.

When he woke before dawn, and Margaret wasn't there, he thought she'd decided to leave. But then he heard her in the bathroom. So Alex pulled his clothes on and headed to the stables to turn out Maxwell and Lady. Maxwell stayed close, confused by the early hour. When Alex heard the door to the barn slam shut, he'd grabbed Maxwell by the reins, already saddled for a ride. He'd guided Maxwell to open land, and hauled the corral gate shut.

Now, as he rode up to the back of the property, he surveyed the paddock, and he could see Lady grazing in the middle of the grassy field. As far as Alex could tell, the back gate looked secure. He didn't see Maggie anywhere. The place looked quiet. Alex dismounted at the bottom of the hill, to walk the rest of the way. He'd settle Maxwell and then Lady, make a final call, and be on his way.

Chapter 26
Margaret

The main lobby peaceful, a handful of early risers were scattered with cups of coffee, and an older couple with matching bright-orange windbreakers perused tourist brochures at a display near the concierge desk. Margaret passed by them on her way to the courtyard where she'd had breakfast the morning before, then around the fountain to the pathway that led to her room. Her bag remained on the dresser, a sweater draped over the desk chair, her bed still made from yesterday. Her stomach turned as she stuffed her sheer white cardigan inside her weekend bag and zipped the top shut. She headed inside the bathroom to gather her toiletries and makeup. She avoided her reflection in the mirror, afraid to face what she'd done, how stupid and impulsive she'd been, never taking into consideration Danny might be lying about the amnesia. That he'd left her. And he'd left Jacob, too.

You are so naïve.

"Stupid," she uttered under her breath, as she shoved a few more items inside a monogramed travel pouch. The letters MP were monogrammed in white in the center of the quilted, black velvet bag, a gift from Henry. Margaret Pierson, Henry's wife.

I don't deserve you, Henry.

There were no tears as she drove back across Sedona to the resort. She'd forced herself to forget Danny. Forget she ever found him. She wouldn't give him the satisfaction.

"What an animal," Margaret said, and pulled her nightgown from the back of the bathroom door inside her room at the resort.

She held the cream-colored, satin gown to her chest. Another gift from Henry, one he'd given her for Christmas. She could picture the matching robe in her closet at home in Laguna Beach. Home. Their beautiful hillside home above the Pacific, where they'd been so happy together as a family. What had she done?

Margaret twisted around, flipped the water on in the bathtub, and drew the switch atop the spigot to trigger the shower. She tucked the shower curtain inside the tub and undressed, folded her dress and nightgown on the counter. Under the showerhead, Margaret scrubbed her skin nearly raw with a bar of soap. She shampooed her hair twice, rinsed every inch of her body over and over, and then shut the water off, and grabbed a clean towel. She used the blow dryer for a few minutes, left her hair damp, tied it back with a band, dusted facial powder across the bridge of her nose and along her jawline, and dabbed clear gloss on her lips. She scooped up her belongings and padded out into the bedroom, still unclothed. She grabbed her weekend bag and tossed it on the bed, unzipped it halfway, added her gown, toiletries, and dress, but then thought better and pulled out the blue dress. Margaret marched to the wastebasket beside the desk and tossed the dress. She glanced at the phone and tried to ignore the red light. Then she went through her weekend bag and found a clean sports-bra, fresh underwear, a pair of khaki shorts and a white t-shirt. She grabbed the novel she'd read halfway through from the bedside, jammed the White Pages back inside the drawer on the nightstand, and caught the clay lamp before it crashed onto the wide-planked wood floor.

She stood back and glanced out the window at the red rocks.

"What a mess," she said, the sky so blue above the desert, she squinted then turned away.

I'll talk to Henry. He'll know what to do.

Margaret wrapped the strap to her weekend bag over her shoulder, slid the book inside her purse and slipped her sandals on, then let the door slam behind her. She passed by the fountain where people lounged underneath the umbrellas for breakfast, but

Margaret headed straight to the lobby and slipped her key across the counter to the desk clerk.

"Good morning, Mrs. Pierson." The same middle-aged man with a closely trimmed beard, who'd checked her in, worked the desk again today. "We don't have you checking out until tomorrow. Was everything okay?"

"Yes, of course," Margaret said, pulling her credit card out of her wallet. "But, I need to check out early, I've got to get home."

The clerk waved away her credit card. "We have your card on file," he said. "Let me cancel your room for tonight."

As Margaret waited for him to finish on his keyboard, she wished he could cancel everything that happened.

"There you go," he said, and handed her the printout. "Hope you'll visit us again."

Probably not, Margaret wanted to say. But, she managed a tiny smile instead and headed toward the front entry.

Outside, the bellhop held the door for her on the SUV, right where she'd left it before she raced up to her room. She handed him a few dollars then she slipped inside the car, and dropped her bags on the passenger's seat. "Thank you," she said, as the young man closed her door and she started the engine. She entered her home address into the GPS and followed blindly along as the voice guided her to the edge of town, toward California, back to Henry.

It wasn't until north of Phoenix when Margaret noticed the gas gauge on low, so she exited the interstate and found a station. After she filled up, Margaret pulled her car around to the side of the service station and parked. She used the restroom, and then poured herself a cup of coffee inside the store. At the counter, she noticed the front page of a newspaper with an article about the upcoming events taking place in New York City.

"Can you believe it's been ten years?" a man said, from behind her.

Margaret glanced over her shoulder as the man pulled the newspaper from the stand.

"Seems like yesterday, doesn't it?" The man, dressed in jeans and a lime green golf shirt, wearing a Diamondbacks baseball cap, folded the paper and tucked it under his arm with one hand, as he held a cup of coffee with his other, trying not to spill it. "I was in New York on business," he said. "Midtown, so I wasn't near the towers, but still, it was quite a day."

"You were lucky," Margaret managed to say, her voice sounded funny to her after being in the car, silent, the only sounds from the engine and the GPS. This man in the bright green shirt had broken her trance.

"Yeah," he said, his eyes, a soothing grey-blue. "I was lucky, but I knew some folks who weren't. So sad."

"Family?"

"Business associates. Two men I'd worked with before."

"I'm sorry." Margaret paid for her coffee.

"Don't forget to get a paper," the man said.

"I was only reading the front page," Margaret said. "But, thanks."

Margaret closed her purse and walked out of the store with her coffee. When she reached the car, she placed the Styrofoam cup on the roof to find her keys at the bottom of her purse. She noticed the man from inside coming toward her, waving a set of keys.

"Hey," he shouted. "Did you leave these on the counter?"

"Oh, my God," Margaret said. "Yes, thank you so much."

Margaret met the man halfway as he handed her the keys.

"No problem," he said. "I distracted you."

Margaret smiled. "I'm really sorry about your friends."

"Yeah, it was hard on their families to lose them. What an awful day. My wife called me on my cell phone, but I was in a meeting when the first plane hit, so I didn't know right away. By the time I called her back, she was frantic, since she wasn't exactly sure where I was in the city." He glanced over his shoulder to a van parked at the pumps. "You realize what's important when something like that happens."

"Yes," Margaret said. "What's important," she repeated.

"Well," the man said, turning back to Margaret before he walked away. "Drive safe," he said. Margaret could see the outline of two small children in the backseat of the van, the sun hitting the tinted windows. "Remember, your coffee is on top of your car," the man said, and then laughed. "Don't want you to forget anything else."

Margaret smiled and nodded, holding up her keys to show him as he glanced back. Margaret stepped around her car to retrieve the coffee. Just before she got inside, she noticed the man pulling away from the pumps toward the interstate. The two kids in the backseat waved, so she managed a smile again. A woman with short blonde hair, the man's wife, Margaret supposed, rode in the passenger seat. Was she any better than Margaret? Her husband had come back. He'd called her as soon as possible.

Margaret thought about what he'd said inside the gas station again. "You realize what's important when something like that happens."

Did he mean he hadn't been a good husband before? Had the tragedy of 9/11 made him take stock of his life, hold tighter to the ones he loved, help others in need, run after someone who left her keys behind, tell her to drive safe? Did he show more compassion, more humanity now? Was he a better man than before? Margaret stood there, coffee in hand, and watched the van until it disappeared onto the interstate.

She got back inside her car and shut the door. But she didn't start the engine at first. She kept her eyes straight ahead out past the edge of the pavement, across the lowlands, the desert landscape less scenic now, to where a track of houses were being built, a block wall surrounded the newly framed homes, piles of construction supplies and lumber sat inside a chain-linked area with a single trailer for the site office.

Why didn't Danny call me? I left so many messages that day. Did he listen to them?

Margaret placed the coffee in the cup holder, and continued to survey the new construction before her. Beyond the new houses, she noticed a half-finished strip mall, across from a gated golf course community. Along the gated entry, palm trees had been recently planted, the fronds still tied to keep the trees from losing moisture and blowing over before rooted in the sandy soil. Another town sprouting up along Phoenix's wide borders, reminiscent of the fast growing communities in Southern California, red-tiled roofs, wide streets, pop-up malls and gated communities. Just without the ocean. Did the man with the silvery eyes live with his family nearby? Had he bought them a new house inside a gated community to keep them safe?

Margaret had awoken during the first night after the planes hit and called Danny again. She'd nodded off holding Jacob in her arms, startled when she realized she'd fallen asleep. She'd reached for the phone on the nightstand to see if he'd called while she was sleeping. No messages, nor were there ever any from Danny when she'd returned home from the store or after collecting Jacob from a play date. She'd kept the same number, and continued checking for messages during the weeks and months after the attack. Only calls from concerned friends and a few reporters digging for quotes from widowed spouses for articles about 9/11 and Danny in particular. But even those calls stopped after a while. Their friends from college drifted away, almost as if they didn't know what to say anymore.

Strange, she found no cell phone with Danny's belongings inside the storage chest where he lived now. Had he gotten rid of it? Or left it behind in the building when he escaped?

Margaret glanced in the review mirror when she heard voices passing behind her car. Families with armfuls of snacks came and went laughing, teasing –- loved ones, traveling together, staying together.

Did he ever love me? Did he?

Margaret had no idea. And she knew she couldn't keep asking that question, it was pointless. He'd lived in Arizona all those years, working odd jobs and hiding out on a wealthy person's hobby ranch.

Why? Why not ask for a divorce?

She would've let him go. And Jacob would still have his father.

Margaret sipped her coffee as she drove back toward the interstate. She didn't have the answers and she wasn't wasting any more time wondering about it.

He's obviously crazy. Maybe there's another woman. That girl? No. She's too young. He must have his reasons for leaving, but like this?

Merging onto I-10, Margaret heard her phone ring inside her purse. She dug for it, but the call rolled over to voicemail before she could answer. Henry. She listened to all of his messages now. One after another, more concerned with each call.

"I've tried calling the hotel direct," he said. "But you're not picking up there, either."

Margaret felt guilty for worrying Henry.

"I love you," he said. "I hope everything's okay."

She'd have to tell him. But she wasn't ready yet. She wanted to see him, touch him, and look into his eyes. Then she'd explain everything. But she'd conceal part of the story, to protect his feelings. Margaret knew she owed Henry more than this. She hoped she'd reach home before he left for the airport, but she wasn't even sure what time his flight took off, or if he'd be there when she arrived. She'd already decided if he were gone, she'd fly to Boston, find his hotel and talk to him there.

The phone rang again. Startled, Margaret jerked the wheel, but she caught herself in time and then put the call on speaker.

"Hi, Henry," she said.

"Hi, babe." Henry's voice sounded calmer than hers. "Where are you?" he said. "I tried calling you last night and now they say you checked out. What's going on?"

"I decided to come home to see you before you left for Boston." Margaret hoped she sounded normal.

"My flight leaves at three, but I need to head to the airport before that..."

She'd never make it in time.

"Margaret, is everything okay?"

She sighed, trying to think of where to begin.

"Is Jacob okay?"

"He's fine," Margaret said. "I'm sorry I worried you, Henry." Margaret picked the phone up from the dash, and held it near, still on speaker. "Something happened in Sedona, but I don't want to talk about it on the phone."

"Well, now I'm really worried. Are you okay?"

"No, I'm not. It's big, Henry. But I want to talk to you in person. I'm halfway home. I'll be there by two. Can you change your flight?"

"I need to be there for tomorrow's opening meeting, I'm the keynote," Henry paused. "What's this all about? Are you ill?"

"No," Margaret said. "But I need to see you. It's very important." Margaret imagined Henry in the den or maybe by the sink in the kitchen, dressed in his grey wool trousers she'd pressed for him before she left for Flagstaff. His carry on by the back door, his briefcase alongside, overstuffed as always. She wanted to tell him to stay, to please stay home.

"Are you sure it's nothing about Jake?" Henry said, his voice even again. "You can tell me. College kids do crazy things sometimes. Did he get caught drinking?"

"No, Henry. It's nothing like that. Just please wait for me. Please."

"You're worrying me."

"Wait for me."

Margaret increased her speed, weaving through traffic in Phoenix. She'd turned her phone off, so she could focus, hoping Jacob wouldn't call. She couldn't speak to him right now. She knew the sound of his voice would make her cry.

Your jerk of a dad is alive.

She knew she wouldn't use those words, but right now, she had no idea how she'd explain his father was alive. She needed to get home to Henry. He'd know what to do.

Please, Henry. Please don't leave.

When the tears came, they weren't for Danny. They were for her husband, for Henry. She'd been so wrong. Holding her love back all those years. She'd ignored the truth, the fact that her marriage to Danny was over long before he disappeared. She felt too ashamed, so she allowed others to believe she'd lost the love of her life. But Danny was not the love of her life. He was a stranger, even then. She'd tried to save her marriage, but she couldn't. They'd slept apart. He'd refused counseling, and continued his sharp criticism and bizarre outbursts. She'd decided that final night alone in their bed the time had come to separate.

Margaret could clearly see now. She'd immortalized Danny when he never returned. She placed him on a pedestal he never deserved. He didn't want her, so he'd left. And in a strange way, she felt relieved.

By the time Margaret made her way west through Palm Springs and Riverside, and eventually to Orange County, heading south along Pacific Coast Highway, it was already half-past-two.

Please be home, Henry.

Taking the final turn up the hill to their home, Margaret pulled the band from her ponytail and ran her fingers through her hair.

When she reached the crest of the hill, she turned right along the single-lined street of remodeled homes perched on the edge of the hillside, sundecks leaning against tall crutches, the pillars buried deep in pilings for support. Past the final few houses, Margaret spotted Henry on the porch. She smiled, her hands moist against the wheel. Henry stepped down onto the bottom step and lifted his hand to welcome her.

Henry.

"Thank, God," she said, as she pulled onto the driveway.

Margaret threw open the car door, left the engine running, and rushed into Henry's arms. He held her tight as her tears came again, but this time, safe in her husband's arms. Her emotions spilled out from the deepest part of her soul, soaking Henry's shirt, one of the shirts she'd pressed along with his grey slacks.

She glanced up at Henry and touched his face with her fingertips. "You didn't leave."

"You asked me to wait."

She thought of the man at the gas station. "You know," she said. Henry had his priorities straight, too. "I love you very much."

Chapter 27
Alex

After Alex got back, he lifted the saddle from Maxwell, groomed him, and then released the lead shank and halter, turning Maxwell out to join Lady at the far end of the paddock. Still early morning, he needed to muck out the barn, so he raked the stalls while he made his plans. At the top of the list—convince Maggie to leave.

He hoped to persuade her that he needed time to absorb what she'd said. That way, he could pack up and head north. Maybe Maggie would let go of him if he disappeared again. After all, she married someone else.

He kept flashing on his mother buried near the old farmland where Dutch's family members were laid to rest. Alex loved the acres of rolling fields at the farmstead as a boy.

His grandmother baked bread and cookies in her large, white kitchen at the back of the clapboard house. It's where Alex learned to cook, which spices to roast a chicken, how to prepare a creamy hollandaise for fresh roasted asparagus. His grandmother taught him to apply mineral oil to the butcher-block counters when they were dry. When they stayed over, Alex slept at the top of the second flight of stairs, in a narrow space between two dormers, where several hand-stitched quilts covered an antique iron bed. It's where he escaped to read his bird book or listen to baseball games on the small radio on the nightstand. His grandmother would climb the creaky staircase late at night to bring him cookies or sometimes a slice of warm apple cake.

The solitude of the open fields acted as the backdrop for his favorite playground as a boy. Tall grasses covered the meadows, and in the springtime, wild buttercups, dandelions and stinging nettles grew along the pathway to the stream where he'd search for tadpoles. He'd hang upside down from the tire swing dangling from an old walnut tree out behind the red barn, the chickens and cows, and the tractor, a big adventure to him as a child. Sometimes he'd play outside until the fireflies appeared, or at least until the clanking of the bell for dinner. He'd hurry back to the farmhouse, where he'd share his treasures with his grandmother, small shiny rocks and oftentimes a handful of daisies for the table. His grandmother always smothered him with kisses and it didn't matter if his family ate dinner with them, Alex always felt he and his grandmother were in their own world together. She'd let him dig into heaping bowls of mashed potatoes and gravy with chicken or beef, and sometimes pork chops. Even when his mother, Jean, told him to slow down, his grandmother would wave her off. "He's a growing boy, let him eat as much as he wants." Alex loved the way she stuck up for him against his parents and brother. She'd send him home with a plastic container filled with apple crisp made with fresh fruit harvested from the orchard. She'd tape his name to the lid, proof of being her favorite.

Always melancholy when they had to load up the sedan back to Cleveland, he'd miss those happy days at the farm. He'd climb inside his dad's car, lean against the passenger door and fall asleep. Sometimes when his mother shouted, or his brother punched him, he'd think about running away to the farm. But his grandmother died before his ninth birthday and from that day forward they only traveled to the farm to check on the new tenants working the land. He'd stay inside the car while Dutch spoke to the leaseholders on the front porch, while his dad then traipsed out to the barn or the fields to check something they'd told him about. Depending on where his dad parked the sedan, he might catch a glimpse of the tire swing, swaying in the breeze behind the barn. He'd long for his grandmother, the tears stinging his eyes. He'd squeeze his lids shut until his father returned, and if it weren't only a Sunday afternoon drive, they — he and his family — would sometimes head north to Niagara Falls or the Finger Lakes for the weekend. His parents would nag him the whole way about being too quiet, but he didn't care. He missed his grandmother. He still missed her.

Eventually his father sold the place, and they never went back again. But, Alex showed Margaret where the farmhouse once stood when they drove through on their honeymoon. The developer who bought the farmstead subdivided the land and built five large colonials. They even tore down the red barn. The apple trees were replaced with hedgerows and evergreen trees.

Once Alex finished inside the small barn, he rinsed off the tools and glanced out into the enclosed pasture. Maxwell and Lady were nibbling taller grass along the fence line. Crazy. He'd miss them. They were his closest companions for all those years. Alex shook his head then checked the gates in the paddock were secured.

Back inside the barn, he took a seat at the desk where he kept a calendar. On the wall, he grabbed a business card held by a tack, set it on the desk before him. When he pulled the phone closer, the cord caught the edge of a drawer that never stayed shut. Yanking the wire free, Alex tapped a finger against Bill Tyler's card before dialing the number. Bill's wife answered on the other end, a recorded message.

Sue Tyler had a voice like a teenager even though she had to be in her fifties. She'd had work done to her face, so Alex couldn't tell. One time, she'd recovered at the ranch after a procedure, her nose and chin wrapped in tape. She lounged near the pool in a black one-piece, a floppy hat shading her face, her eyes covered with giant, dark sunglasses as she joked with Alex who'd tried to avoid her, but she'd called out to him, waving him over, so he had no choice. A nurse checked on her now and then. But Alex kept an eye out that time, since she was there alone and seemed loopier than usual.

He didn't mind. Sue Tyler was always pleasant to Alex. She'd bring him oranges or a bottle of wine. Alex sometimes found a basket of gifts at his doorstep, signaling their arrival.

They didn't have kids and Bill seemed much older than Sue. Sometimes Bill reminded Alex of Dutch, something in his confidant manner, the way he swaggered around. But Bill Tyler became far more successful than Alex's dad. He'd seen the world, traveled the globe for his business. Bill made him nervous. He could see through Alex, asked leading questions.

"You're a smart guy," Bill would say. "Why tend horses?"

Alex laughed it off, insisted he'd no interest in desk jobs. When they were in town, Alex kept to himself, got his work done, spent his time off in town.

A tone sounded to leave a message. "This is Alex," he said, clearing his throat. "I have a family emergency and need to leave Sedona today. Maxwell and Lady are fine. I've made sure everything is in order. You'll need to contact the vet to arrange for boarding this week. Since it's Sunday, they won't be available to pick up Maxwell and Lady today. I'm sorry for the short notice. I'll make sure they're secure before I head out."

Alex hung up, tried to jam the desk drawer shut again, where the wire had caught, but it rolled back open like always.

"Where are you going?"

Startled, Alex twisted around expecting to see Maggie. Sonia stood near the door to the portico.

"For God's sake," Alex said, his heart pounding. He hadn't realized how deep in thought he'd been. "What the hell are you doing here?" He rose from the desk, crossed his arms to face Sonia.

Her black hair much shorter, jagged, chopped off, as if someone had taken a dull-scissor and wacked at the ends. She appeared glassy-eyed, high on something, he could tell. Her army green hoodie hung from one shoulder, exposing her pale brown areola beneath the sheer white tank. She'd tucked her black jeans inside her combat boots.

"Sonia, you look like hell." She didn't look good. Something seemed off. Before he could tell her to leave, she lunged at him with a knife.

He grabbed for her wrist, but she pulled away quick, and then swung at him again, missing his chest by a few inches as he stumbled backward against the desk. But he pushed off and dove at her, grabbed for her wrist again. She moved too swift for him. She took another jab as he leapt sideways, the blade long enough to catch his shirt. But he twisted in time and caught her from behind, gripped her hand holding the weapon, and then twisted it behind her back. He wrapped his other arm around her neck in a chokehold, as she arched to get away, but he had a strong hold and squeezed her wrist until she screamed out in pain.

"Let go..." she struggled against him, her voice hoarse and weak. "If I can't have you..."

He twisted her wrist even tighter until she released the knife onto the dusty ground. Alex kicked it away, but continued to restrain her, wrenching her neck as he choked her.

"Nobody," she said, hacking spit. "Nobody can have you." The words came in raspy, half-gasping tones.

Alex squeezed her neck to shut her up, his legs locked in place. Her feet went out from under her when she tried to kick him. She struggled and jerked her body, but with each movement Alex further restricted her mobility, thwarted her ability to escape. He kept her lifted high from the ground, her feet dangled in the air as she continued to thrash about. Alex arched his body backward as he compressed her windpipe, overpowered her each time she tried to pull free. She scratched at his arms and face, dug her nails into his skin. She bit at him, but he jerked her back with such force, her legs went still, and her arms fell dead against her sides.

Alex yanked Sonia back once more, and held her suspended in the air, her lifeless body, limp against him. Then Alex leaned forward and released her onto the ground. Her face hit the dirt with a hard thud. Alex staggered backward, away from Sonia, and collapsed against a wooden post near the stalls. Breathing heavy, Alex tried to steady himself, but couldn't. He ran his hands through his hair, smoothed it back, over and over, trying to calm down, gain composure. But everything spun crooked around him. He tried to assess what lay before him, Sonia, sprawled out, motionless, on the barn floor.

"Oh, God." Alex straightened up, glanced over his shoulder at the door to the portico. Wide open. He turned his attention back to Sonia, who hadn't moved. Alex squared his shoulders, stepped away from the post toward the door, pulled it shut then turned the latch. He crossed past the stalls to Sonia, and nudged the side of her leg with his boot. Nothing.

He headed for the phone, but stopped shy of the desk.

Where's Maggie?

Alex fled for the door and let it slam behind him. The entrance to the pool house stood wide open just like he'd found the barn door. Alex ran inside. His eyes darted from one corner to the other.

"Maggie?" he shouted, "Where are you?"

He checked the bathroom, behind the futon, and then noticed a towel on the floor near the sink draped over what looked and smelled like vomit. He covered his mouth and nose, and flipped the lock on the slider. He nearly tore the curtains from the rod to open it.

"Maggie!"

He leapt over a good-sized rock at the edge of the patio and a few small cacti near the pool, and almost fell in, as he peered into the water. He half-expected to see Maggie at the bottom of the deep end. He continued to search the patio area near the main house, and then jogged along the front driveway and down the side of the property toward the barn. Alex glanced through the trees and shrubbery. "Maggie," he yelled several times. He saw no sign of her anywhere. When he checked the pool house again, he noticed her sandals were missing. Did she even come back inside after he left? God, he hoped not. Then he ran up to the front gate. No car parked out front.

She must've left. She's fine. Maggie's fine.

Alex headed back to the pool house, trying to catch his breath.

He went straight to the kitchen sink and stuck his head under the faucet to scrub the sweat from his face and hair. The bandage was missing from his forehead. Sonia probably tore it off. He jammed a few large sterile pads in his pocket, dried up with a towel. Then tied his hair back using a thick rubber band from the counter. He tossed the towel atop the one covering the vomit, banged his knee against the end table, and ignored the lamp as it crashed against the terra cotta tiles.

Alex pulled open the storage chest in front of the futon, tossed the thick wool blanket on the floor, and reached for a wooden box under a few shirts. The lid had an artisan carved Mexican figure with two flowers on each side. Alex released the latch and a faint lemony scent from the wood oil of a Linaloe tree drifted into the room. He rummaged through folded papers to find his wallet tucked beneath. His grandfather's pocket watch fell from inside a white business envelope with local telephone numbers scratched across the front. The solid gold case had loosened over time, the secondhand dangled above the 30-second mark, the hour and minute hands stuck at three o'clock. Alex always meant to take it apart and repair it with a watchmaker's toolset he'd bargained for at a pawnshop. The watch could have been damaged any time after he lifted it from his brother's jacket. He knew the watch kept perfect time before. After 9/11 Alex didn't open the watch for almost a year. When he did, the watch didn't run when wound.

He slipped the watch inside his front pocket behind the bandages, the wallet into his back pocket, and then folded some of the papers into the other. He ensured nothing stayed behind that could trace him to Cleveland, grabbed a jacket from a hook by the front door and shut it tight behind him.

Inside the barn, Sonia still lay in the same position. Her nose and mouth were twisted into the dirt, as if someone took her by the head and screwed her face into the ground. One arm tangled underneath her body, the other bent the wrong way at her side. Hooves hit the ground in the shaded area. Lady, her footing quick—like a prance.

She must need water.

Alex hurried outside to the paddock to fill the trough a few more inches.

"There you go, girl," he said, twisting the spigot.

He spotted Maxwell grazing in the center of the field, all the gates still secured. Once the trough was full, Alex shut off the hose, then wound and hung it near the grooming area. Lady wouldn't be combed today. Alex glanced back as she dipped her head to drink.

She'll be okay. The vet will certainly check her hooves.

Alex dumped a mass of feed into the food bin and went back to the barn, careful to shut the door behind him.

The phone rang and startled him.

Probably Bill.

Alex felt the room spin and tilt as the timeworn answering machine picked-up after four rings then clicked over to a recorded greeting. Sue's voice echoed through the rafters as Alex stood over Sonia. Suddenly ill, he swallowed hard to keep from throwing up. His stomach convulsed a few times, but he kept it together with deep breaths. His heartbeat pounded inside his temples, the back of his neck felt stiff and sore, and his horrible headache worse than ever. Alex squatted, almost falling forward onto Sonia. The room spun in different directions around him, but he managed to grab Sonia by the legs and dragged her inside Maxwell's stall.

The machine signaled the caller to leave a message. "Alex? This is Bill Tyler. If you're still there, I got hold of the vet's office and they're sending someone over now. You'll need to unlock the gate. Sorry to hear you've got family problems. Keep us posted. I won't be able to get out there until next weekend."

The answering machine clicked off as Alex released Sonia's body inside the stall. He rolled her over against the rails, her eyes wide-open, her mouth agape, filled with dirt. In fact, near unrecognizable, Sonia's expression seemed lodged somewhere between frightened and peaceful, and neither vein of which Alex had seen before. She often acted angry or childish when their eyes met, so this sudden cast of victim struck Alex as eerie.

He felt like he might get sick again, so he turned away against the railing to catch his breath. He grabbed the thick wool blanket folded over the railing and twisted around to cover Sonia's face and limbs. He waited, as if expecting her to somehow awaken.

"Sonia," Alex said, his voice hoarse. He tapped her ribcage with his boot. But she still didn't move. A creepy stillness filled the barn that made Alex back away and then trip over his own boots, catching himself against the grille of the stall door. He inched through the gate, out of breath, a lump in his throat, tears burning his eyes.

I need to get out of here. Now.

He pulled the stall door shut and then noticed a shimmer of metal buried in the sawdust near the desk.

The knife. Leave it. She went crazy, that's all. Now go. You've got to go.

184

He noticed now, the knife looked familiar. The same chef's knife he used at the restaurant, he recognized the handle. He wouldn't touch it. And hoped only Sonia's fingerprints were on it.

It was self-defense. I had no choice.

Alex paused near the desk and considered calling for help again. Instead, he jammed the top drawer shut, jerked open the bottom drawer to find his money. He kept his pay inside a small coffee can. It rolled forward as he pulled the drawer open. He'd saved a decent amount, since he'd cashed his September check from Bill, and Carlos had left him a full envelope on his last shift. He still owed money to the doctor at the hospital, but that seemed senseless now. His thoughts were racing, some making no sense to him. He headed out to the portico without glancing back. The latch clicked on the Dutch door, both top and bottom closed in sync.

Outside, he zipped his jacket and grabbed the handlebars on the dirt bike, pulled it away from the wall, and rolled it along the side path toward the front of the property.

Damn, the gate key.

Alex rested the motorcycle on its side in the gravel and rushed back to the pool house. The key hung on a hook beside the front door, but then Alex spotted a photo on the tile near the futon. He shoved the storage chest aside with his knee and reached down for the picture of Jacob.

He glanced at the young boy, smiling at him with a toothless grin—Jacob's first day at kindergarten.

Alex squeezed the bridge of his nose, his headache throbbed, and his eyes watered as he jammed the photo in his back pocket and pulled the hood of his jacket over his head.

Sorry, kid. Your dad screwed-up bad.

For the first time since leaving Ohio, Alex felt like he'd done everything wrong. He coughed back his emotions, Jacob fading into the past again as he closed the door. For a split-second, Alex wondered if he should go back for Sonia. Drive her body out into the desert.

But, there's no time, the vet's coming.

The bike started up after Alex used the throttle and kicked the engine over a few times. He backed off the choke as the bike warmed up. The engine smoked a bit, but Alex headed toward the street anyway then pulled up alongside the gate, the motorcycle idling while he turned the key in the lock. A block away, Alex drove the bike onto a dirt pathway to the National Forest trails.

No houses appeared for several acres in either direction, so he felt certain nobody saw him. He gunned it, switched gears and ran the motorcycle faster than Maxwell that morning. No matter the speed of the bike, he felt chased, his past catching up to him, the world closing in on him. So he drove on even faster, unafraid of falling again, his head pounding, every bump sending daggers through his skull. But he kept on. By midday he saw patches of scattered clouds in the distance. Red rock vistas, and colorful canyons to the north stretched out before him.

The further he escaped, the further Sonia's face, contorted and covered with dirt faded.

He focused on the desert floor ahead of him. What would the point be to agonize over what happened in the barn? Alex began to hit rough ground near Secret Mountain then crossed over the highway toward Oak Creek Canyon, where he'd hiked before. The foliage denser now, the red rocks seemed almost within reach. A clear stream flowed down through the canyon, the terrain jagged and rocky.

As Alex climbed the trail, the bike sputtered, low on fuel, and then the engine died altogether. Alex rolled to a stop.

He hopped off and pushed the motorcycle away from the dirt path behind a thicket of trees. He laid it down near a cluster of grander rocks, then jogged back to the trail and headed north, through the canyon. On the pathway, Alex hid his faced or cut away from the trail altogether to avoid hikers. He maintained a decent pace, stopping only once for a sip of fresh water near West Fork. Summer flowers and greenery filled the lush twisting gorge. Alex wanted to rest, but continued his trek deeper into the forest, as far away from Sedona as possible.

Chapter 28
Margaret

They switched planes in San Francisco with an estimated arrival time in Boston at 7 a.m., giving Henry just enough time to hail a cab to the hotel for his 8:30 speech. Margaret said a little prayer, clenched Henry's hand, and hoped for no problems when they landed. She glanced over at Henry in the window seat, impervious to her concerns at the moment. He seemed deep in thought as he watched out the window. Margaret turned her head and settled against the headrest, choosing to believe they were fine, that their conversation had drawn them closer. Exhausted now, she couldn't keep her eyes open. She relaxed against the leather seat as the plane rumbled forward along the runway to take off. She drifted into a deep sleep as they ascended then leveled off, the engines settling into a steady rhythm.

When she awoke later, a soft blanket covered her lap, her seat adjusted into a semi-reclined position, the first class cabin now dark, except for the glowing screen of Henry's laptop. He sat hunched over the tray table wire-rimmed glasses perched on the tip of his nose, engrossed by the bright display. Margaret touched his shoulder as she adjusted her seat forward.

"Hey, baby..." Henry said, with his eyes fixed on the monitor. "You slept for quite a while." Henry smiled her way now and then glanced back at the screen.

"What time is it?" she said, as she stretched her arms to rouse herself, then relaxed back in her seat. She gathered her hair at the back of her neck and pulled it to one side smoothing it between her hands into a twist, then let it drop along her right shoulder.

"We land in about an hour," Henry said, closing his laptop. "They served a meal earlier...you hungry?"

"A little, but I can wait."

"I think you should eat, they have breakfast."

Henry pushed the button for the flight attendant who came right away and then brought Margaret a breakfast tray and coffee. She nibbled at a bagel while Henry slid his computer and papers back inside his briefcase.

"Reviewing my presentation," he said, as he patted Margaret's wrist. "Just to make sure I know what I'm talking about." She could see his warm smile out of the corner of her eye. Everything was okay. He still loved her.

"I hope you can focus," Margaret said, as her eyes filled with tears again, a condition that seemed permanent after the past few days. She felt like a basket case. But, Henry's kindness kept overwhelming her since arriving home. Lucky to have him, Margaret never felt so sure. She loved Henry more than ever.

When she arrived home with her dramatic story about Daniel being alive, Henry remained composed, not passive, but calm, as if he'd expected the news.

Margaret spilled her heart out, explaining everything, but left out the more intimate details. Why hurt him? Besides, she never wondered, like in her first marriage, about other men, because Henry loved her so completely and made sure she knew it every day. This was different. An act of confusion and shock, she'd been caught up in the moment, something that would never happen again.

Inside their house on the hill, Henry pulled her close and wiped away her tears.

"We'll sort this it out together," Henry said, as he held her on the living room sofa. He'd arranged for a later flight, prior to her arrival, and even booked a ticket for her. Before they left for the airport, Henry called his lawyer and explained the situation, asking for advice.

"Margaret's traveling to Boston with me," he'd clarified by speakerphone in their bedroom while Margaret repacked her bag.

"I don't want her alone this week." The attorney agreed, and said he'd find out which authorities should be notified and the course to take in this type of situation. He also said Margaret should notify her former in-laws as soon as possible.

"I can't talk to them right now," Margaret said, when Henry hung up. "I'll call them from Boston." Margaret felt she needed to collect her thoughts first, process it all and besides, she still felt shaken from the emotional afternoon with Henry.

She glanced at him now, his brown eyes so gentle, filled with love. Her husband. Henry. The confusion of her past over now, she knew Henry would always be the love of her life. Right where she needed to be, next to her husband, Margaret would prove to Henry and herself that she was a good woman. The choices she'd made in the past did not define her.

Back at home, before leaving for Boston, Margaret told Henry she'd been protecting herself. "I was afraid of showing you all my love." Her words flooded the room like waves breaking along the shore below their hillside. "I guarded my heart after Daniel disappeared, after I they said he was dead," she said. "I was afraid of another tragedy, of being vulnerable." She wiped away her tears with both hands and leaned against him, her hand on his chest as she glanced up into his eyes, his arm around her shoulder.

They talked about the tragedy and confusion of 9/11. "I couldn't tell anyone after the buildings came down, that Danny and I were headed for a divorce," she said. "It was all so dreadful and everyone was devastated, and I didn't want to hurt his parents." She paused to collect her thoughts, to share the truth. "My feelings for Daniel got mixed up with Jacob's broken heart and Daniel's family." She rested her head against his chest as she glanced out the window across the room. The sun shone across the floor, casting projections of dusty light along the rich grains in the wood. "I was completely undone when I lost the baby," she said. "I began to immortalize Daniel and reinvented him in my mind."

Margaret tilted her chin to meet Henry's gaze again, trying to see if he might be hurt or angry. She knew they needed to get to the airport soon, but she had to tell him everything, to hear it all herself. He touched her with tender hands. So she continued.

"As the years passed, I believed my own lies, and put him on a pedestal." Margaret took a deep breath. "I wasn't fair to you, Henry."

Henry lifted her chin. "I'm fine," he said.

"But, I didn't give you all my love," she said, with a sniff. She wanted to be clear, for him to understand. She turned toward Henry, tucked her leg underneath and held his hands in hers. "You're the man I love, Henry. There's nobody else but you."

Henry stayed quiet for a moment, Margaret's heart pounded waiting for him to say something.

"I love you, too," he said, and pulled her closer. "I knew you were struggling, but I also knew in time, you'd trust your feelings again." He wrapped his arm around her. "I know you love me. I've always known."

They'd finally left the living room and went into the bedroom, where Henry helped Margaret out of her shorts and t-shirt. She stayed in his arms at the foot of their bed, the furnishings so familiar, a silver framed wedding photo on the nightstand, Jacob's senior portrait on the dresser, she never felt so sheltered and loved. When he tried to pull away to get ready for the airport, she held him tighter. He ran his fingers through her hair, the sun trickling in through the tilted shutters. Then he lowered her onto their bed and made love to her, gentle at first and then with a hunger they both seemed to feel at the same time, and Margaret finally released the love she'd held in for so long, feeling a kind of peace and wholeness she'd never felt before.

"I love you," she whispered, when they finished. And she meant it with her whole heart. Like never before.

Now, on the way to Boston, Margaret began to realize the long road ahead in dealing with an estranged husband. There would have to be a divorce and what about the matter of the life insurance money? It all seemed overwhelming. Thank goodness Henry had convinced her to let the attorney begin the process. And arranged for her to got to Boston where she could rest and come to terms with the situation.

"Once we're settled at the hotel and you've slept a bit, you can call Dutch or Michael," Henry said, before they took off from Southern California. "They need to know."

Margaret kept thinking about the man at the gas station near Phoenix, as they waited to board their flight in Orange County, how he'd told her about his wife being frantic awaiting his call. It seemed unfair to keep the news of Daniel being alive from Dutch and Michael for any longer than necessary. She knew she had to come to her senses and make the call as soon as possible.

"I've got to talk to Michael as soon as we get to Boston."

Henry nodded. "Yes, Michael should be the one to tell Dutch."

Now, after a connecting flight in San Francisco, and more than halfway to Boston, Margaret sipped her orange juice and placed a cloth napkin over the breakfast Henry had requested for her. She really had no appetite and wanted to sleep again.

"I don't know what to do about Jacob," Margaret said, rubbing her eyes. "I'm so worried this will set him back."

Henry turned to meet Margaret's eyes, she could tell he'd been lost in his own thoughts, and hoped just work. His brown hair mussed, she used her fingers to comb a few strays from his forehead, smoothing the hair along his part. He smiled with his lips closed, his eyes shining in the low light, he pulled her hand to his mouth, and kissed her knuckles.

"There's no reason to tell him right now," Henry said. "Let's deal with Dutch and Michael first, see what they want to do."

"You're right," she said, wishing the flight attendant would retrieve her tray. "But, I'm worried Daniel might want to see Jake. I wish I hadn't told him where he's going to school. You don't think he'd go up there, do you?" She glanced at Henry, who shrugged. "I left so fast, I didn't have a chance to tell him to stay away."

Henry leaned closer to Margaret. "Let's not get ahead of ourselves," he said. "He left years ago, there's no reason to think he'd have any interest in being a dad all of a sudden. And it sounds like he has some hidden issues. People don't leave everything for no reason. Like you said last night, he could have easily filed for divorce."

Margaret glanced at Henry, knowing he made sense.

"He never reached out, Margaret. Never contacted you in all those years. My hunch is he might disappear again, sooner than later, and that's why it's important to tell his family."

Listening to Henry, Margaret felt better. Danny made his decision years ago, and had showed no sign of wanting anything different.

"Just rest, darling. We'll land soon and you can worry about it then." Henry got the flight attendant's attention to remove the tray.

Margaret pulled the blanket up around her shoulders, closed her eyes, and tried not to think about Danny or his family. Instead, she pictured Jake at school, getting settled in, unpacking the ridiculous amount of stuff they'd bought. She smiled to herself, knowing her son probably hadn't even unpacked yet. It would be Monday morning before she could hear his voice. She only hoped Jake had been too busy to notice she hadn't called. She opened her eyes then and leaned closer to Henry.

"Did you call Jake this weekend?"

"I left him a voice mail and he sent me a text about how busy he was," Henry said. "Said he'd call this week."

Margaret closed her eyes again, knowing she'd call Jake before then. "Thanks for being there Henry," she whispered, and kept her eyes shut. "You're a wonderful dad to him."

Chapter 29
Margaret

Margaret awoke just as the plane made its final descent. Reluctant to wake now, Margaret knew she had to face reality and call Michael once they arrived at the hotel in Boston. She dreaded the call, dreaded Michael's voice on the other end. She wished she could hide a bit longer, the airplane being a shelter from the rest of the world. Before she knew it, they were on the ground, taxiing toward the gate.

"I'll get the bags," Henry said, as they unbuckled their seatbelts. "You go ahead. I'll meet you in the terminal."

Margaret scooted ahead to join the other first-class passengers while Henry retrieved their carry-on bags from the overhead compartments. She waited near the agent's counter, turned on her phone, and noticed she had a text message from Jacob.

I love this place!

The note made Margaret smile. Just a kid, a boy trying to be a man, off to college to learn, meet new people. Then she frowned knowing she'd have to tell him about Daniel sooner or later. But she didn't want to drop such a huge bomb his first week at school—and not over the phone. She'd wait until parents' weekend. And even then, she wasn't sure how she'd tell him or how he'd take the news.

She glanced up to see Henry coming out from the jet-way. He wore his grey plaid sports coat, so handsome. He dragged the two bags behind him. One of the wheels on hers spun out of control. She'd meant to get the bag repaired for months, but always seemed to forget until another trip. Henry shrugged it off with a smirk, which made her laugh out loud. She covered her mouth shocked by her reaction. But then Margaret realized it felt good to laugh, to be with Henry, to feel so normal. So loved.

Henry had his briefcase strapped over his shoulder. Ever the clean-cut, well-groomed, successful man, his confidence became something good for Jacob to see. Henry had proven to be someone Jacob could look up to and respect.

He paused a ways from where Margaret stood to wait for an older woman to pass by, and Margaret thought about the dinner they'd had with Jacob the night before leaving for Arizona. Henry had given Jacob great advice.

"You're going to have moments where you feel strange, and that's normal when you're off alone in a new place, surrounded by people you don't know yet," Henry said, as Jacob hung on every word from across the table. "But, don't panic," Henry, continued. "Instead, introduce yourself to others." Henry reached across the dinner plates to shake Jacob's hand. "Look them right in the eye, project confidence, even if you don't feel that way...because you will, eventually." He shook Jake's hand, a bit exaggerated, as they both laughed. "Just like that, Jake, just be yourself."

Jacob asked Henry about his time in medical school, how'd he gotten through so many years of education. Margaret was glad Jacob had Henry to talk to about his plans and goals. In many ways, Jake could talk to Henry easier than he could with Margaret. She sensed her boy needed Henry right now, in a way she couldn't be there for him. They talked about the tough class schedule Jake would face as an engineering student, how to commit to his studies, get help if needed and balance his time.

Whenever Margaret brought up those same topics, Jacob rolled his eyes, ignored her as if she didn't know anything, hadn't graduated from college, or landed a good job right out of school.

With Henry, Jake listened to every word, as if speaking to a genius. "Yes, sir," Jacob would say. "Thanks for the advice."

Margaret didn't feel bad about being snubbed. It seemed a normal way to break away for Jacob. And she knew in her heart, he needed to do that.

Henry finally stepped forward to join her in the terminal. Margaret put her arms around his neck after he rolled the bags to a stop. She squeezed him tight, kissing him on the lips and cheeks. "Thank you for taking care of me."

Henry smiled down at her, holding tight to the bags. "Everything's going to be okay, Margaret."

When she stepped back and looked into his eyes, she could tell he meant it. He'd stand by her and be her husband. If it took the rest of her life, Margaret would give him the love he deserved. She smiled at him as he winked at her, and then she reached for the handle on her bag to head for the exit with her husband—with Henry.

The cab arrived at the hotel and conference center with thirty minutes to spare before Henry's meeting. They checked-in and took their bags upstairs. Margaret kicked off her flats and climbed into bed in her navy leggings and soft, grey cashmere sweater from the flight.

Henry kissed her on the forehead before he unzipped his bag and found a crimson silk tie, and then drew it tight around his collar. Margaret pulled the comforter up to her chin as she watched Henry go to the mirror across from the foot of the bed. She loved how he blushed when he hurried, his English ancestry showed through in his lighter skin and now that she thought of it, even in his reserved manner. He ran his fingers through his hair, flattened a wild strand near the cowlick at the back of his crown, the same place Margaret often trailed her fingers, after they made love. Henry would drift into a deep sleep. His years of performing emergency surgery, often in the middle of the night, had trained him to nod off quick when he had the chance.

"I'll see you in a few hours." Henry glanced at Margaret in the mirror. "You can wait to call Michael, if you feel you need me here."

"I think I'm fine." She straightened the pillow behind her neck, her cell phone next to her on the nightstand. "He's probably commuting to the office, so I'll call him later, too many distractions. And he'll need time to think about everything before he tells Patty and his dad." But, she really just didn't want Henry to hear her talking to Michael. It might get emotional, and she wanted to protect Henry as much as she could from the fallout.

"Good idea." Henry lifted his briefcase from the desk and turned to face her. "None of this is your fault, Margaret."

He looked so handsome, she wished he'd climb in bed with her and sleep away the morning together. He seemed serious, so she didn't say anything, only listened.

"Daniel left," he continued. "You did nothing to make him choose that path."

But, she wasn't so sure that was true.

"He was a coward," Henry said. "Just be straight with Michael. He needs to know. It's their responsibility now. Not yours."

Margaret nodded. "I know. I'll tell him. You better get going or you'll be late."

Henry's cell phone sounded right then and he checked the screen. "They're looking for me." He keyed in a message and then glanced back at Margaret. "You'll be okay?"

"Yes, I'll be fine."

As the door closed behind Henry, the latch clicked into place, and Margaret thought about the barn door and helping Danny back to his house. His filthy, long, disheveled hair fell into her face as she dragged him along. Shocked, she could feel his ribcage, so thin and wiry, his skin leathery and weathered, his hands callused, and his fingernails caked with dirt and grease. He wasn't the Danny she knew, and she felt regretful now, that she hadn't figured it out right away. Danny had become some other person.

Michael wouldn't even recognize him. She'd have to explain Danny's appearance, what he did for work, where he lived. She shook her head. Would Michael believe her?

Margaret checked her phone for Danny's address and the restaurant where she'd first spotted him—details for Michael and Dutch. She placed the phone in her lap and leaned her head against the headboard, willing herself to call.

An emergency vehicle passed on the street below, and Margaret heard a tap at the door across the hall. "Maid service." The woman's voice sounded muffled through the door. Even so, the room felt peaceful. Defused light coming through the sheer drapes on the window. The walls were wrapped in muted bluish green, a nod to Boston Harbor. She could close her eyes and sleep for hours. Maybe she should wait for Henry to come back.

No. I've got to do this myself. Danny and I were married. He's Jake's father. And Michael might get crazy.

She closed her eyes, picturing her son's face, his smile and then Henry, holding her tight. How senseless it had been to sleep with Danny. Henry would leave her if he found out. Their family would be ruined. Margaret avoided her reflection in the mirror across the room, tilted her head toward the window. Soft morning light shimmered through the creamy-colored sheers like sunlight dancing across the ocean. Sickened by Danny abandoning her and Jacob, Margaret felt even more disgusted by her own actions. The pool house had seemed more like a motel room, few personal possessions, and only bare necessities—easy to abandon at a moment's notice.

Margaret sat straight up in bed now.

"I bet he's long gone," she said, seeing her reflection in the mirror, avoiding nothing, looking straight at herself.

Danny had left.

Horseback?

None of it made sense. But she felt too emotionally drained to care anymore. Maybe she was in shock, she didn't know, she'd been so tired since telling Henry about Daniel, about how she felt. Every minute since she left Sedona, Margaret had let go of Danny, little by little, for good this time. She never wanted to see him again.

Chapter 30
Margaret

Michael answered on the first ring. Not a surprise. Margaret knew he'd take the call. He always did, even when busy. Michael always wanted to talk, but Margaret stopped wanting to years ago. The picture taped inside the card he and Patty sent last Christmas showed Michael with an inflated smile, Patty, by his side, impossibly thin, and all of them, even the boys, dressed in khakis and white t-shirts. Happy. Was he happy?

"Did you change your mind about coming to the memorial?" Michael said before Margaret had a chance to say hello. She had no intention of going to New York. He knew that. So why did he ask?

Just say it. Tell him.

"No, Michael," she said, instead. "I'm not coming." Her voice sounded strange. Formal. Aloof. Cold.

Tell him.

She cleared her throat. "Where are you right now?"

For a moment, a flash, Margaret wondered if Michael needed to know. Did anyone? All of sudden she wanted Henry again. She felt heat rush to her face. If Danny disappeared again, wanted nothing to do with his past, was it cruel to inform the family, to tell Jacob?

Henry. Oh, my God.

But it was too late. "Maggie, are you okay?" Michael had picked up on her tone. He always could. "Why are you calling so early? Is something wrong?"

"Actually," Margaret said, her mouth suddenly dry. "Henry and I are in Boston."

Yes, I'm with him, Michael. Of course I'm with him. He's my husband.

She heard Michael breathing on the other end. He liked Henry. He'd told her so. Right before they went to Hawaii.

"He's a good guy, Margaret."

She remembered Michael's eyes that night, sincere, forgiving. But Michael continued to drive by her house on his way home. She'd seen him as she glanced up from a magazine, his car moving past the front window in slow motion.

"Patty and I were just talking about you this morning." He sounded casual, like things were good. He's fine. Patty's fine. Everything's fine. But Margaret knew better.

"What are you doing in Boston?"

She squeezed her eyes shut. "Henry has a conference." Michael told her once, she sounded like she was from Cincinnati, her voice a bit southern, as if raised across the murky Ohio River in Kentucky, not northeast in Cleveland. Margaret heard it now, the flinty, soulful mid-range of her voice. Had she always used this willowy cadence with Michael?

"Oh, Michael, I'm so sorry."

"What's going on?"

She knew she sounded confusing. But that was exactly how she felt now, confused.

"I'll tell you everything," she said. "Just give me a minute."

"Take your time," he said, his voice gentle. "I'm just sitting here in the parking lot watching the rain."

The rain. When they'd come up for air, the windshield was dotted with a thousand tiny, perfect raindrops. She remembered.

"I'm sorry for grabbing your hand that day," Margaret said, shocked by her own admission. She hadn't thought of the day when it all began in so long. She felt tears in her eyes now. They'd been so young.

"I'm not," Michael said. "I don't regret any of it."

They were both quiet then. Margaret's mind raced back to a time when she felt vulnerable, and lonely.

"I've told myself over and over," she said. "You seduced me." But she knew otherwise. "That was a lie." Everything came back to her so fast now.

"Maggie, we were just kids."

"But, we hurt him."

"No we didn't," Michael said. "Nobody knew."

"I think he did," she said.

Margaret stood up and walked to the window, pulled the sheers aside to reveal the harbor below. The sun glittered across the water, calm sails rested against tall masts, a single scull floated by, the rower's movements in perfect rhythm, as his body thrust forward and back pulling the ores against the early morning tide. She thought about rowing with Henry in Newport Harbor, not far from Laguna Beach, the smooth sound of the ores swishing against the currents. The peace she always felt with Henry, no matter what they did together.

"There's no way," Michael said. "I know my mom said things, but only because Jacob looked like me, that's all."

"Not anymore," she said, her voice flat now. "He's his father's son."

"Did you call to hurt me, is that what this is about?"

"No, of course not." She dropped the shears and leaned back down on the edge of the bed, her feet flush against the floor. "I'm sorry."

"You already said that, Maggie."

Tell him. He needs to know.

"You didn't tell Henry, did you?"

"This isn't about that, Michael," she said, and pushed her hair behind her shoulders. "There's more. But first, I need to say something." She let her hair fall against her back as she held the phone closer to her face. "I want to apologize for hurting you."

"Water under the bridge, Mag, you know that. We settled all this years ago. I love Jacob, whether he's mine or not. Why are you worrying about this now? He's doing great, Maggie. He's a good kid. Let it go."

She could see him in his car, his broad shoulders, and his dark hair. She could hear the rain falling against the windows, his hand tapping the wheel.

"It was my fault, too," she said. And it was true. Yet, she'd always believed otherwise.

"Okay, so we both wanted it, so what?"

His voice sounded flip, but she didn't care.

"I guess I just needed to say it out loud." Margaret sat up straighter, to see the outline of the clouds through the sheers. "I'm sorry I didn't stop it sooner, I should have."

"Maggie, I know." He sounded kinder now.

She heard a loud swooshing noise in the background on his end.

"The rain is really coming down hard," he said. "I'm sorry too, Maggie, I didn't mean to be an ass."

It sounded like hale to Margaret. She remembered the autumn rains, how they could rip the colorful leaves from the branches, plaster them across the lawn, stick to windshields and sidewalks, and with an early snow, they'd be trapped underneath until spring.

"We both had different reasons for what we did, Maggie, and I'm okay with it, I really am."

That night, almost ten years ago, on Danny's birthday, Margaret paused at the bottom of the steps after she'd told Michael it was over. She held tight to the banister for a moment, hoping she'd done the right thing. They'd fallen in and out of the affair for so long, it'd become a convenience for both of them, a way to avoid their lives. When she heard his laughter from the living room, she knew he saw her and acted as if it didn't matter. He'd gone right back to his big stories with the other guests.

She told herself, he'd come after her. Upstairs, she cried inside the walk-in closet.

"I was in love with you, Maggie."

She thought of stopping him now, but she didn't.

"Bad timing," he said. "You were right. It would've torn the family apart."

"Are you happy, Michael?" Margaret thought about the Christmas card.

"I am."

She felt dizzy about what she still needed to tell him. But he kept on.

"Remember when I'd come over and mowed your lawn after Danny died?"

"Yes." Margaret let her hand stroke the top of the bed covers. She could picture Michael in the backyard, crisscrossing with the mower. The next year, she hired a gardener.

"I'd watch you in the kitchen, cooking dinner for Jacob," his voice quieter now, the rain calmer. "You were so beautiful."

"Michael, don't..."

"No, it's okay," he said. "That's when I started to let go of you. I love my wife, Maggie. I do. That's why I stopped coming by."

She wouldn't tell him she'd seen his car all those times. It didn't matter anymore. They'd both made their choices over the years, believed what they wanted to believe.

"Maggie?"

"I heard you," Margaret said. She wanted to say how'd she'd felt back then, but the words were buried too deep. Maybe Danny made the feelings come back.

"Did you ever love me, Maggie?"

She noticed him in high school. An upperclassman, Michael ran with the popular group, the athletes and cheerleaders, his good looks a constant topic of discussion amongst Margaret's girlfriends. But Michael never noticed her beside him on the sofa at a party when his friend dated her friend. How she'd leaned against his arm, smelled his cologne, and a hint of sweat from the game. Even after the affair began, she never mentioned her crush on him.

She heard his phone click onto the speakerphone. Maybe she'd call him back later if he needed to go. Henry might agree she shouldn't tell him about Danny.

"You don't have to tell me," Michael said.

She wouldn't say it. She'd decided long ago to keep the lie.

"It doesn't matter, now," she said.

"But it does," Michael said. "It always did."

If she'd told him she loved him back then, would he have left Patty? She'd been too afraid to find out.

"Michael, I just wanted to say I'm sorry."

202

"Right," he said, his voice sharp, resigned.

She'd ended it so long ago, what was the point?

Margaret glanced through the sheers once again, the sun above the horizon, atop the masts and the bridge, suspended between the buildings, windows tinted copper under the glimmers.

He's alive. Tell him.

A million tiny snapshots flashed through her mind. The verdant Pennsylvania landscape Michael described when he'd called from the road on his way to New York. The dusty motel before Danny disappeared, the bright red sofa where she'd leave her clothes. Michael, face down, the skin on his broad shoulders glistening in the low light, asleep under a white sheet, the bedspread on the floor. The sad, shrewd eyes of the homeless man near the apocalyptic center. The kitchen, painted yellow. Michael's hollow expression when he'd come home without Danny.

"I found your grandfather's pocket watch." The rain tapped against the windows six hundred miles away. "Your brother has it," she said. She waited, but all she heard were raindrops and Michael breathing. "He's alive," she said. "Danny's alive."

Chapter 31
Alex

To the east, the sun rose and streams of light filtered through the Ponderosa pines. Alex moved to higher ground yesterday, away from the main trail, paranoid of helicopters. Burrowed between two boulders, surrounded by a thicket of trees, Alex shivered most of the night beneath leafy branches. The pitch-black night had dragged on, as coyotes howled and wildlife crept along the undergrowth, crackling branches and twigs underfoot.

Was it Tuesday?

He'd lost track of time, but he knew he hiked all day yesterday, further into the wild, fearful of being tracked. He took no chances, glad for the sunrise so he could continue north.

Alex stood up, stretched his arms tall, achy from the hard ground and days of hiking. He bent to adjust his boots, feeling the blisters already. He straightened his jeans as he stood back up. The skyline shifted around him and the buzz returned to his head. His headaches were intense the day before, but he'd kept going.

He steadied himself against a large rock nearby and studied the sky. No helicopters today. Maybe they found what they were searching for.

Maybe, lost hikers.

But, Alex hadn't seen anyone since he'd left the trails.

He trekked the short distance to a stream he'd found last night and drank from cupped hands. He splashed his face to wake up. With the sun to the east, he'd head upstream. The mountain terrain steeper now, but the climb necessary if he wanted to escape Arizona. He scaled the rocky terrain all morning until he realized, he'd somehow taken a wrong turn and had traveled in a wide circle.

He'd wasted precious time and lost ground. So he followed alongside a highway for a while, afraid of going adrift again. He kept to the forest, hiking amongst the pines so he wouldn't be spotted. Heading up a knoll, Alex moved faster, though he was exhausted, the grade even steeper than before. Alas, he reached the pinnacle, high above the wide valley below.

"Oh, my God."

Flagstaff. He'd thought he'd hiked long past this area, further north. Lowering onto his haunches, he shook his head, scooped a handful of pebbles, and tossed them down the hillside before him. He reached for his wallet and counted his pay. He might as well hike down for provisions, get better equipped for the long journey ahead to Oregon. Besides, he hadn't eaten a good meal in days. He'd almost been glad he felt nauseated after dizzy spells, so food hadn't crossed his mind. Water was enough.

Alex took his time down the final hillside, his eyes darting in all directions. When he reached the edge of town, the safety of the pine forest behind him, he cut through parking lots to stay clear of the roadway. Still early, he found a discount store open, and bought a large backpack, filling it full of supplies—a tarp, fishing line, hooks, a knife, socks, a warmer jacket, a package of lighters, granola bars, other dry foods, and a few more necessities.

After he paid, Alex found a restaurant down the street serving breakfast, chose a booth, ordered eggs and bacon. He wished he had a cigarette to go along with his coffee. The bitter taste burning his tongue, he watched out the window as a group of young men, five in all, bounded across the street, jay-walking, all wearing blue athletic shorts, high tops and backpacks, several wearing the hoods up on their sweatshirts, like Alex. They piled into the diner and took the corner booth next to him.

"What can I get you boys?" The same fortyish, stout waitress, who waited on Alex, brought them waters and menus. Two of them ordered milk. Everyone wanted coffee as they studied the menus. The waitress headed behind the counter to pour the drinks, then grabbed a plate of food from the cook's station and delivered it to Alex.

"There you are, three eggs, sunny-side up, with bacon." Her mouth outlined in dark red, with pale pink lips. "Forgot to ask what kind of toast you wanted."

"Wheat is fine."

"Coming right up." She topped off his coffee then stepped over to the corner booth, filling all the boy's cups. "I'll be right back with your milk to get your order." Her grey hair, tied into a long braid, hung down her back, grazing the top of the bow on her red apron, her white peasant blouse stained with strawberry jam near her waist. She wore nurses shoes and thick, taupe-colored nylons. Alex wondered if she knew the boys. The way she spoke to them seemed familiar, like they were regulars.

"Here's your toast. Jelly's right there by the window." She motioned to a caddie, with various jellies and preserves in small plastic containers. A sticky syrup bottle and hot sauce sat pushed up against the jelly holder. The place smelled of grease and fresh, dark-roasted coffee, and Alex could hear the sizzle of the grill whenever the cook tossed a slab of ham or strips of bacon onto the hot oil.

"Thanks." Alex lowered his head.

"Quite a cut you got there."

Alex glanced up at the waitress, her hands on her hips.

"Yeah, looks worse than it is."

"Looks painful, bleeding a little there," she said, pointing his way.

Alex took the paper napkin from his lap and dabbed at the cut. "It's fine."

"Burned my arm real bad a few months ago, took forever to heal."

Alex didn't glance up again and she walked away.

He heard the boys talking about school, their classes, and glanced over, all of them slouched in the booth. He studied each of their faces. Were any of them Jacob?

"You boys ready to order?" the waitress said. Alex hadn't noticed her walk up to their table. He lowered his eyes again and pulled his hood tighter over his head, glancing out the window.

The young men ordered breakfast and went back to their discussion. "Someone told me he's tough," one of them said, as he stirred some milk into his coffee.

Another guy pulled his hood off and commented, "Thermo's tough, no matter who you get."

Thermodynamics. These guys are engineering students, like Jacob.

Alex could see mid-sized buildings beyond the strip malls across the street. Northern Arizona University. Maggie told him, Jacob started there this week. Alex finished his breakfast. He grabbed his backpack and the bill from the edge of the Formica table, and then stopped near the boys.

"You guys engineering students?"

They glanced up at Alex, and one of the boys with a tangled mess of brown hair responded, "Yup, except Dwayne, here." He pointed toward a stocky, dark-skinned, young man. The whole group laughed.

"He's undecided," said another.

Alex figured it must be an inside joke. He almost wanted to defend the kid, but he didn't have time.

"Can you point me toward the engineering buildings?"

The same boy with the messy hair told Alex where to go. "You'll see a hotel at the corner, cross there," he said, pointing down the street. "Head straight onto campus and the buildings will be in front of you to the right."

"Got it," Alex said, turning toward the register to pay.

Outside, he headed through parking lots, to stay clear of the sidewalk along the main road. He kept his head down when he crossed the street and found a pathway onto campus between newer buildings jutting up against other older structures. He passed along an open quad, feeling exposed in the crowd of students. The campus was nice. He found a grassy area, stood near a tree, and remembered Maggie saying Jake lived in a dorm with other engineering students.

He pictured her now, hovering above him, her eyes closed, as she made love to him. She was beautiful, the moon glimmering against her silky skin from the skylight. Her body felt wonderful against him. She'd run after him when he rode away on Maxwell.

I hope she doesn't come back looking for me.

He was afraid of what she would find. Somebody would discover Sonia's body soon enough, if they hadn't already. He knew the helicopters he'd seen were probably searching for him. But he couldn't worry about that right now, he wanted to see the campus, see where Jake went to school.

A group of young men came out of a building across the way. One of the boys looked familiar. Alex shifted behind the thick trunk of the tree, but kept his eyes on the group as they moved further away from him. The young man he'd noticed was taller than the others, with curly, sun-bleached hair. Alex couldn't take his eyes off the boy, and wanted a better look, so he stepped out from the shelter of the tree into the open. Right then, as if he knew, the boy stopped and glanced over his shoulder. Even from several hundred feet away, Alex knew he was Jacob. The boy stared right at him. But then someone hollered his name.

"Come on, Jake, let's go."

Jake turned with quick strides to catch up to the group. He glanced over his shoulder once more, but by then, Alex had moved to the left, enough to still see his son, but so Jacob couldn't see him anymore. Alex's breath caught in his chest as he watched the young man stuff his fists deep inside his pockets, walking faster until he disappeared between the buildings. Alex almost ran after him, but turned back, slamming into a girl on the pathway.

"Watch it," she said, and moved on.

Alex surveyed the area. Something seemed off. The quad was clear of students now. Where was everybody? His eyes darted from one building to another, and for a moment, Alex couldn't remember which way to go. His heart raced. Running now, Alex headed toward where he thought he'd come onto campus, cutting across the grass and between two buildings.

Ahead, he saw a man coming toward him, too old to be a student. Alex darted a different way and ran down another path. Where was the road? The motel where he'd crossed the street? The diner where he'd had breakfast? Alex couldn't catch his breath now.

"You okay, man?"

Alex twisted around, facing the man he'd seen before.

"You lost?"

Alex shoved the man hard, sending him flying onto the concrete.

"What are you doing?" the man yelled.

But, Alex couldn't make sense of the moment. The man's voice echoed inside his head. The world spun around him. Alex ran. He sprinted as fast as he could, nearly dropping his backpack before he came upon the street at last. He heard voices behind him, but didn't look back. Darting across the street, Alex heard several horns blaring, but kept going.

Slipping between cars through a parking lot, Alex glanced up, trying to see the forest, but there were only buildings and people. He crashed into the side of a car, and a woman shouted something at him as he took off, looking up again. The mountains? Where are they?

In an alleyway, his vision blurred, Alex saw an opening and the hillsides, so he stopped for a moment, leaned against the brick wall of a warehouse to rest. When he could breathe again, he realized he couldn't see right, like peering through a long, narrow tunnel, the center foggy and bright, with outside edges dark as night. He rubbed his eyes, burning with tears. But he had no time to cry. He had to get away. He headed across an opening toward the hills and followed a side road where the highway led up toward the mountains. Traffic surrounded him, but Alex kept walking, slower now, so he wouldn't attract attention.

Vehicles sped past, as Alex kept his head covered to avoid police. He felt conspicuous out in the open, but continued to hike along the edge of the steep hillside. The trees were in sight now. His thighs burned, but he picked up his pace.

Alex glanced to his left when a red pick-up truck slowed beside him, then pulled off the road ahead. The driver motioned to Alex. Alex checked behind him. The vertical line of cars had slowed behind a delivery truck about halfway down, so he hurried uphill to the pickup, nearly lost his footing on the rocky embankment, but grabbed hold of the passenger door, the window rolled down.

"Get in," the driver said.

Alex pulled the door shut as the driver took off to keep ahead of the traffic.

"Thanks," Alex said, short of breath.

"Where're you headed?"

"Hiking." The dashboard held heaps of folded maps, newspapers, clipboards, and the floor was cluttered with empty plastic water bottles. Alex still had tunnel vision, so he tried to control his breathing.

"Those don't look like hiking boots."

Alex glanced down at his dusty work boots, sweat dripped from the tip of his nose onto his chin. With the sleeve of his sweatshirt, he dried his face then rested back against the seat, inhaled as much fresh air as he could from outside, but it didn't matter, his heart wouldn't slowdown.

"Take you as far as Snowbowl."

"Sounds good." Alex didn't care as long as they were headed uphill. Shoving the backpack aside with his boot, he watched out the passenger window as they gained ground, further from Flagstaff, breathing easier with each mile.

"First thing I do at the end of the day is kick my boots off," the driver said, his window wide open as well, papers flapping in the cool air. "Gonna be flip-flops only when I retire."

Alex glanced over at the driver, a giant man with a thick neck, broad rounded shoulders, huge arms with dried grout stuck to the reddish hairs along his forearms. Hard to tell, but he looked to be pushing sixty. Grey curls escaped his red cap with the same insignia Alex saw on the door getting in.

"Laying tile up a ways," the driver said. "Owner's some rich guy from Scottsdale. Place is huge. You do construction?"

"Did in the past, mostly labor."

"Huh. Thought with boots that worn, you'd be in the trade."

"Wrangler," Alex said. He'd never called himself that before. Felt more like an estate manager all those years. But, since he'd gotten the hang of tending to Maxwell and Lady, he guessed he'd earned it, and even liked the idea of being a cowboy. He missed the horses now, hoped the vet had shown up.

"Now, that's something I could never do. Nope, horses and me don't get along. But, my wife, Arleen, she loves animals, all kinds. We got three dogs and a mess of cats. I hate it. Keeps her happy though. If she had her way, she'd keep horses and pigs, the whole thing. No way, I tell her, dogs and cats are where I draw the line. That woman, she's crazy. You know?"

"Hmmm." Alex stared out the window glad to be riding instead of running, even if the guy wanted to talk the whole way up the hill. The blisters on the sides of his feet burned inside his boots. He kept the window down. Let the wind blow against his face, the sun peeping through scattered puffs of white clouds against the brilliant blue sky.

As the driver rattled on about the tiling business and the slowdown in the building industry, Alex could tell the temperature had dropped the higher they went. The clouds grew more dense— silvery billows painted with broad-brush strokes drifted over the San Francisco Peaks, the volcanic mountain range jutted out from beyond slighter ranges—the rocky slopes blanketed with aspen, spruce, and ponderosa pine. Alex knew from his books, the highest summit, Humphreys Peak was also the highest point in the state. He'd need to find a way around if he was going to make it out of Arizona.

"I'm Roger, by the way." The man reached across the vinyl bench to shake hands.

"Dan," Alex said, crossing his right arm tight against his chest to meet Roger's strong grip, the man's hands were huge, too.

"You live around here, Dan?"

"Tucson."

"Getting away, I guess."

Alex pulled the hood tighter around his face. "Just checking it out. I like the mountains." Alex wished he'd used another name, but Dan was all that came to mind right then.

"Well, you're in the right place. If you hike all the way up, you can see Flagstaff, the Grand Canyon on the other side. 'Course it's easier taking the chairlift. I can drop you there."

"Appreciate it."

Lofty trees were abundant now. Wild flowers, Zinnias and Dahlias and thick foliage blanketed the ground between rocky patches. Alex was relieved to have supplies, but he couldn't wait to retreat back into the shelter of the forest, where nobody would see him, like Jacob did at the university.

I know he knew me. I knew him, too.

Alex wished he could tell his mother the boy was his. Jacob was his son, no doubt in his mind. The young man was the spitting image of him in college. Jean had tried to punish him, in so many ways, for so many years, for something that happened when he was even younger than Jacob was now. For a mistake, a terrible mistake, he made when he was just a kid, a drunken kid. He'd never do that to Jake, still a boy, a tall, good-looking young man, but still a kid, Alex could tell.

Alex squeezed his eyes shut.

He turned his head into the wind, suddenly flooded by the reality of how he'd abandoned his son.

I did the same thing. I punished Jacob for something that wasn't his fault.

Alex opened his eyes wide now. "God damn it," he shouted, then slammed his fist against the dashboard, knocked a clipboard thick with papers into the air. It bounced against the steering wheel with a loud pop, the papers flying everywhere before landing near Roger's boot on the gas pedal.

The tires swerved across the road, Roger caught the wheel in time, and then straightened the truck out. "What the hell?" he said, as he steered the truck back into the right lane before an oncoming traffic hit them head on.

Alex threw himself back against the seat, grabbed his head with both hands. "I'm sorry," he cried out. "I'm so sorry." Then dropped both arms into his lap, cracking his neck back into place with a quick twist, pain radiating up from his spine over the top of his head like whiplash, but it wasn't new, it was the same awful throbbing he couldn't escape.

"You crazy?" Roger said, his growl even louder, like an angry bear. "I'll dump your ass right here," he said, as he gripped the wheel.

"No, don't to do that," Alex said, trying to get control of the adrenaline rushing through his body. "I just remembered something, that's all, something important." He folded his arms over his chest, held himself still. "I'm good now."

"Christ," Roger said. "Nearly veered off the road." The man breathed heavy, his face nearly red as his cap.

Alex shut his eyes again. Tried to relax. Hoped Roger wouldn't kick him out right there in the middle of the highway.

Still shaky, Alex was clear enough now to know he was not in his right frame of mind at all. His head pounded worse than before, like a sledgehammer. He wished he'd remembered to grab the pain medicine before he took off on the motorcycle. Everything he had in the world was in the backpack at his feet. He'd lost it all. His family. His son. Maggie. He could hardly stand it any longer.

Keep it together, man. You need to get to Oregon.

Hands slick with perspiration, he wiped them on his jeans, every bump of the truck sent a fireball of pain deep inside his skull, pulsating like ribbons of heat shooting through the hemispheres of his brain. Alex could almost see the waves of pain when his eyes were closed, magenta and midnight blue, specks of orange light like dagger holes in his skull.

He tried to rest, breathe in and out, to no avail. Alex opened his eyes again. Now, in his line of sight, black paisley shaped blotches had formed and floated by in his peripheral vision. He tried to rub away the shadowy spots, but when he glanced out the window at the sky, the blotches remained, making it difficult to see. He'd almost rather trade back for the cylindrical vision he'd suffered earlier. Things were getting worse, he could tell.

"You okay?" Roger said, his voice lower now.

"Yeah, I'm fine." Alex shut his eyes one more time as he leaned back again, trying not to panic.

"Just take it easy," Roger said, sounding like a friend now. "Almost there."

Alex took a few more deep breaths, convinced now that he'd probably hyperventilated, so he focused on breathing in through his nose, out through his mouth, slower each time, better, but the pain was still there. Back inside the forest, he'd find a safe place to sleep for a while. He could make it through, if he just got some rest.

You're fine. Stop thinking so much.

He touched his bag on the floor of the cab without opening his eyes.

Jacob carried a backpack, nearly the same one, in fact, when he glanced over his shoulder at Alex. There was something in the boy's eyes, the way he looked straight at Alex. His eyes did not stray. As a young boy, Jacob would stare at Alex the same way, especially when he drank too much. It was unsettling and even when Alex was completely inebriated—when he met eyes with Jacob, he'd have to look away, and oftentimes leave the room. It was like the boy saw right through him. Big sad eyes Alex dreamed about for months after he left. But now, Jacob seemed like a normal kid, an ordinary 18 year old. His eyes were the same, though, melancholy, haunted. That's how Alex knew. Jake was his son.

Jake's physique, identical to Alex in college, long and lean. He even moved like Alex, heavy footed, more of a lumbering stride, and his hair thick and wavy, too. The moment he'd spotted Jacob, he knew.

Did Margaret feel the same way at the restaurant the other night? Had Jake sensed it, too? Or had Maggie warned the boy, told him about his dad being alive? Alex hoped Jacob had turned around because of an intuition, because he could feel the energy.

God, I'm so sorry, kid. I really messed up bad.

Alex found himself saying a silent prayer, asking God to watch over the boy, keep him from going astray like Alex had done.

God, please keep him safe.

When they arrived at the ski area, Roger pulled his truck to a stop near the ticket booth. Several people mingled with cameras strapped around their necks, hiking gear and backpacks just like Alex. He'd blend right in with all the day-trippers. Alex got out, closed the door then glanced through the open window giving Roger a quick head-nod.

"Right," Roger said, and then took off fast, the wheels on his truck kicking up dust as he turned onto the highway.

Alex could hardly blame him.

Chapter 32
Alex

Alex watched the red truck disappear up the hill, and then headed to the lift area. The blotchy spots before his eyes had faded somewhat and Alex wondered if he should go straight to the trails or take a chance on the lift.

Another group passed by to the ticket booth, so Alex went inside the park area's restroom, filled his canteen at the sink, a sheet of thin metal acted as a mirror and Alex could just make out the outline of his face, his skin sunburned, his lips dry, his hair disheveled covering the wound on his forehead. He washed and dried his face, then grabbed a roll of toilet paper from atop the towel dispenser, stuffed it inside his pack, then used one of the stalls to relieve himself.

Outside, he noticed a police car parked nearby, but there were no officers around, so he headed to the ticket booth, stayed close behind a group of men and women to the lift. They paired up, but he rode alone after hanging back for a moment.

The lift operator, a young man with dreads, skin-tight jeans and a brown flannel shirt, someone who looked like he might be friends with Sonia, gave Alex a long, peculiar look as the chair jerked and began ascending above the grassy slope. Alex glanced below, as the lift went higher, still no sign of any uniforms.

Fifteen minutes later, as the sky-ride reached the pinnacle, Alex grabbed his backpack and headed to the trail area. The air cooler at this altitude, he zipped his jacket tight and tucked his hair inside the hood. A ranger led a discussion about The Navajo, the rising peaks as a holy landmark. Alex kept his head down, and moved in the opposite direction from the group. Others snapped photos of the views, so he cut away again to the edge of a steep hillside. He glanced along the horizon where a volcanic field of rock spanned out into the distance.

Alex hiked along the rocky ridge, knowing from his trips to the library, the land surrounding the dormant volcano was considered sacred.

Where earth meets heaven.

Photographers had set tripods to shoot the Northern Rim of the Grand Canyon, seventy miles away. But Alex moved along, with no time to glance toward the canyon, like the tourists. He found a trailhead, and then hiked down the path at a quick pace, until he neared a clearing. Pines and spruces lined the edges. He headed for the wooded area, faster now. Voices came from behind him, so Alex started to jog, cautious not to trip. Deeper inside the woods, tall trees shaded the grounds, branches and leaves crunched underfoot. He could smell pine and sap, as he kept a swift pace through the thicket of trees, checking his compass for the arrow pointed north.

After an hour or more, Alex felt exhausted. His head throbbed worse than ever, so he paused near a stream. He pulled off his boots, his blisters stinging in the icy water of the rocky creak. Afterward, he leaned against a rock and wrapped each foot with an elastic bandage. He knew he should keep going until dark. The scab around his stitches seemed fine, but the wound needed to stay clean, so he squatted back down near the stream, splashed his forehead, washing away the sweat.

Bent over the surface of the water, Alex blinked several times before he realized it wasn't his own reflection he saw in the water.

It was Brian.

He stared at Alex. His skin greyish, pupils dilated, mouth wide open, a thin, black snake slithering out from his throat.

Alex stood frozen in place.

Brian screamed from under the water as he propelled upward toward Alex, who fell backward against the embankment. Alex dug his hands into the muddy grass, pushed onto his feet, and stumbled away from the stream, then turned and ran into the woods, barefoot, tripping several times on branches and rocks.

He sprinted through the forest, Brian hot on his heels, but when he glanced back, he saw no one. The woods spun around Alex, his head ready to split wide open, so he caught hold of the trunk on a lofty pine, dozens of trees in all directions, limbs tapered like lanky teenager legs. The wind howled and yapped, pine needles whistled high pitched warnings, legions of fallen leaves caught in the gust performed three-sixties, and then floated to the ground, like tiny paratroopers landing between derelict forest relics of moss covered logs, sticks and twigs and other tinder. Alex held on tight, his face stuck to the sap covered bark.

"Let me go," Alex cried, breathless, ripping his tangled hair from the branches, his cheek scraped raw. Weary from running, from trying to escape the seriatim of his past, Alex heard the ultimatum.

"Face us," the voices said. "We are all around you, there's no escape."

Alex whispered into the woods. "It wasn't my fault." He dropped to his knees, like a child, rolled onto the ground and pulled his legs toward his chest, fetal. "Let me be."

He wept for his friend, for Brian, for having left him alone, for Sonia, for his son, Maggie, for everything.

"I'm sorry," he said. "God, please forgive me." The light faded fast around him and Alex blacked out, his face in the dirt, like Sonia.

The earth beneath Alex had shifted away from the sun, and the forest had grown dim as he rotated onto his back, blurry and disoriented, thousands of stars dangled from the dark blue canopy above the trees. After a few moments, Alex remembered where he was, the air even colder now, he shivered as he got to his feet. He needed to go. His head felt thick as he reached for his forehead. The cut was dry, but still tender to the touch. He heard the chop of a helicopter, somewhere above him. Dogs barking.

Alex staggered away, not knowing which direction to go, the dogs drowned out now by the chopper overhead. The hum of the blades confused him, but he continued to move toward the edge of the darkened woods, to get his bearings, find a way out. He shoved his way past some branches near a clearing when the lights hit—giant stadium lights, or flood lights, he wasn't sure, but he couldn't see, blinded, he tried to block the brightness with his hand. He managed to find the edges of the light if he turned his head a bit and caught sight of three off-road vehicles. For a moment, Alex figured it was a bunch of college kids messing with him. But then, Alex saw rifles drawn, the lights still making it difficult to see, but he could make out several men in uniforms along the edges, a man's voice yelling from a tunnel, but then he realized it was coming from a speaker, louder than the yowling dogs.

"Daniel Waterson?" the man shouted. "Are you Daniel Waterson?"

Alex dropped to his knees, the sting inside his head so intense he could only whisper. "Yes. Yes, I'm Daniel Waterson." Instinctively, he raised his hands over his head.

It's over. No more.

"Get down on the ground," the man yelled. "Get down."

Did they hear me?

Alex was too weak now to repeat himself, the man's voice echoed inside his skull.

"Down on the ground," the man kept yelling.

"But, wait." Alex remembered his Ohio license. "I can prove it," his voice gone now, he stood once again to reach for his wallet in his back pocket.

Alex heard a sudden blast.

He flew, the flash ripped through his chest, blew him backwards. Stars shone all around in the wind. Alex smelled rain, the scent of creosote bushes. Arizona poppies. The desert rain, each droplet a sweet perfume. He landed against a Ponderosa pine, the reddish-brown bark smelled of rich butterscotch, and the evergreen needles seemed reminiscent of fresh rosemary. The same woody, fragrant rosemary he and Margaret planted together in their garden. The scent had stuck to their hands even after they washed up.

Alex stared back into the lights.

"Truth," he whispered.

The clouds made the lamps seem misty against the dark sky, and the fog distorted the earth around him.

"I'm Daniel Waterson," he said, knowing they couldn't hear him. But he said it again, anyway, for himself. "I'm Daniel Waterson." He reached inside his front pocket, found his grandfather's watch, and wound the gold chain around the tip of his finger. "Waterson." The world seemed to blur out of control around him. Daniel searched for the opening now. Scratched at the surface of ice. Begged for mercy at the time of the end. But he was alone as all light dimmed to black.

"Danny, open your eyes."

A warm breeze danced across his face. The pain gone now, he kept his eyes shut, the moment too precious to let go.

"I've been waiting for you."

Brian.

Daniel lay on his back, the grass cool beneath his legs, he heard water lapping nearby, could sense his friend beside him. When he opened his eyes, the sky shone more brilliant than he'd ever seen before, brighter than sapphire, richer than cobalt.

Brian sat close to Daniel, holding his bent knees to his chest, face to the heavens. His teenage body slight, his shoulders narrow, arms thin and long.

When Brian finally glanced over at Daniel, his smile was broad, his teeth crowded along the bottom, one tooth overlapping the other, just as Daniel remembered. Brian stood up, walked the short distance to the lake, and paused near the edge. The water, blue as sky, the wooden dock, sturdy, sanded clean. The homes around the lake, gone now, replaced by thickets of trees, tall and wide, encircling the water. Abundant orchids, daylilies and wisteria filled the air with sweet fragrance.

Out of the corner of his eye, Daniel saw Brian take off, run the length of the dock, his arms and legs extended wide as he flew off the end and disappeared under the shimmers of currents.

With no time to spare, Daniel chased after Brian, dove off the dock as far as he could jump, and swam beneath the surface in a frantic search for his friend. He spotted Brian's arm and then his legs, grabbed hold of his torso and pulled him to the fresh air above. Brian gasped and coughed as they reached the shallow edge of the lake.

"I knew you'd save me," Brian said, and then floated on his back for a second before kicking his feet away from Daniel.

"Wait," Daniel said.

Brian disappeared across the lake, beyond the trees, his body lifted into the sky, toward the heavens.

Daniel knew Brian was too far away to hear him now, but he spoke to him anyway, and to whoever else might be listening. "I ignored my conscience that night." Daniel smoothed his hair back, as his eyes filled with tears. "I abandoned you," he said. "I chose to ignore you, Brian." He watched his friend floating, arms extended at his sides, the clouds almost translucent above him. "I went with my brother and his friends, so desperate for their attention, I turned my back on you."

How could Brian be so kind?

Daniel lowered his head, a shameful sinner at the foot of paradise. The reflection of the sky so luminous against the water, Daniel began to cry.

"But even worse," Daniel said, his tears rippling against the water. "I was ashamed of you as my friend," he shook his head now, glanced back at the sky. "When faced with right and wrong, saving you or serving my own ego, I let you sink."

Daniel remembered closing the door to the basement, and never looking back.

"I was rotten." He knew he had to say it.

"I wasn't a good friend," Daniel said. "Yet, you give me this gift of redemption."

Brian had always forgiven him. Let him win when they raced across the lake, turned a blind eye when Danny cheated now and then when they played cards or video games.

"I've cheated so much in my life."

Daniel paused. Could Brian somehow hear him?

"Brian," he shouted, "I want you to know that you died because I was a fool."

Daniel watched Brian until he vanished beyond the white billowing clouds. "I'm sorry," he shouted into the sky. "I'm sorry, my friend."

Daniel climbed up the embankment from the lake, returned to the grassy knoll and rested, waited. Somehow he knew there would be further penance. He was ready.

"God, forgive me," he prayed, his voice humble. "I should have gone to Brian's parents, told them the truth." He closed his eyes, ashamed. "I've lived my whole life like a wrecking ball, destroying everything in my path."

Daniel broke down, crying into the grass. He pictured Sonia's lifeless body in the stall, tossed against the railings like nothing better than a bale of hay, the dusty blanket covering her face.

"I killed her," he said, his voice raspy, throat thick with tears.

Daniel sat up straighter, cleared his voice and nodded toward the sky, as if God was there with him, listening, waiting for him to admit every wrong, every sin.

"I deserted my family," he said, his voice strong now. His eyes wide open. Aware of everything he said. "I left my son." Daniel held back his tears now, determined to tell the truth, if only for him to hear. "I drifted from the truth, allowed myself to be selfish, to go astray," he said. "I know what I've done is despicable, terrible sins, but I ask for your forgiveness."

Daniel lay back against the grass, his arms at his sides, his eyes wide and clear, a flock of birds crossed the vault of heaven, high above the trees, headed toward eternity, he knew he was near God, near heaven.

He knew because of Brian. He was still only a boy, his body frozen in time, how glad Daniel was to see his friend again, to touch him, to hear his voice.

A light breeze rustled through the leaves as a blanket of serenity fell over Daniel like never before.

He remembered his grandmother's whispers as she tucked the quilt around him in the big iron bed between the dormers.

"Always speak to the Lord before you sleep, he will hear your prayer and comfort you."

221

Daniel closed his eyes again. "Forgive me, watch over Brian, and my family." He began to drift to sleep. Whatever came next, he did not know. But, the fear was gone from his heart.

Chapter 33
Michael

At first, Michael didn't recognize his brother. The homicide detective said to take his time, whatever time needed to be certain. Certain the man lying before him was, indeed, his younger brother.

Head and shoulders propped against pillows, the man's face familiar to Michael, of course. But with the heart monitor and IV lines, a breathing tube taped to his dry, cracked lips, gauze wrapped around his forehead and across his shoulder, Michael struggled to find something, anything conclusive to identify him as Danny. Daniel Waterson, the brother, son, husband and father who disappeared, thought to be among the thousands who'd died nearly ten years ago at the World Trade Center in New York City.

It took Michael several minutes in fact, to get past Daniel's battered appearance, the tangle of long, filthy hair, the obvious wounds, and the fact that this man was far older than Michael remembered Danny, and so lean, his ribs protruded out from under skin deeply weathered by the hot, arid Sonoran desert.

But, as he examined the unconscious man before him, three distinct factors helped convince Michael, without a doubt, that the half-dead man before him was his brother, Daniel.

The first identifiable sign Michael looked for was the scar on the right side of Daniel's neck, a burn mark from when they were kids. They'd made off with a box of fireworks from their dad, who'd taken the boys to a roadside stand to buy a mix of sparklers and fountains to celebrate 4th of July at their family cottage in Michigan. While their dad, Dutch, napped on the sofa,

Michael lifted the box and motioned for little Danny to follow him outside onto the porch. Michael placed a Piccolo Pete in six-year-old Danny's hand.

"Hold it tight," he'd said.

His brother's eyes wide with excitement, Michael lit the fuse and seconds later, red-hot flames shot upward toward Danny's face, missing his cheek by only a few inches. But the fire had singed the side of his neck before the boy dropped the fiery tube on the white painted boards of the porch. Veritable, high-pitched whistling blasted out from the wild Piccolo, masking Danny's screams, as sparks flew amongst old, grey wicker chairs and clay pots of yellow marigolds and bright pink petunias, nearly threatening to burn down the entire cottage.

But like a fierce, angry bear with a sharp thorn in his paw, Dutch shot through the screen door, almost ripping the entire doorframe from the hinges, all blurry-eyed and red-faced from his nap, shouting expletives as he kicked the fireball onto the lawn, let it peter out, then dowsed the remaining flames with the garden hose as Danny collapsed on the porch.

Michael remembered now being more annoyed with his brother than afraid of his dad. He'd shouted something inane at Danny. "I told you to hold on tight." Then felt the crisp smack of his father's hand across the back of his neck. He'd shut his mouth after that and sat down on the bottom step of the porch while Dutch tended to Danny.

Later, after the emergency room, Michael glanced at Danny at the other end of the backseat, propped against the passenger door, white gauze taped to his neck, his cheeks still reddened from bawling the entire time the doctor worked on him. Michael was as riled by Danny now as he was then. But that's how it always was between them. Like night and day, they were so different. It was hard to believe they were related. Michael still wondered how they'd grown up in the same house.

With an innate passion for sports, Michael loved any athletic pursuit where he could run fast, and catch, toss, kick, pass, or hit a ball. Still to this day, he often coached his kids, and tossed a football or baseball in the yard with them. He liked the fresh air, and breaking a sweat. But Daniel was different. He was the bookworm. A kid happy to watch TV all day, never leave the house, hang out by himself or with his loner friends. Their mother shoved him outside during the summer, and locked the door behind him until dinner. Michael would ditch him to keep him away from his friends.

Michael stepped back from the bedside for a moment, wiped the sweat from his brow with both hands.

"You okay?" the detective said, from where he stood on the other side of the bed.

"Yeah," Michael said. "Just give me a minute."

"Like I said, take your time."

"Right." Michael felt sick, like the air was too thick inside the room. He glanced at the air conditioner blasting away from under the window, the type at older motels. Seemed odd, a modern hospital with a room like that, but maybe it was for fugitives, the other rooms were updated, but this space, near the stairwell, seemed to have been left off.

The guard outside the door had all but searched Michael when they first arrived, kept a serious eye on him while the detective explained the circumstances. The younger cop stepped aside for them, took a seat on a folding chair near the door. Michael noticed his gun, the Billy club, or was it called a baton now? He'd heard that term before on TV police dramas. But he didn't ask, instead he'd followed the detective inside the sparse room. A single bed, plenty of medical equipment, the shades pulled closed on the window, a single chair near the side of the bed, no phone, no TV.

Michael couldn't tell now if there were bars installed on the window. He wanted to be alone with Danny, but knew enough not to say anything then. Instead, he shifted nearer to the bed again.

That July 4th, when everyone else was free to run and play, Michael had to pay penance by doing yard work. All the while, tucked inside a red and white hammock, tied between two lofty Sugar Maples, Danny sorted baseball cards, his dark blue t-shirt blended so well with the patriotic fabric, it seemed as though he was stitched inside an American flag. Lake Michigan sparkled under the bright sunshine all day, and right across the street, the shoreline called out to Michael to dive into the cool water, but there would be no flips off the end of dock for Michael. Instead, he mowed the lawn, weeded the beds, and rolled the wheelbarrow full of clippings back and forth to the compost pile at the far end of the yard. But every time Michael passed by Danny, he got even with a swift kick beneath the hammock.

Near his brother's bedside now, Michael shook his head. The same irritation welled up inside his chest, forced him to take a deep breath and let it out again. "What the hell, Danny?

The detective stepped away, leaned against the wall near the window, his arms crossed while Michael examined his brother.

The same embossed scar, Danny always formed keloids on his skin as he healed. The doctor told their mother when they'd gone for a checkup it was rare to see keloids on light skin, more common in people of color. Looking at Danny now, it seemed as though he had plenty of color, similar to the Native Americans selling jewelry by the side of the road. His skin was like worn leather. But the scar, still unchanged, about two inches in diameter, jagged, raised edges, an ugly pinkish color right above the collarbone a few millimeters shy of the carotid artery.

"For God's sake," their mother had said, her voice shrill as she screamed the words inside the car after they'd left the hospital. "He could have been blinded or even worse, he could have died."

"Well," Dutch said, as he drove the car toward the highway. "Maybe not died."

"You heard what the doctor said." Their mother, Jean often turned bright red when she was angry, her skin a creamy color and cheeks rosy under normal circumstances, but right then, her face was nearly crimson, the vein on her forehead bulged as she glanced over her shoulder at Michael in the backseat. He tried to look away, but he couldn't, her face terrifying, like he'd never seen before. "It just missed the artery," she'd said, and then glanced back out the front windshield, her eyes now on the road, her right hand directing Dutch which way to go. "Here, turn here, go right," she said, her voice still strange, not at all acting like the refined and elegant mother Michael knew her to be. "If he'd fallen just right," she continued, waved her hand again, as Dutch made the right turn, as requested. "That damn thing could have cut right through his neck like a knife, and he might have died."

226

"He's alive," Dutch said. "That's what matters."

He watched his mother cross her arms over her white summer sweater, the one that always smelled like flowery perfume when she draped it over the back of the chair in the kitchen. "I want those fireworks gone."

"Yes, dear." Michael caught eyes with his father in the rearview mirror as he glared in Michael's direction. Dutch never liked when Jean was upset, and neither did Michael.

"You got us in trouble, stupid." Michael tried to whisper, but Dutch heard him, swung his big arm over the seat, smacked Michael on the leg, hard. He shut up again. Stayed quiet all the way home. But he retaliated later with every jab he took beneath the hammock.

Danny took his punishment well, never cried out for Mommy. Although, Michael wished he would. He'd have taken the belt over yard work anytime, faster, and no punk brother on watch from the hammock.

Jean made it clear after her rant that the boys were not to bother Grandmother Lacey about what happened. "You go straight to bed when we get home," she'd said. "I don't want you worrying my mother."

Jean always referred to Grandmother Lacey as her mother, never called her Grandma, or even Grandmother. It was always, 'my mother'. As if she was some separate entity, not a regular grandmother, like their father's mother. Dutch's mom was Grandma. Even Jean called her Grandma. But Grandmother Lacey was another type, and Michael never liked her, she wasn't grandmotherly at all. She paid little or no attention to Michael and Daniel when they visited. Sure, sometimes she'd have gifts for them, but they were placed in the guest room at the end of their beds and all toys were to be kept inside the bedroom. She really only spoke to Jean when they were there, out on the porch or in her bedroom with the door closed. Private conversations. Michael didn't know why, never asked. He just figured Grandmother Lacey was strange. In fact, he'd often thought his brother was just like her, odd as he was, even teased him about it.

"Weirdo," Michael said, that day in the yard. Tossed a few clumps of weeds on Danny's head as he went by. "Why don't you go stay in your room all day like her," Michael said, and nodded toward their grandmother's windows along the forbidden wing of the old cottage. He'd nearly let go of the wheelbarrow when he thought he saw her peering out from behind the sheer curtains. After he paused to regroup and get a better grip on the handles, the shadow disappeared, she'd moved away from the window. "You're as freaky as her," he'd said to Danny. "Like a freakazoid."

But when he'd glanced back at his brother in the hammock, Danny brushed the dirt from his hair, as if he didn't even notice him.

Michael breathed in deep again. He'd never felt comfortable hospitals.

Better here than at the morgue, I guess.

Michael chuckled.

He noticed the detective watching him again.

Michael's nerves were frazzled from the flight to Phoenix, the headache at the car rental counter and the long drive north to the address Margaret had given him.

When he arrived, police swarmed the grounds. Said some guy, called Alex Gershom, lived there. Michael almost left, thought he had the wrong place, but the detective stopped him.

"What's your name, sir?" the man had said. Dressed in a dark sport coat and khaki slacks, instead of a uniform, Michael could tell he was in charge.

"Michael Waterson." He didn't hesitate, even reached out to shake hands, as if he was visiting a client. He'd left his own jacket inside the rental car, the temperature too high for coats. He wondered how the man could tolerate wearing lightweight wool in that type of heat, not a drip of sweat on his forehead, his hand cool and dry when they shook hands.

The detective interrupted Michael when he once again tried to explain he had the wrong address. "I think you might know Alex Gershom," the detective said. "We have reason to believe he's actually Daniel Waterson."

Michael stood in the gravel outside the gates certain the officer was wrong. Danny wouldn't live in such an elaborate home, especially if he was trying to hide. And Margaret said he stayed in a tiny room out behind a house. This was an estate. Not a house. She hadn't said anything about Danny using another name. Or had she? The conversation was quick. Maggie wanted to get off the phone. Had cried, in fact, she'd sobbed. He hadn't known what to do. Didn't know if she'd gone crazy. But somehow, he believed her. She was too upset to be lying. In his gut, he knew it was true. Daniel was alive. After he hung up, he'd driven straight to the airport, got on the first flight west, connected twice before landing in Phoenix.

The man was still talking and Michael realized he hadn't heard a single word. He tried to step forward toward the house again, but the detective grabbed him by the arm, led him further away. Michael saw the yellow tape along the front gate. That's when he blacked out.

When he came to, he was actually still upright, leaning against the detective, his head spinning. The detective helped him inside the backseat of a black sedan, not the rental car he'd driven, a different car with the engine running. Inside, the leather seat was cool, the air chilly compared to outside.

"Wait here," the detective said. "Cool off, I'll get you some water." Before Michael knew it, the detective handed him bottled water through the door. "The heat can sneak up on you out here."

Michael gulped swigs of water, tried to explain again that he had the wrong address. Even got back out of the car. "I need to find my brother."

"I'll take you to him." The detective asked if he could see Michael's identification and check for concealed weapons. Michael nodded, and then realized when it was too late, he'd agreed to a pat down. "He's at the hospital here in Flagstaff, but they might move him to Phoenix, so I'd like to head over right now, if it's okay, so you can get a look at him, maybe ID him for me."

Michael hadn't responded for a moment. His heart raced. "Is he still alive?"

"Yes, he's stable, but he needs surgery," the detective said. "I need you to take a look at him, see if you can identify him as Daniel Waterson."

Michael would learn later about the woman they'd found in the barn at the estate. That Danny was suspected of murder. But when they first arrived at the hospital, all Michael knew was that there was a man there, who had two driver's licenses in his wallet, one for Alex Gershom, and the other, Daniel Waterson.

Michael took another look at this man who claimed to be two people, leaned in closer, even though he already knew the truth. "He's Daniel Waterson," Michael said, his eyes on Danny's face. "He's my brother."

They were just kids back then, at the cottage. He thought his mom liked Danny better than him that weekend. That maybe she always did. God knows she always protected Danny, like he was some angel. He had this way, a kind of gift for being able to charm women. Even their Grandma in Ohio preferred Danny to Michael, always cutting a bigger slice of cake for him, sneaking cookies to him in the loft. Michael saw it. Dutch had even talked to him about it once.

"He's the youngest, the baby, don't worry about it," Dutch said, when Michael had stormed out of the farmhouse kitchen, stomped straight down to the creek and was tossing stones into the water by the time his dad caught up. "Just the way it is," Dutch said. "You'll understand someday when you're a parent," he explained, The baby is always the favorite." Michael wasn't satisfied with what his dad said. "But, here's the good news, son," Dutch said, as he rested his strong hand on Michael's shoulder. "Don't tell anyone, but the truth is, you're my favorite."

They stood together for a long while, silent, his dad skipped a few rocks across the top of the water. Michael reached for a few pebbles himself and mimicked the way his father had tossed the stones, held his wrist flat the same way, and then flicked the rock sideways, watched it bounce across the currents.

"See there," Dutch said. "You're a quick learner, and you're athletic like your old man." He smiled at Michael, a big, broad smile. The type of smile Michael always craved from him, even now. Approval from his father meant the world to him. He knew his dad would be proud of him for going to find his brother now. "Let your little brother have the women," Dutch said, with a wink. "You and me, we've got something different. We're men's men. And son, it's a man's world," he said. "Your brother, he's what you call a lady's man, and they don't do as well."

After that day, whenever Danny brought their mother bouquets of buttercups from the yard, and Jean would go on about how sweet he was at dinner, Dutch would wink at Michael, and somehow Michael didn't care as much anymore.

But even so, Michael had still tried to get his mother's attention, and knew he'd win her over in the end. It's what drove his competitive nature, made him want to win, with sports, in business, and even with Margaret.

After Brian drowned, Michael didn't need to try very hard to be favored by his mother. She grew to resent, even hate Daniel, after Brian died. Even Michael began to feel sorry for Danny.

He realized long before Danny left for New York, before that fated day when the planes crashed into the towers that he'd gone too far with his jealousy toward Daniel. It wasn't enough that he'd made his brother take the fall for Brian's death back in high school. After all, he'd been there, too. He knew Brian stayed at the dock after Danny came up to the house without him. But, Michael had done nothing. The thing was, Michael wasn't drunk that night, not like Danny and Brian. He'd been the one to hand them beers all night, maybe to see if they could handle their alcohol, or just so they'd get sick. He didn't remember now. But, he did know, he was the one who got them drunk. And he also knew, he'd seduced Margaret when Danny first started going wild.

Michael saw it coming. He followed his brother several times, worried about him. Michael witnessed his reckless behavior, how he drank so much, drove too fast, slept with strange women he'd pick up at hotel bars where they stayed for business. Michael knew all about it. He saw it happening and never did anything to help Danny. His own behavior wasn't much better, and in fact, Michael was glad, maybe even relieved, when Margaret broke it off for good, said she wanted to save her marriage.

Michael knew why Daniel never came back to Cleveland. It was because of him. He'd driven his brother off. Taking Danny down had become an obsession.

With Danny as his target, Margaret had become Michael's main fixation. He'd wondered how he didn't notice her in high school. She was beautiful when Danny brought her home to meet the family. Intoxicating. Maggie was stunning, but more than her physical looks, it was her essence, the softness in her voice, the way she tossed her head back when she laughed. Michael found himself falling for Maggie, every time she listened to him, laughed at his jokes. She was the perfect audience, even told him to date nicer girls, marry someone special, that he was worth it. When Daniel announced their engagement, Michael's heart shattered into a million pieces. He was in love with her, too.

His heart beat fast now as he stood next to his brother's bed. Michael had already confirmed Danny's identity, but it wasn't only the scar on Danny's neck that proved he'd found his brother. There were other reasons, too.

The next indication at almost the same moment Michael thought of the scar, were the prominent veins on the back of Danny's hands. Michael could almost see the blood pumping through the thick blue-green lines. Michael had tortured Danny about that, too. Called him, Hulk, freak, even an animal. Anything to get a rise out of Danny, but it never worked, because Danny always walked away, sulked by himself in another room. Eventually as adults, Danny would just have another drink when Michael tried to bust his balls.

Michael tried to ignore the tattoos on his brother's arms. Sure, it flashed through his mind, Danny at a tattoo parlor. Made him nearly break down right there and cry. But he didn't. He held himself together. Instead, he focused on being certain. Like the detective had said. That was easy when he looked at Danny's hands. The tattoos were not an identifying factor. To Michael it was a personal matter between brothers. He knew exactly why Danny got those tattoos.

After the wedding, when Danny married Margaret, Michael went out with some friends the next weekend. He got stupid drunk downtown at an Indian's game. Danny was somewhere in Canada by then with Maggie, and Michael couldn't stand the thought of them up there in the woods together. So he drank a ton of beers at the game and afterward, ordered shots of tequila on a bar crawl with the same group of friends. After they took the Red Line to Cleveland Heights to search for more bars, but Michael walked inside a tattoo shop instead, paid good money to have the Chinese letter for strength tattooed on his upper arm. He wouldn't do it again, even though he couldn't remember the sting, having been so inebriated, but what he did remember, was the look on Danny's face, fresh off his honeymoon with Maggie, as she said she liked the tattoo.

"I love the simple lines," she'd said, and traced the black symbol with her fingertip. "Did it hurt?"

"Not really," Michael said, smirking at Danny. "I wanted something strong." He'd flexed his muscle as Maggie examined the tattoo. "Kind of a crazy night, but I'm glad I did it."

"You're an interesting guy, Michael." Maggie smiled and tilted her head, glanced into his eyes. "Like peeling back an onion, you've got so many layers."

Michael knew right then, it wouldn't be hard to get her attention if Danny didn't watch himself.

He couldn't look at Danny's tattoos now. It all seemed so pitiful.

"What happened, Danny?"

Michael shook his head.

The scar.

Those hands.

Funny what you remembered about someone.

Danny always had bigger hands than Michael. He could palm a basketball. But Danny had no use for those types of skills since he never liked sports, other than from the sidelines of an armchair in his den. Danny inherited their father's large bones, and his prominent cheekbones like so many from the Netherlands.

Michael, on the other hand, took after his mother's side of the family. An athletic build, yes, but not lanky and durable like Dutch and Daniel. They were both solid. If Michael paused his workouts for long, he went soft fast. His dad had great posture even now as an elderly gentleman, maybe a bit thicker around the middle, but still quite sturdy, even robust for a man his age.

Danny's hands were proof even without studying his face. The only difference, the calluses, nicks with new keloid scars, the hands of a builder or a bricklayer. Not Daniel. Not the Daniel he knew anyway. The most strenuous thing Danny ever did was flip steak on his backyard grill.

But he was obviously a different person now.

People could change.

Michael knew firsthand, because he was different now, too. He wasn't the same loud mouth guy who needed all the attention. Over the years, he'd grown up, tired of the same old stories, living in the past, his glory days.

So one day, he stopped, like an alcoholic who decides never to drink again. Michael ended his braggart behavior.

It was after he'd lost Daniel, called Margaret on his way to find him, figured out he'd lost her forever, and then later when Patty got sick, it all began to sink in. He needed to change. So he did.

Patty wouldn't let him tell anyone about her condition. It was enough for the family to mourn the loss of Daniel, and besides, she'd been ill for a while, long before Danny disappeared. The medicine never worked, so several months after Danny disappeared, she went in for surgery and received treatment with radioactive iodine to kill what was left of the over-active tissue.

Even though they cut away the tumor on her thyroid, Michael thought for sure, he would lose her. The boys would grow up without their mother. She was so weak afterward. But like a miracle, she began to rebound, even gained some weight back, and eventually became healthy enough to give birth again, to their third son, who was still so young—their baby, the one who was a bit spoiled just like Dutch said.

Michael vowed then to be a good husband, to love Patty the way she deserved. But out of the blue, last year, Patty was diagnosed with Leukemia. She was thinner than ever before from the chemo, but despite all the side effects, she was still the best mom to their kids. Dutch knew about it now, but Michael hadn't told Margaret, there was no reason, she'd moved on with her life by then and Patty didn't want her to know anyway. She didn't want anyone to know. He realized for so many years, he'd been an ass. Promised every day, he'd be a good person if God would let

Patty make it through. Michael only hoped his prayers weren't too late.

The tubes and white tape masked Danny's face, but it didn't keep Michael from knowing him. There was no reason to even see his face, because Michael had known the moment he walked into the room. Even more than the two physical facts, Michael knew this was his brother, because he'd know Danny anywhere. Every breath his brother took, Michael remembered him, recognized him. He'd always know Danny, no matter what. They were brothers, and Michael loved him, he did.

When he first came in the room, a nurse was prepping Danny for surgery. The nurse mentioned she'd shaved his beard, but would come back to cut his hair, after Michael had time to see him. No matter. Danny's long hair couldn't obscure the fact of whom he was, and just like Margaret, Michael had known Danny right away.

Michael's eyes filled with tears now. His brother was hooked up to machines, fighting for his life. And Michael wanted Danny to live.

He sat down in the chair near the bed, hunched over, and dropped his head in his hands. "It's Danny, he's my brother," he said, between sobs. "I'm certain."

Danny was alive.

He'd walked away from his life.

And Michael might be the only one who'd ever understand why.

Chapter 34
Daniel

Daniel opened his eyes, mouth parched, dim lights overhead. There were voices nearby, muffled. When he eased his head to the right, he noticed the door ajar, held open by the arm of a man, leaning into the hallway, broad shoulders, grey dress slacks and wingtips. Inside the room, to the left of the door, in the corner, Brian stood dressed in translucent silvery robes, his eyes peaceful. The door swung open wider, and blocked Danny from seeing Brian for a moment, then shut all the way. Brian had vanished, and so had the man in the wingtips.

When Daniel woke again later, his eyes searched the room for Brian, still gone. But next to him, slumped in a chair, arms folded across his chest, eyes and mouth shut, same wingtips and trousers, Daniel knew him right away.

"Michael?" His voice raspy, throat sore, he gasped for air. "Water," he whispered.

His brother stood up before he could choke out another word.

"It's okay," Michael said. "You're going to be fine."

Michael's hair was grey now. Fine white strands mixed with dark brown, same face, exactly the same, in fact.

"Where's Brian?"

Michael seemed puzzled, his forehead wrinkled, a deep line formed between his brows that Daniel hadn't noticed before.

"Brian died when we were kids, Danny, remember?"

236

Daniel glanced toward the corner trying to make sense of what he'd seen before. He remembered now, they swam together again, one last time.

Was it a dream?

It all seemed so real.

He tried to speak again, but the words caught in his throat, he couldn't get enough air. He grabbed for Michael.

"Stay calm," Michael said, and used some type of damp pad to moisten his lips and dry mouth. "They removed the tubing, so you'll feel dry, but you can't have water yet, only these swabs for now." Michael held the swab for him to see before he ran it inside his mouth, across the top of his tongue and along his lips again.

A temporary fix, but water was what he needed.

Michael placed a new swab in Danny's left hand, and that's when Danny realized he couldn't raise his arm, locked against the sidebar of the bed.

"Sorry," Michael said, and motioned to the guardrail. "I forgot about the handcuff." He grabbed the swab from Danny, ran it over lips several times. "They've got you on lockdown, your ankles, too."

Daniel could feel the shackles on his feet now.

"You know you're in a lot of trouble, right?"

"Why are you here?" Daniel said.

Danny felt the cotton sheets beneath him. His chest bare, his upper right arm felt stiff, strapped against his side. A large white dressing was taped to his upper chest and shoulder. An IV line poked his arm. He couldn't raise his right arm either, could only move his hands, so he tried to reach for Michael's sleeve.

"Where are we?" he said.

Michael took his hand and placed it down against the mattress again, held it there with his own. "You're in Flagstaff at the hospital," he said. "You had surgery for a gunshot wound to your shoulder." Michael nodded toward Daniel's right arm, and then squeezed his hand. "Don't make any sudden moves, you've also got a drain for your head injury."

His skull felt different, the burning pain had subsided, but he could feel the heat in his shoulder now, and he could see in Michael's eyes that his injuries were serious.

"How long have I been here?"

"Three days or more," Michael said, and glanced over his shoulder at the doorway. "You don't remember being awake before?"

Daniel stared at his brother.

Did Margaret call him?

"Maggie," he said, his voice weak. "Is she okay?"

Did Sonia hurt her after all?

"She's fine," Michael said. "She's with the detective at the police station for questioning."

Questioning? What's he saying?

Daniel tried to get up again, but Michael held him down.

"Stop, or you'll hurt yourself, stay still now." Michael let him go once he relaxed again. "Try to be quiet." Michael glanced at the door once more. "The officer could come in anytime," he said. "They only let me in here because you were unconscious."

Daniel closed his eyes, tried to make sense of what Michael said. He wanted to go back to the lake, to lie in the grass, to wait for God.

"No, don't go to sleep, not yet." Michael was over him now, near his face, he could feel his brother's breath on his cheek. "Open your eyes, Danny."

Danny was his real name.

How long had it been since he'd heard his brother's voice? Why did it sound so comforting now?

"I'm awake." Danny squeezed his eyes open again, but struggled to focus on his brother's face.

The woods.

Danny remembered the bright lights now, the dogs barking, and the loud blast.

"I called a lawyer," Michael said. "So don't talk to the police before you meet with him, be careful what you say." Michael spoke in a low, husky voice, his breath smelled like scotch and peppermint. "Did you really kill her?"

Panic rose inside Daniel's chest.

238

Michael slipped the monitor from Daniel's finger. "Your blood pressure will trigger the nurses." He slipped the device on his own finger and checked the monitor. "Mine's not much better."

"Mike," he said, tried to clear his throat, nodded toward the swabs on the tray nearby.

Michael took a new one, doused the inside of Daniel's mouth and lips again. "Better?"

Daniel nodded, using his tongue to lick the fluid from his lips. He realized Michael was talking about Sonia.

They found her body.

He pictured the scene, Sonia crumpled inside Maxwell's stall.

The horses would be with the vet by now. They were safe. Bill called them. Of course he did.

"I choked her," Daniel said. "I killed Sonia."

Michael moved back several inches, stood up straight.

"But, why?" he said, his voice a whisper. "Who was she?"

"It doesn't matter why, Mike." He remembered the truck ride up the highway, the ski lift operator, and the blast, so loud. "I did it," he said. "I killed her."

Michael leaned back in. "Quiet, they might hear you, you don't want to say that around the cops."

"It's the truth."

"Just talk to the lawyer first." Michael covered his own eyes, but the tears escaped onto Daniel's bandages.

Daniel realized this was real. He was alive. His brother was right there, crying. Had he been dreaming before? When he saw Brian?

"I'm sorry, Michael."

Michael wiped his nose on the back of his hand. Daniel could see his eyes again. Michael's thick brows were mixed with grey now, too.

"I'm the one who's sorry," Michael said. "I'm the reason you left." Michael shook his head now.

Daniel had more to say, but waited.

"I was thinking about that night," Michael said. "When Brian fell under the ice." Michael stared straight into Daniel's eyes. "I was sober, never drank a single drop all night." He wiped his nose again. "I got you guys drunk, knew Brian didn't go home, and the ice was thin, I should've helped him, it was all my fault."

Michael stood still as tears streamed down his face.

"I got you guys drunk on purpose," he said, again. "I let you take the blame, never told anyone the truth."

Daniel didn't know what to say. Michael had seemed drunk that night. "What?" Daniel shook his head.

But, Michael just stood there, took a deep breath. "It's true."

Daniel glanced across the room to his left, the silver blinds were closed on the window, a bit of sun sparked along the edges of the sill, a line of light shot across the beige linoleum floor, red and grey patterned wall paper covered the adjacent wall with a door open to a bathroom, where he could see the sink and the mirror and over to the right was the other door, to the hallway, he assumed, to where the officer must be on guard.

He was a prisoner, chained to the bed, he tried to scream, but when he opened his mouth nothing came.

Michael swabbed his mouth again. "You must have known the truth," he said. "You knew about me and Margaret."

So it was true. Daniel did know that much. He'd seen them together in the kitchen. But, he'd never thought about Brian, about his brother getting them drunk. That was the first time he'd ever had a drink.

After that horrible night, after Brian drowned, Daniel snuck into his father's study all the time, to sip from his collection of whiskey and bourbons. When he went away to college, he kept it up, a steady supply came from a guy on the floor above him, a transfer student from Kentucky who always had plenty of alcohol stashed in his closet.

Daniel never stopped drinking and before he left for New York, and escaped to Arizona, his was worse than ever. He drank throughout the day, a flask, and the bottle under the seat in the car, another in his desk drawer at the office, hotel bars, and dark taverns on back roads.

He was drunk all day, every day, he'd just learned to hide it, to be quiet at meetings, hold it together until he was home.

240

Maggie always got the fallout, and when the rage would escape, his moods were out of control. He knew he was sick. But he didn't care. He'd killed his best friend. He'd ruined so many lives.

"I seduced Maggie," Michael said. "It wasn't her fault, I knew she was lonely, I knew you guys were in trouble."

The streak of light from the window cast a thin trail through the air, dust particles floated in the beam, and Daniel remembered the brilliant colors of heaven, how he wasn't afraid anymore.

Daniel glanced back at his brother now. He tried to see his face, but Michael's head was down, looking at the floor. He could see his brother's hair had thinned toward the back, a small circle with strands of grey and brown combed across.

"I fell in love with her that first time you brought her home."

"We played croquet," Daniel said. "I remember." And he did. He remembered the way his brother showed Maggie how to hold the club, and hit the ball, how he'd held her wrists and circled around her, giving instruction, sat next to her before Daniel could in the dining room.

"That's why you left, and I don't blame you," Michael said, "I was a shit to you, your whole life."

"Jacob." Daniel could see his son's face now, how he'd turned to catch eyes with his dad.

"He's your son, Danny."

Daniel already knew that, he'd seen the boy. Jacob was his son.

"Does he know about me?"

Michael nodded. "He saw the news before Maggie could get to him."

The door opened wide and Michael stepped aside as the officer came toward the bed. "What's going on in here?"

"He just now opened his eyes," Michael lied, his face stained with tears.

"I heard voices." The cop wore a dark uniform, silver badge above his left pocket, two pens and a pad of paper in the other, a radio microphone tucked between the buttons on his shirt, a thick belt with holster and gun, a black club tucked into a holder on one side, a wedding ring on his finger.

Daniel wondered if he and his wife had children, lived nearby, if he was a rookie—he seemed young. He was stocky, dark brown closely trimmed hair, how Daniel kept his once. The top was spiked, and he almost looked like a younger, more athletic Carlos. Hispanic. Handsome like he took care of himself, worked out, ate right, probably had a wife who loved him, worried about him when he was on the job. He wondered if this young man was one of the officers who'd hunted him down in the woods, flashed bright lights on him, aimed their weapons at him, did he know the officer who'd shot him?

Everything came fast now. Daniel's mind was in overdrive. His senses were alive and he felt clearer than he had in weeks, maybe even years. He shifted in the bed, could feel something taped to his lower back, noticed the line feeding out and off the side of the bed, hooked to a plastic container, the sheet and thin blanket covered him to mid-waist. He wasn't cold. In fact, he was a bit too warm if anything. Maybe he still had a fever.

Margaret had put cool towels on his forehead, had run her fingers along his skin, made love to him with the moon shining in from the skylight, her hair shiny as it fell against her skin. He understood now that she'd only tried to show him the love they once shared, so he'd snap out of his lost mind. She'd almost succeeded, but in the end, he didn't want to go back.

He hoped Margaret wasn't afraid now at the police station, a cold metal chair, one of those wooden tables with a lamp overhead. Were they interrogating her? Did they think she had something to do with Sonia's death?

Daniel met the officer's eyes. "I was telling my brother I wanted to confess."

A sudden stillness fell over the room, only the buzz of the hospital equipment and the light above his head. The officer asked Michael to step away, to move over toward the door, to stay quiet, not speak to his brother. "Sir, you need to move aside, right now."

"Michael, do what he says."

Daniel nodded to Michael, and his brother gave up his post and moved away, wiped his face with the inside of his hands and then folded them in front of him, and lowered his head again.

"Sir, I need to read The Miranda Rights to you, but first I need to know if you are fully awake, are you aware of what you just said, of where you are and of what this means?"

"I know what I'm doing, yes."

Daniel could see the young officer was looking him over, noticed the blood pressure clip unattached next to his finger.

"I'd like to call for your doctor or nurse to make sure you are okay before you say anything else." He pushed the button on the side of the railing, and a female voice said they'd be right there.

Daniel closed his eyes for a moment, his mouth felt dry again, he wished he could have a drink of water, soak the walls of his throat with fluids. It was hard to breathe deeply, so he kept his breathing shallow, afraid to cough, knowing the pain he felt in his chest would be worse if he did. He focused on each breath until the nurse came in, hooked him up to the heart monitor again, swabbed his mouth and lips, checked the level of fluid in the container dangling from the side of the bed, felt for his pulse while she watched the second hand on her watch and then checked the bandages on his chest and forehead.

She had light, golden hair like Maggie, pulled back into a ponytail, younger, but pretty like Maggie, too. Feminine. Wholesome. It was then that Daniel realized his long hair was gone. Shaven. He could feel the smoothness of his skin against the pillowcase.

She seemed to have noticed. "They shaved your hair before surgery, it was so tangled they decided to take it all off. You've had two procedures this week, they removed most of the bullet and debris from your shoulder, and the next morning opened your skull to relieve the pressure in your brain. The surgeon can explain everything when she comes in for rounds this evening. You're stable, but still in the ICU for observation. We might move you to another room tomorrow. We'll see how you do tonight. Are you thirsty?"

243

Daniel nodded. Her fingers were cool against his arm as she adjusted the IV line.

"I'll bring you ice chips when I come back with a new IV bag." She squeezed the bag hanging on a tall metal arm next to Daniel's bed. "Be just a few minutes, can you hold on till then?"

"Yes, I'm okay."

"Are you cold?"

"No, I'm fine." He was warm, but it was okay, he didn't want to stop her from leaving.

"You seem alert, how's your pain?"

"I'm okay."

"I can give you something more for pain if you need it, just let me know, I'll be here all night, just push this button." The nurse pointed to the side of the railing. "My name is Sally, if you need anything."

"Thank you."

She spoke to the officer for a moment in a low voice, too quiet for him to hear what she said, and then squeezed past Michael near the door to leave. Daniel closed his eyes again, pictured his grandmother's house, the bed where he would sleep, could almost smell the applesauce cake in the oven.

"Sir," the officer said.

But, Daniel couldn't open his eyes now. He was too tired and drifted off again, dreamed about the orchards, running between the rows of trees.

"You have to tell the truth, Danny." He heard his grandmother's voice at the end of the orchard.

She stepped from the trees, a basket at her side, the same apron she always wore when she was in the kitchen, her hair up in a twist with a long gold comb holding it in place, wisps of silver hair that had escaped blew in the breeze.

"You need to do the right thing and put this all to rest now," she said.

Daniel felt the breeze against his own skin now, his grandmother slipped back behind the trees, the fruit ripe and low on the branches, he caught sight of her hand on the basket before she disappeared altogether and he was back in the hospital room.

244

"Are you okay, sir?" The officer stood nearby. "Do you want to make a statement now?"

Daniel nodded and the man read to him from a small black notebook—his rights. The officer explained that he'd record what he said and would need his signature on a form. He asked if Daniel understood.

"Yes, I understand."

Michael stood nearby as a witness, Daniel realized, his brother was asked to stay for his confession.

It was okay. In fact, it felt right. Daniel was ready to come clean about everything. And he realized now, he'd already forgiven Michael. Now they could make things right, together. He didn't want a lawyer to talk him out of a confession, and he wanted his brother in the room. Things needed to be said.

Michael wasn't guilty for anything more than being a competitive older brother, for falling in love with Margaret. She was easy to fall for, her tender voice and gentle nature. Maggie was the kind of woman a man wanted to protect and somewhere along the way, Daniel got lost, drank too much, forgot to love her, turned himself over to his insecurities, the voices so loud inside his head, he'd gone deaf.

As far as Michael's confession about the night Brian died, it was something Michael would have to deal with on his own, with God. Daniel knew he was responsible too. His brother wasn't the only one who'd made poor choices that night. Everything else—Michael was right—was stupid, all of it. Both of them had been fools.

But worse than anything, Daniel had ended Sonia's life with his own bare hands. He could have stopped, but he didn't and now he needed to tell the truth.

Daniel told the officer everything. How he'd walked away after the planes crashed into the buildings, assumed a new identity, had hidden away—deserted his wife and child.

He told him about Sonia, how she'd stalked him. That she didn't deserve to die. "I killed her," he said. He didn't cry. Her life meant more than him being weak. "She came at me with a knife and I pulled her into a headlock, squeezed her wrist until she let the knife drop, and then I pulled my arm even tighter around her neck until she was gone. I remember it all, very clearly. I left her in Maxwell's stall and took off on the motorcycle."

Daniel stopped then—turned his head away from the officer.

Michael had stayed silent the whole time.

Daniel closed his eyes again. The room felt cooler. He heard the nurse's voice on the speaker nearby, pretty Sally, said she'd be right in. Within minutes her hand was on his wrist and he opened his eyes to see her hang a new IV bag of fluids on the hook, and then she held a plastic spoon to his mouth, the ice slipped onto his tongue, instant relief.

Her eyes were hazel, not blue like Maggie's, and she wore thick black mascara, her brows penciled in light brown, more make-up than Maggie ever wore and her scent was lighter, citrusy, like lemons, probably from the soap she used between patients. Not the same spicy perfume as Maggie.

Daniel closed his mouth, let the ice melt on his tongue as he signed the report with his left hand still cuffed to the bedside rail, then he shut his eyes again. He let a single tear escape down his cheek—for Sonia, Maggie, Jake, Michael, Dutch and his mother.

He was finished now. And at the time of the end, when he waited in the meadow again, Daniel would know the lies had ended, forever. He'd pay for his sins, and while he was still alive, he'd spend every day for the rest of his life, doing what was right, being the man he was meant to be.

Across the room, Daniel could hear the quiet voices of his brother and the officer, Sally rearranged the IV pole near his bed, the wheels squeaked against the floor, the hum of the air-conditioner kicked in by the window and Daniel breathed in deep, his chest rose and then fell as he released the air from inside his lungs in a slow, deliberate fashion. He could breathe again.

The swish of the door against the linoleum meant Michael and the young officer had moved into the hall, and as the door inched shut again, Daniel kept his eyes closed.

Sally's cool hand on his wrist now, his pulse pumped in even beats under her fingertips before she straightened the blanket across his lap. As Sally pulled the door wide open again to leave,

Daniel peaked out from under heavy lids, and there stood Maggie, several feet beyond the young officer and Michael now in deep conversation with another man. Henry was at her side, concentrated on his cellphone.

Their eyes met, and Daniel saw the glisten of tears as he held her gaze, her golden waves of hair fell against a sheer, cream-colored sweater, which illuminated her sun kissed skin.

Maggie tilted her head, her eyes shown bright under the hospital lights, a faint smile formed across her lips as she nodded to him then wiped away a tear as the door crept shut all the way, the room empty and still.

Caron Kamps Widden is the author of *Restoration, a novel* set in Saratoga Springs, New York and *The Lies We Keep, a novel* of suspense set in Sedona, Arizona. She has written short stories and articles for literary magazines and newspapers, was an editorial assistant for *Orange Coast Magazine,* and a reader for *Zoetrope: All-Story*.

When it comes to writing, Caron enjoys exploring the complexities of family relationships, writing from both the male and female perspective. Her stories are rich in emotion and delve deep into the intricate dynamics of love and heartbreak.

After a recent expat assignment in Antwerp, Belgium, Caron and her husband settled back in the states in a small town near Cleveland, Ohio. Caron has lived all over the country, but grew up on the west coast. She was born in Oregon, raised in California and spent summers in Washington State. She has three grown children and keeps thinking she needs to get a dog.

Made in the USA
Middletown, DE
14 October 2016